# There
himself and the mare

It seemed as if they were locked in a desperate struggle with birth and death, and sweat ran freely down into his eyes and dripped off his chin....

Suddenly the mare jerked, gave a cry and a gigantic heave, and the foal neatly slid out, knocking Sara backward in the straw and landing almost perfectly in Mitch's arms.

"Hot damn, he's alive," Mitch crowed exultantly. "Sara darlin', he's alive."

Sara turned her head just then and smiled at him, a watery, blazing triumphant, ecstatic grin.

He looked into the shining glory of her face and everything in his immediate world shifted, rearranged itself. It was as if he'd been asleep all his life, and suddenly awakened.

He fell in love with Sara at that exact moment in time.

## ABOUT THE AUTHOR

Bobby Hutchinson considers herself very fortunate to be a writer. She says, "I get to write books about all the things I might like to have chosen for a career if I'd taken a different path through life. Writing is a way of choosing alternate realities and living in them for a magical period of time."

Bobby and her husband Al recently moved from Vancouver to an isolated lakeside farm in British Columbia's southern interior.

## Books by Bobby Hutchinson

HARLEQUIN AMERICAN ROMANCE
147–WHEREVER YOU GO
173–WELCOME THE MORNING
223–FOLLOW A WILD HEART

HARLEQUIN SUPERROMANCE
166–SHELTERING BRIDGES
229–MEETING PLACE
253–DRAW DOWN THE MOON
284–NORTHERN KNIGHTS
337–A PATCH OF EARTH

# Home
# to the Cowboy
## Bobby Hutchinson

# *Harlequin Books*

TORONTO • NEW YORK • LONDON
AMSTERDAM • PARIS • SYDNEY • HAMBURG
STOCKHOLM • ATHENS • TOKYO • MILAN

For my sons, Dan, Dave and Rob—
all of whom are cowboys in their dreams.

Thank you to Susan Wales, DVM,
and to Wendell and Helen Stephens
and Don and Terri Omans of Paradise, Montana.

Published April 1989

First printing February 1989

ISBN 0-373-16290-1

# Chapter One

Sara Wingate took one look at the muddy penful of squealing, milling hogs, and her heart sank. There must have been at least a hundred and twenty prime Yorkshires in the large wooden enclosure, and every single one of them looked mean and ornery.

*C'mon, Sara, you're a vet, and pigsticking is just one of the less attractive parts of the job,* she lectured sternly, but the silent pep talk wasn't much help. Pigsticking ranked right up there with having a root canal in her lexicon of pleasurable pastimes in life, and this was going to take the rest of what had been a really great summer afternoon.

"Well, Floyd, let's get this over with."

Floyd O'Malley, her assistant, had a perennially flushed, usually cheerful face. Today it was sullen, and even his rusty crop of wildly curling hair seemed less electric than usual. He muttered dismally under his breath as he and Sara assembled the necessary equipment.

"Abominable, ungrateful, nasty creatures, are pigs," he intoned, his usually mild Irish brogue thick and pithy with disgust at the forthcoming venture.

They struggled into heavy waterproof suits and rubber boots. Sara felt the sweat begin under her arms and trickle between her breasts even before she'd finished zipping up the coverall. *Just what the elegant Montana woman wears on a hot day in June,* she thought wryly as she tugged on the knee-high boots.

They were ready to begin far too soon for Sara's liking.

The operation ought to have been simple; in theory, it involved two people, a ten-inch needle and a defenseless pig.

The object of the exercise was to obtain a blood sample from each animal, which would then be tested for common diseases.

The problem was, Sara had never yet seen a pig that agreed to cooperate in the routine, and she doubted the pigs on the Carter ranch were any exception.

Wearing what she hoped was a confident, jaunty expression, with Floyd trailing morosely at her side, she opened the gate and waded into the swarm of porkers.

INSIDE THE OLD FRAME ranch house, Mitchell Carter had been eating lunch when the green pickup with the white letters on the side drove into the yard. He got up and glanced idly out the window over the sink when his mother announced the vet had arrived.

"Doc Stone's still got the same old truck, I see. And isn't that Floyd . . . Floyd, what's his name? Family had a rundown place up the valley south of Plains. O'Malley, Floyd O'Malley?" Mitch commented as his father hurriedly finished his coffee and headed for the door.

"Yup, it's Floyd all right, but it ain't Doc Stone. We're gonna have to change vets." Wilson Carter plopped his straw hat on his nearly bald head with an air of finality. "Doc Stone hired himself this newfangled woman here a few weeks back, daughter to the lady Dave Hoffman down at Bitterroot married awhile ago. When I phoned yesterday to get the pigs done, it was either use her or try and get the guy all the way from Thompson Falls to come down, and that could take a week or two. So I said fer her to go ahead this time. Floyd surely knows somethin' after all these years watchin' Doc, but I figure I'll take my business to Thompson Falls after this.''

Wilson slammed the door, making Mitch's mother wince nervously and purse her mouth.

"I wish your father wouldn't bang the door like that all the time," she said in the weary, edgy voice Mitch couldn't seem to get used to. She began to clear the dishes, walking slowly with shoulders slumped the way she'd been doing lately.

Mitch planted a hasty kiss on her soft cheek and hurried out the door after his father, feeling trapped. He found himself getting caught up in senseless hassles between his mother and father these days, and the only way to avoid them was to escape.

Heading for the horse barns, he found himself detouring instead toward the pigpens, reluctant curiosity about the woman vet temporarily overcoming his abhorrence for pigs.

Climbing up the wood-sided pen, he slung a long, Levi's-clad leg over the top rail and balanced there easily, tilting his worn brown Stetson down lower over his face and wondering disgustedly how anyone could stand the deafening noise and the sickening stench that rose in equal portions from the hog pens. Why would any female in her right mind deliberately choose to make her living at a job that included pigs?

Down in the midst of the action, Sara was wondering exactly the same thing.

Floyd was reluctantly wielding the snare, a pole with a wire loop attached. He looped the wire around a pig's snout and then reeled him in and held him still while Sara jabbed the needle into the neck and prayed she'd hit the vena cava on the first try, extracting the blood sample so they could move along to the next unhappy creature.

Sara was certain Floyd was uttering vile curses, although she couldn't hear them amidst the unholy squealing. His mouth moved petulantly, and his washed-out blue eyes were full of rancor as he stalked one pink porker after the other, lassoed a snout and did his best to put a headlock on an angry animal.

"Hold him, Floyd, hang on, darn, missed, once more..." Sara knew her hollered encouragement was also drowned out by the din, but it helped to vocalize as a panting Floyd did his best to hold several hundred pounds of bacon steady for at least two seconds so she could get the needle in.

Sara guessed Floyd was somewhere past fifty, and he simply wasn't an athlete, unless hoisting beer mugs to his mouth counted. This wasn't going well at all, and to make matters worse, she was painfully conscious of a rangy cowboy perched on the fence rail, silently watching the entire fiasco.

Sara groaned. If ever she didn't need an audience...

Well, Wilson Carter had probably sold tickets for the event. Where else could Montana cowboys get a firsthand look at mud wrestling in the afternoon?

"Atta boy, Floyd, now hold the miserable...gotcha."

The cowboy nodded at her somberly when she glanced up. His face was almost entirely shielded by the brim of his hat, but there was something mocking about his laconic, easy grace, sitting there so clean and removed from the rigors she was undergoing. She found herself resenting him.

The next pig was a whopper. Almost twice the size of the others, he also was no fool. Obviously somebody in a rubber suit had stuck this monster before, and he was having no part of a repeat performance. Floyd had the snare on his snout, but the pig was orbiting the pen with Floyd in tow, obviously immune to the pain of a nose hold.

Floyd's complexion was livid purple, and his mouth moved unceasingly. He tightened the snare and somehow managed to throw a shoulder lock on the renegade. Sara readied the needle, but at the final instant the pig gave a mighty heave, tossing Floyd head over heels into the muck. Then, with what Sara could only label deliberation, the pig turned and trotted right over Floyd with his mean little hooves, never missing a squeal.

Sara scrambled across the milling bodies, extending a hand to the portly man lying flat on his back.

"Floyd, you okay? You hurt?" she hollered, but the words were indecipherable in the din. Floyd slowly hauled himself to his feet, screwing his face into a grimace and holding his right shoulder with the other hand. Sara helped him over to the gate and together they struggled through it. The cowboy had leaped down from the fence, and he helped her force the gate shut before the hogs could escape.

"Here, lean on me," he instructed Floyd, hollering to be heard. Glancing at Sarah, he gave a small, courtly nod and bellowed, "How d'ya do, ma'am. I'm Mitch Carter." Together they half supported Floyd, walking slowly on either side of his limping form over to the truck.

Mitch Carter was several inches taller than her own generous five eleven, Sara noted with interest. A few years older than her twenty-nine, as well, although it was hard to tell.

Somewhere in his early thirties, probably: there was a sense of maturity about him. And his worn Stetson shielded a deeply tanned, clean-shaven face with eyes as green and deep as a pond, a nose that must have been broken once or twice, judging by the interesting bumps along its otherwise straight bridge, and a narrow, hard-looking mouth that would have benefited from a smile or two.

They made their halting way over to the truck, depositing Floyd on the bumper.

"Thanks, Mitch. I'm Sara, Sara Wingate," she volunteered. Here, at least, they were far enough away from the pens so that conversation was possible in a normal tone of voice. Except she sounded breathless at the moment. Mitch Carter was one handsome cowboy up close.

Flustered, she turned her attention to her groaning assistant.

"Where are you hurt, Floyd?" Sara demanded anxiously.

"Ohh, me shoulder's dislocated, without a doubt," Floyd moaned piteously. Sara helped him unzip the filthy rubber suit as Mitch silently bent over and tugged off the muddy gum boots. Sara wiped her hands down her own suit in a futile effort to remove some of the grime and gently touched Floyd's shoulder, making him wince dramatically.

"Oh, the pain, the pain. It travels right up into me head, and the hand on that side is numb." Floyd howled, making a great show of favoring his shoulder.

Mitch looked past Floyd, straight into Sara's clear gray eyes. He noted their fringe of long, curling lashes, the attractive planes and angles of her open features, and wondered if she knew about the streak of mud on her tilted nose and across her cheek. He recognized the exasperated, uncertain expression she wore, however.

She wasn't exactly sure whether or not foxy old O'Malley was faking it. Mitch strongly suspected he was.

Mitch raised a laconic eyebrow at Sara, and they exchanged a telling glance before Mitch shrugged. No way of proving the shoulder was or wasn't injured, and no point in taking a chance.

She had lovely browny-gold hair, Mitch noted absently. It looked nice, even carelessly pinned back into a sort of bun. Wavy, thick hair.

"I'll get somebody to run you into the medical clinic in Plains, Floyd," Mitch decided. He turned and strode toward the house.

Sara watched him walk away, admiring the long, loping gait, his wide shoulders, which beneath the blue shirt narrowed dramatically at the waistline, and his snug, worn Levi's that stretched tight across a well-developed male posterior. Fine gluteus maximus development, she concluded clinically.

Floyd was apologizing to her a little too fervently for not being able to finish the pig testing, and Sara tried to be sympathetic, hating herself for feeling suspicious instead. Six weeks of working with Floyd O'Malley were enough to make anyone suspicious, however. He had an uncanny ability for slipping out of nasty jobs, and he'd just done it again.

How in the dickens was she going to finish the testing by herself? Not even a quarter of the pigs were done, and the thought of coming back again in the morning made her shudder. Better to get it over with now, when she was already smelly, dirty and half deaf.

"Hey, Floyd. Dad'll give you a lift into town, he's just getting the station wagon," Mitch called as he approached across the yard. As Sara watched, her injured right-hand man suddenly became much spryer, hurrying away from the truck and across the gravel.

"I'm awfully sorry, Sara, awfully sorry," he half sang over his shoulder as the station wagon backed from the double garage. He hurried toward it and climbed through the door Mitch held open for him.

The car didn't drive off immediately, however. Wilson Carter detoured across the wide expanse of farmyard and pulled to a stop a few feet from where Sara stood.

He stuck his head out the window, careful not to dislodge his hat, and narrowed a frowning glare at Sara with eyes several shades lighter green than his son's.

"I want those pigs finished today, miss. Mitch here will give you a hand holding 'em," he stated. Then, in a spurt of gravel, he was gone.

For a moment, Mitch couldn't believe he'd heard right. Had the old man actually said that, knowing full well how Mitch despised having anything to do with swine?

He stood, well-worn boots planted wide apart in the gravel, and watched the station wagon disappear down the rutted driveway.

Anger filled him: the frustrated, impotent anger his father was able to stir in him a dozen times a day with his unbending dictums over how every single thing on the ranch should be done, and when.

At thirty-four he was too damned old to start being treated like a kid again.

Mitch felt the blood rise in his face, and he also felt Sara's eyes trained on him from where she still stood, bulky in that suit and boots, covered from head to toe in everything that naturally landed in the bottom of a pigpen.

"Well, Mitch? You up to this procedure?"

He was aware of her voice, pleasantly low pitched and a little husky. There was a definite challenge there.

After sending one final, malevolent glare after the cloud of dust that was all that remained of the station wagon, he reached a hand up unconsciously and settled his hat more firmly on his head in the gesture he'd always used in rodeo just before the chutes opened to release him and some maniac bronco he was determined to ride into submission.

His hair was very dark, Sara noted, at least the parts she could see under his hat. Somewhere between black and brown, long over his ears, sort of silky looking.

"Let's get at it," he growled. "It's either that or butcher the whole infernal herd while Dad's in town."

The idea had merit, and they both considered it longingly for just an instant.

"Better pull on this suit. It's none too clean in there," Sara suggested. She thought he was going to object, but he glanced again at the mess she was in and, with a few well-chosen cusswords, pulled the rubber coverall over his lean length and zipped it angrily.

"Boots?" Sara held Floyd's mucky gum boots aloft, grasping them by the tops to avoid the manure. "I think these might fit you."

She was actually enjoying herself for some perverse reason, probably because of the aloof way in which Mitch had sat on that fence just a short time ago, removed from it all, making her intensely uncomfortable. There was a certain poetic justice in having him join her.

He hesitated again, and both he and Sara studied his dusty leather boots.

"Damn it to hell." With an exclamation of disgust, Mitch finally leaned back against the truck's bumper and, bending one knee, smoothly pulled off his booth, exposing a green sock with a large hole in the toe.

There was something touching and vulnerable about a man with a hole in his sock.

Sara silently handed him first one rubber boot and then the next, stifling a sudden urge to giggle at the sulky glower on his handsome features. The suave cowboy of a few minutes ago had been transformed by the shapeless vet's garb, except for the worn felt hat that seemed to be part of his head. Sara suspected he'd draw the line at taking the hat off, and she was right.

The hat stayed, crammed down tight on his skull with the gesture he'd used several times before, as if he were adjusting his helmet before going into battle.

"Let's do it." Mitch carefully placed his leather boots up on the truck's tailgate, cast a baleful glance down at the filthy rubber boots on his feet, cursed under his breath and led the way toward the pigpens.

Once inside the pen, Sara demonstrated the snare for him, and after a few minutes, Mitch got the hang of it much better than Floyd ever had. Mitch was stronger as well and superbly well-coordinated.

The pigs didn't stand a chance, and she suspected they sensed it, because the whole procedure began to go the way it was described in the textbooks: smooth, efficient, rapid, professional.

Dirty, noisy and stinking. Exhausting, filthy work.

But their eyes would meet over the top of a struggling, squealing hog, and one of Mitch's thick eyebrows would lift in a wordless query. Sara would cross her eyes and shrug.

*What the hell are two nice people like us doing in a place like this?*

She'd meet his green gaze and her clear gray eyes would crinkle at the corners, humor making them dance as she looked at him and grinned, unaware that mud was now smeared across most of her face or that half her wavy hair was flopping down her neck.

Incredibly enough, a giddy kind of wordless rapport blossomed and flourished between them as the afternoon progressed, a closeness that might have taken weeks to develop under ordinary circumstances, or might never have developed at all. Several times, some grotesque or utterly ridiculous action on the part of the pigs would start Sara giggling, and she'd watch in fascination as Mitch's hard mouth widened and softened, just the way she knew it would when he laughed.

Then they'd have to pause in the middle of the noise and heat and stand helplessly amidst the squalling bodies milling around them, until control returned.

And at last, it was done. The number of labeled vials of blood exactly matched the tattooed numbers on the animals. Sara held a triumphant thumb high in the air and pointed at the gate. Mitch made her a chivalrous bow, and then like maniacs they bolted for freedom, one trying to outdo the other in their stumbling race for the gate, impeded by the pigs and the sloppy fit of the gum boots.

Mitch got there first, but he turned back to clear a path among several milling bodies, and then they were outside the pen.

"This way," he called, leading the way over to a tap with a hose attached. "Let's wash these damn outfits off so you can at least handle them to put them in the truck."

Twisting it on, he turned the nozzle on Sara, washing away the worst of the muck from her coverall and mischievously sending spurts of water into her hair and down her neck in the process. But the cold water felt wonderful, and Sara held her hands in the stream and tipped her face up to the sky to let the drops cascade over her skin.

It was a childlike gesture that made something inside of him feel tender and warm.

Then she did the same for Mitch, carefully avoiding the hat still pulled low on his forehead.

"There's a rough shower down at the barn, with towels and soap, if you want to use it," he suggested as they wrestled their way out of the rubber suits a few moments later.

"I feel as if I'll never get the stink off me," she moaned.

The thin T-shirt and jeans Sara had on under the coverall were literally soaked with sweat, glued uncomfortably to her body, and she thought longingly of the clean ones she always kept in the truck. A shower would be heavenly, refreshing before she started the long drive back to the clinic.

"I'd love it. But what about you, don't you want a shower, too?" The moment the words were out, she blushed crimson as a Montana sunset. Would he think that was an invitation?

"I mean, don't you want to use it first?" she stammered.

His lopsided grin came and went along with a teasing glint in his eyes. "Tell you what. I'll give you the first fifteen minutes in there, but I warn you, after that I'm coming in. Oh, and while you're in the shower, I'll go up to the house and tell Mom you're staying for supper."

Sara was shaking her head negatively before he was finished speaking. "I couldn't possibly do that, Mitch. It's not fair to your mom, and also my family are expecting me home."

He frowned. It had never occurred to him that she might be married. He tried to remember exactly what his father had said about her that morning.

"What family?" he demanded bluntly, noticing again how the sweat-dampened clothing outlined her tall, strong body. She had wide shoulders and lovely full breasts, a shape perfectly balanced by curving hips and slender waist. Her arms and legs were long, and she moved gracefully.

This was one lovely lady. His heavy eyebrows came together in a frown. "Who's waiting for you, Sara?"

There was a peculiar intensity to the query that puzzled her.

"Why, Mom and my stepfather, Dave, probably, and Gram Adeline for sure, back at Bitterroot," she supplied. She smiled and shook her head fondly. "Gram always insists I eat a full-scale meal at the end of the day, and she usually stands over me like a watchdog to see that I do. She has this theory about—'' Sara beetled her eyebrows together and made her voice reedy and querulous ''—dern fool diets and foolish women who starve themselves.' Gram's eighty-two, so I guess she's entitled to her pet theories.''

Mitch nodded, his frown gone. "I'll get Mom to give her a call, then, and tell her you're having a good dinner here and that we'll make sure you eat your carrots so your eyesight stays healthy."

"But, I, your father, that is . . ." Sara hated babbling like this, but she didn't fancy choking down dinner under the sour surveillance of Wilson Carter, either.

"Pop's bark is worse than his bite. He's not bad, once you get to know him." His impetuous invitation began to seem more and more a good idea. "And my mom is probably like your grandma. Her idea of a real good time is feeding people."

It was true; Ruth had always loved to cook for him and his brother Bob and their friends.

But that was long ago. Before.

Nowadays there were never guests at the round oak table, and meals alone with his parents were one more of the numerous things Mitch found increasingly difficult since he'd come home.

Besides, he simply wanted to spend more time around this Sara.

His insistence didn't annoy her, the way another man's might have done. She tilted her head and gave him an appraising look.

He flashed his one-sided grin and raised his eyebrows questioningly, and she smiled too and gave in.

"Okay, but make sure it's not a problem for your mother. And I'll call Bitterroot myself as soon as I shower."

Fourteen minutes later, she rubbed dry with one of the oversized towels she'd found stacked neatly on a wooden shelf in the utilitarian washroom at one end of the huge, clean-smelling barn. She hurriedly pulled on clean underwear and the fresh denims and bright pink T-shirt she'd brought from the truck and used her brush as best she could on her wet, waving mass of hair.

When she opened the door and stepped outside, Mitch squinted up at her and nodded approval. He was propped on his heels against the wooden wall of the building, a glowing cigarette held in his right hand between index finger and thumb, half cupped inside his palm. His hat was carefully brushed clean of mud and firmly in place, and she noted that his boots were, too.

He rose to his feet in one effortless motion as Sara hesitantly walked toward him.

"Mom's whipping up biscuits in your honor, and she said come use the phone in the kitchen as soon as you are done. She gave me what for because I made you use the shower down here instead of sending you up to the house."

"This one was great. You're sure it's all right about supper?" Sara felt shy all of a sudden, and once again that unsettling awareness that had overcome her earlier was back.

He had a way of giving her his undivided attention, eyes meeting and holding her own, seeming to convey quite different messages than the words they exchanged out loud.

"You must drive your mom crazy, asking people to eat at the last moment like this," she went on, using conversation to fill in what could be an awkwardness, an admission between them of . . . what?

*Stop being a fool, Sara. This is your first exposure to a real, honest-to-goodness Montana cowboy, and you're reacting like a fourteen-year-old from a parochial school.*

"It's good for her," he said shortly. "I'll be up as soon as I shower." He moved past Sara to the door, noting the way her skin shone from its recent scrubbing and the fact that her thick hair was beginning to dry in wispy little curls over her ears.

He passed close by, and he could smell the harsh green soap they'd always used in the barn shower, along with a warm and subtly sweet scent, like wild grass in hot sunshine, that must be Sara's own. He breathed it in, feeling as if he'd discovered an intimate secret about her.

Sara made her way slowly across the wide expanse of graveled yard over to where the rambling wood-framed farmhouse with its flaking coat of white paint squatted in a circle of lawn. She hesitated several moments before she made her uncertain way to the screen door at the side of the house where the kitchen must be, judging from the delicious smell of baking biscuits wafting into the heavy evening air.

She was puzzling over Mitch's comment about his mother.

Why should having Sara arrive for dinner unexpectedly be good for Mrs. Carter? What was wrong with her in the first place that she might need such therapy?

Feeling a lot less than confident and wishing fervently she hadn't let Mitch bulldoze her into this, she smoothed a hand over her still-wet hair and finally knocked softly on the screen door.

# Chapter Two

"Goodness, come right in dear. Mitch said...it's Sara, isn't it? Sara, eh...?"

"Sara Wingate, Mrs. Carter. I do hope I'm not putting you to a whole lot of bother. I told Mitch..."

"It's a pleasure to have you, Sara. And please call me Ruth, won't you?"

Nervously wiping her floury hands on her faded apron, Ruth Carter nodded and smiled, motioning her guest into the large, cheery kitchen.

"Sit down, I'll pour you some lemonade. I just have to..." Ruth's voice trailed off as she hurriedly rescued a pan of biscuits from the oven of the large, modern electric range.

The entire kitchen was well equipped, old and new blending in charming proportions: heavy old oak cupboards fitted with gleaming stainless-steel sinks, a microwave resting beside an antique wooden bread box, an old coffee grinder on a shelf above a food processor.

Sara watched Ruth Carter curiously as the older woman moved around the kitchen. Ruth seemed about Sara's own mother's age, perhaps a few years past fifty, but the two women were very different.

Jennie Wingate-Hoffman was attractive, vigorous, meticulously groomed, full of fast quips and bubbly good humor.

In contrast, Ruth's hair was combed and carelessly pinned back from her face, unstyled, with wide streaks of white weaving through what must have once been a pure golden wheat color.

Her delicate and pretty features were devoid of makeup, and around her eyes and mouth were deep lines, grooved into the mushroom-pale skin. She looked as if she'd recently been ill, and her smile, warm and sweet and rather shy, still seemed somehow forced, as if she weren't in the habit of using it. Her clothes, too, looked as if they'd been donned for covering and little else. The cotton housedress was as faded as the apron, and it hung on her too-slender frame as if it might have been purchased for a much larger woman.

"Lemonade, heavens, I'd forget my own head these days..."

Ruth poured a tall, icy glass for Sara and then, after a distracted glance around the kitchen, a smaller one for herself. With an unconscious sigh, she slumped into a chair at the circular table, across from her guest.

"Supper's nearly ready; I hope Mitch thinks to call his father up from the cattle barn. Wilson bought a new steer today and he's down there admiring it. Sometimes I envy men." Ruth's voice was both weary and querulous. Sara didn't have a clue what the proper response should be to a remark like that, and she began to feel slightly uncomfortable.

"Could I please use your phone, Ruth?" she asked after a few moments had passed in silence.

It was a relief to get up and dial the number and hear the sprightly and businesslike voice of Gram Adeline announce, "Bitterroot Resort, can I help you?"

Sara grinned as she always did at Gram's newly acquired professional telephone manner.

"Gram, it's just me. How you doing? Learned how to make a Singapore sling yet?"

Gram had decided some weeks before that Dave needed a relief bartender, and she needed something to challenge her mind. So now every wall in her room was papered with her carefully hand-lettered recipes for exotic drinks, which Gram memorized as she bustled around. She saw absolutely no discrepancy in being eighty-two years old and learning to be a bartender. And her family knew better than to try to dissuade her, despite their well-founded reservations about actually having her behind the bar.

What Gram made up her mind to do, she did with a vengeance.

"Singapore sling, let's see now..."

"Gram, never mind, I'm just teasing. I'm calling to say I won't be home for supper. I'm at the Carter ranch, and they've asked me to stay and eat with them."

"That's nice, dear. Isn't that the place you had to do the pigs? How'd it go?"

"It went, uh, I guess as fine as pigs can go. I'll fill you in on all the details when I get home."

"All right, dear. And Sara?"

Sara grinned again. She'd bet her afternoon's wages on what was coming next.

"Yes, Gram?"

"You mind your manners, now." There was teasing humor in the old voice. The words were a litany from Sara's childhood, and they bound the two women together in fond memories of long-ago times.

"I will, promise. Bye, Gram."

She hung up slowly, aware that Ruth couldn't have helped overhearing the conversation.

"My gram lives with Mom and Dave at Bitterroot. She helped raise my sister and me after my dad died, and she still treats me as if I were ten," Sara explained.

"How lucky you are, to still have a grandmother around. My sons never met their grandparents. Both my mother and my father died young, and Wilson was an orphan," Ruth said.

"Do you have any grandchildren?" Sara asked innocently, and then she watched with alarm as Ruth's eyes slowly filled with big tears, which then trickled down her cheeks.

"Three dear little granddaughters, but Kate took them back to Seattle after..." Ruth's face contorted into a mask of grief, and she seemed unable to go on as sobs overcame her.

Sara felt panicky. What on earth should she do? What had she done to bring on this storm of grief? She got hastily to her feet and went around the table, putting a clumsy arm around Ruth's shoulders and patting her helplessly, fumbling at a box of tissues on the table and finally extracting a handful and offering them.

Ruth's body shook with weeping, and then slowly she seemed to get herself under some control.

"I'm so sorry, dear, such a thing to do when you've never even met me before. It just comes over me, and Wilson...Wilson won't let me talk about it. And talking helps, you know. Anyway, my daughter-in-law, Kate, she took the little girls back to her home in Seattle right after my oldest son, Bob, was killed last November. There was ice on the hill in the north pasture, and the tractor tipped and rolled, and Bob..." Ruth's voice caught on another sob. "He was trapped underneath. Wilson couldn't get him out until it…it was too late. Anyhow, I miss those little girls something fierce.''

Sara felt shock and overwhelming pity. She'd never felt as helpless in her life as she did this instant, trying to think of what to say to comfort Ruth.

Why hadn't Mitch warned her? Yet how could he have? They'd only known each other a few hours, and there wasn't any tactful way to announce that your brother was dead and your mother half out of her mind with grief.

Male voices sounded outside, and Ruth hurriedly blew her nose, scurrying into the bathroom just off the kitchen. Sara could hear water running as Wilson Carter and Mitch came through the kitchen door. They were discussing the new steer, but they stopped when Sara rose to her feet and walked toward them. It seemed imperative that Ruth have the time she needed in the bathroom.

Both men took their hats off, and Sara took note of Mitch's thick, springy dark hair. It looked softly disarranged, marked by the place his hat had rested, and he ran his fingers through it, setting it even more on edge. He gave her a tight-lipped smile that didn't quite reach his eyes, and Sara sensed tension between the old man and his son.

Sara smiled back at Mitch and determinedly held out her hand to Wilson.

''Hello, Mr. Carter.''

He was the same height as Sara, and as trim and muscular as a much younger man. His face was ruddy and leatherlike from the sun, but a sharp line across his forehead showed much lighter skin where the hatband rested.

''Hullo,'' he growled, taking her outstretched hand after a slight pause, giving it a single shake and then dropping it. ''We don't stand on much ceremony around here, young woman. My name is Wilson, you call me that. Mitch tells me the pig testing went along all right.''

"Yes, we're all done. I'll have the results in a couple of days."

"Humph. Well, damn good thing Mitch was around to give you a hand, is all I can say. Can't expect a woman to do a job like that on her own."

Sara's mouth opened with a suitable retort to that and closed again as Wilson went blithely on.

"I dropped Floyd off at the medical center in Plains. Don't figure there was too much wrong with his arm, either. He managed to open the truck door with no problem before he remembered the derned thing was supposed to be out of commission."

Sara nodded, noting the mischievous wink Mitch gave her from behind his father.

"That sounds like Floyd, all right," she commented ruefully.

Wilson peered around her, his gaze searching the kitchen anxiously.

"Where's Mother got to? It's past time to eat around here," he said loudly, and Ruth appeared on cue from the bathroom, her cheeks unnaturally flushed and her eyes a little swollen. She went fluttering over to the stove and lifted various lids to check on the vegetables.

"Go sit down. Not here in the kitchen, Wilson, in the dining room. All of you, go now. I'll just mash these spuds," Ruth said.

"Can't I help with something?" Sara asked, but Ruth gave her a watery smile and shook her head. Wilson, conscious of his role as host, said loudly, "C'mon, Doc, take a seat out here so the rest of us can sit, too. I guess they still call you Doc, even though you're a woman, huh?" He guffawed loudly at his joke, and Mitch shot him a narrow-eyed, quelling glance that Wilson blithely ignored.

Mitch carefully held Sara's chair, and she slid gratefully into it, wondering if things were going to improve or only get worse. It had been a big mistake, accepting this invitation.

The dining room was obviously in use for her benefit, and just as obviously, Wilson Carter wasn't particularly thrilled at having her at his supper table. Mitch quietly took the chair right beside her, as if providing a bulwark between her and his father.

Altogether, Sara decided it was vastly different from any meal she'd shared before. The food was delicious, but Ruth popped up and down, anticipating everyone's needs as well as serving, seeming not to take more than one or two bites of anything herself. Her activity was punctuated by Wilson's monologue on the new steer and the need for repairs on the fence in the west pasture. Once, in an exasperated voice, he broke off his discourse to order, "Mother, sit still and eat your food. Makes me edgy, you jumping up and down all the time."

Ruth seemed to shrink further into her skin, but she stayed sitting as they finished golden fried chicken, fresh garden salad and the flaky buttermilk biscuits she'd made in Sara's honor.

"You're a tremendous cook, Ruth," Sara said sincerely, and Ruth smiled, a real smile this time, her pale skin flushed with pleasure.

"Oh, any farm woman can cook. You don't need training for that, the way you must to be a vet. How much schooling does it take to get your degree, Sara?"

"Four years of college and another three at vet school. Seven, altogether."

"Must have been quite an experience. I suppose they teach you to do operations and all that?" Ruth queried timidly.

"They sure do. In our third year we had surgery twice a week." Sara humorously described a few scenes from that training period, even succeeding in making Ruth laugh at one point when she told of a hilarious operation she and her surgery partner had performed on a ten-foot boa constrictor from a local zoo. Both Mitch and his father smiled at her story, but Sara noticed their smiles seemed more for Ruth's laughter.

"Understand you're doin' most of Doc Stone's practice," Wilson commented a little later, buttering one last biscuit and popping it whole into his mouth. "Seems hard to figure how a young girl could take over from a man with all Doc's experience. Makes some of us old-timers a mite nervous, trusting you with our stock. No offense meant, you understand."

Mitch had been quiet till now, eating his meal with honest hunger.

He looked up quickly and scowled at his father.

"For heaven's sake, Pop," he snapped.

But Sara had encountered this same attitude at least once a day since she'd first started working for Doc Stone, and she no longer found it as insulting as she had in the beginning. What Wilson was saying straight out was simply what most of the old-timers in the area felt, and she appreciated the chance to meet it head-on.

"It's okay, Mitch. I understand what your dad is saying. I've still got a lot to learn," she admitted forthrightly. "But I've also had an excellent education as well as practical experience. In vet school a lot of the learning is done first-hand, working with qualified vets. And you get a chance to be what's called an extern, a student who lives in the clinic and takes the calls during the night. I did that, and it helps build confidence as well as supplying experience. I also worked every summer at a country practice, where we treated nearly every livestock problem imaginable. So I feel secure about the trust Doc Stone has put in me, and I'll do my best to earn a reputation around here as a good vet. Everyone makes mistakes, of course. But I'll do my absolute best." She met Wilson's eyes in a forthright challenge. "The thing is, you ranchers have to give me a chance to prove myself, like the fair-minded men I think you are. Can I count on you to do that, Mr. Carter?"

Wilson had been listening closely, and she'd caught him off guard with her challenge. He frowned at her in annoyance, and then, when she didn't look away, he reluctantly nodded.

"I suppose everybody deserves a chance," he allowed. "But mind you, that fancy degree won't cut no ice if you don't do a good job with my stock," he warned.

"Agreed," Sara purred, and Mitch grinned, feeling absurdly proud of her ability to match his father's bluntness. It hadn't even taken her an hour to get the best of the old man.

Mitch felt he could use a few lessons.

Ruth was clearing the plates away and serving deep-dish apple pie and huge mugs of strong, steaming coffee.

"Mitch and, and . . . our Bob—" her voice quavered, but she managed, just barely, to keep control this time "—they both went to college, but neither one seemed to use their education much," she remarked to Sara, passing a pottery jug of sweet cream for pouring on the pie.

"Bob, now he always wanted to be a rancher, like Wilson—" she swallowed and hurried on before the ever-present tears could overcome her "—but you, Mitch . . ." Her eyes rested fondly on her son, and Sara saw him give his mother an affectionate wink as he poured cream liberally on his huge slice of pie and began to eat it. "You always had that touch of wildness in you that scared me half to death. Riding wild horses every chance you got, roping your father's bulls when you were still a boy." There was now fierce pride and animation in Ruth's tone, and it transformed her. Sara marvelled at how attractive she was when the sorrow faded from her eyes and her expression became animated.

"You see Sara, Mitch is a rodeo cowboy. He was a professional till just last year, didn't he tell you? He won prizes, too. All Around American Cowboy two years' running, and he's made two TV commercials."

Mitch moved uncomfortably beside Sara, refusing to meet her eyes. The lobes of his ears were fiery red, and Sara loved his embarrassed reaction.

"You didn't mention any of that to me," she said sweetly. "All Around Cowboy, huh?" She was gently teasing him, but the disclosure explained a lot of things. It accounted for his athletic build, for instance, and the impression he gave of rangy toughness and trigger-sharp reflexes. Modern cowboys were superb athletes.

"Two TV commercials as well. What were you advertising, Mitch?" It was wicked to put him on the spot this way, but she had a suspicion he could handle whatever she served up.

Now he met her eyes squarely, more than a hint of a twinkle there. "One was for smokeless tobacco and the other was for beer. Basic necessities of life. Far as I know, they only play them during the breaks in grade B movies at three a.m. on Wednesday mornings."

"I've probably seen them both, then. That's my favorite time for watching television," she replied laconically, and he laughed aloud, a gruff, short bark of sound.

Sara was impressed, though. There were obviously depths to this man she hadn't yet seen, and she was curious about him all over again.

So he'd been a hero in his field.

Her sister Frankie would know him. She decided to phone Frankie later tonight. It was too long since she'd talked to her sister, anyway, and Frankie could probably tell her a whole lot about this sexy cowboy.

Undoubtedly, Sara mused next, he was also well aware of his dangerous aura of sexual attraction. Rodeo cowboys had always been a major romantic fantasy among her female roommates in college, and she knew from her sister that not many cowboys on the rodeo circuit ever lacked female companionship for long.

But she, Sara, knew better than to fall for that patented charm, she reminded herself sternly. She'd known what rodeo cowboys were like when she was still a teenager, thanks to her sister.

Frankie had been married to one. Even now, she worked with them every day.

Professional cowboys were charming and endlessly lovable, and unreliable. Quixotic. Irresponsible.

It was something in their blood, a strength and a weakness. Frankie had always said they were strong in going and weak in staying, and no one knew cowboys better than Frankie Kesler.

Mitch's shoulder brushed against her, and warm awareness coursed through her veins despite her internal lecture. So much for not being affected by cowboys.

Ruth had gotten up again, but this time it was to bring several photos from a shelf on the far wall. She rubbed her apron against the glass and handed the first to Sara.

"That's Mitch on his prize mare, Misty, when he won the award the first year. That was taken in Wyoming, wasn't it,

Mitch? You should take Sara down to the horse barns later and introduce her to Misty.''

It was a profile shot, seemingly unposed, with a wide, rosy sky at sunset as a backdrop. Mitch was twirling a lariat over one shoulder, wearing a white Stetson, a cowboy shirt, a rough leather vest and chaps over his jeans. He was both intent and yet relaxed, exuding confidence. The hand nearest the camera held the reins with careless grace. The beautiful dun-colored mare was at full gallop, and man and horse were one powerful unit.

It was a classic portrait of the traditional American cowboy at work, and both Mitch and his horse were nothing less than breathtaking in their beauty.

The others were less dramatic and less natural, posed photos of Mitch holding various trophies aloft, grinning self-consciously, and one of him accepting the keys to a shiny new truck as one of his prizes.

Wilson had been uncharacteristically quiet until now. He motioned at the photos with the dripping spoon he'd been using to stir his coffee.

"It's a dangerous, foolhardy way to make a living, if you want my opinion. All show. If you win, the money's good, but nobody wins all the time. And when you get hurt or grow old the way we all do sooner or later, then what've ya got?" He snorted scornfully. "A pile a' fancy pictures and a truck with the wheels worn down from all that travelin', that's what.''

It was easy to tell that Wilson gave that particular opinion often. Sara noticed Mitch's mouth tighten and his eyes narrow as Wilson sounded off.

Sara studied the photos, one by one. "That's true, but there's a wild excitement and a sense of tradition about it, as well. It gets into your blood, and then it's hard to turn your back and just walk away," she said absently.

Mitch was watching her. "That's what it's like, all right. How come you know so much about it?" he asked in a low, intense voice.

Sara looked up at him for a second and then shrugged. "I know because my younger sister, Frankie, is a rodeo clown, a bullfighter. She's worked the rodeo circuit off and on since she was a teenager, and she's twenty-seven now, two years younger than I."

She instantly had the undivided attention of everyone at the table.

"Frankie Kesler? That Frankie's your sister?" Mitch's voice was a combination of astonishment and disbelief.

"Yup, Frankie's my baby sister. She was married very young to a cowboy named Brian Kesler. He died in a rodeo accident years ago. He was a bull rider, and he taught Frankie more as a gag than anything to work the barrel for him. She was a novelty because she was female, and also just a kid. After Brian died, she went to bullfighting school down in Texas and learned more about it, how to do it professionally. She's been working the rodeos ever since."

"I've seen her work plenty of times," Mitch said in a guarded tone. "She's not bad," he added reluctantly.

"Not bad?" Sara was instantly defensive. "Frankie's considered by a lot of riders to be the best insurance around against being mauled by a bull. She's a top-class athlete."

"She's also an attractive young woman," Mitch snapped, and now there was an angry, vehement tone to his voice that was brand-new to Sara. She half turned toward him, ready to defend her sister, but Mitch didn't give her a chance to say a word. His green eyes were anything but calm now. They were dark and cold. His tone was as insistent and stubborn as his father's could ever be.

"Every single clown knows the day will come when he gets hooked by a bull and hurt, that's a chance you take when you compete in the rodeo arena. It's a man's rough world, not a woman's. Everything to do with rodeo competition is dangerous, but the Brahmans are the worst of all. A lot of good cowboys, me included, won't have anything to do with the Brahmans. It's absolute total madness for a woman to go risking her life around bulls just to say she can do it. As far as I'm concerned, your sister's out to prove some damn fool women's liberationist point, and she's going to end up badly mauled or dead because of it."

Sara's mouth opened, and she felt raw anger and outrage boiling up in her, but before she could explode, Wilson Carter interrupted loudly, "I agree a hundred percent on that score. I sure as hell wouldn't allow any daughter of mine to have a job like that."

Sara leveled an acidic look at the senior Carter. "Maybe," she said, her voice syrupy sweet, "a daughter of yours wouldn't be the type to let you allow or disallow her any career she chose to follow. Maybe she'd just tell you to mind your own damn business and let her get on with her life. I certainly would."

Wilson's self-righteous expression changed to one of amazement, as if something had bitten him unexpectedly, and Sara thought there was a fleeting look of admiration and hidden amusement on Mitch's features.

Ruth said softly, "I always wanted a daughter, Sara." She hesitated and then added apologetically, "But I have to agree with Wilson, I don't see how I could bear the thought of her fighting bulls. Having Mitch in danger all the time was bad enough, but to have a girl involved in that type of life, I don't know...." She shook her head, a shocked look on her face.

It dawned on Sara all of a sudden that she was definitely alone in this discussion, with the three Carters staunchly lined up on the other side of the fence, and she felt desolate and absurdly abandoned and hurt. After all, she was a guest here, and politeness demanded she not start an outright war. But up till now she'd been relying heavily on Mitch's support during this difficult meal, and he'd abruptly deserted her.

The very worst part of the whole discussion was the fact that all the things they were saying about Frankie and her work were valid concerns that kept Sara awake and worrying lots of dark nights, just as they did her mother and grandmother.

All of Frankie's family had serious reservations about her job, about women as bullfighters, and they were all vocal about it at given times among themselves.

But here with strangers, Sara felt she had no choice except vehement, total defense of her sister's occupation.

Her body felt rigid and stiff with tension, and she eased away from the masculine shoulder that had been touching her own so pleasantly till now.

Close beside her, but as isolated from her as if a thick wall had been erected between them, Mitch felt his amusement at how well Sara managed his father fade abruptly, and he seethed with frustration. Every muscle in his body felt knotted with tension at the way the conversation was going. He was disgusted with himself for getting into a discussion about women and rodeo; it was a thorny issue, and he should have just kept his mouth shut.

He frowned blackly and clenched his fist around his coffee cup. He had to make himself let go before his mother's best china cracked with the force of his grip.

Why had he impulsively asked Sara to supper, anyhow?

He supposed he must have had some fool idea that the fun they'd enjoyed together that afternoon could continue, some wistful notion that her wonderful laughter and sparkling humor would lighten his mother's heart for just this one evening.

He'd wanted things to go along differently than this. God knew, with the old man around, supper couldn't be anything but difficult, but how the hell had this situation gotten so far out of control? He felt as if a bronco he'd been confident he could ride had unexpectedly thrown him into the boards.

"Look." How could he make her understand? He turned in his chair until he was facing Sara. Some part of him noted the high, bright spots of rich color in her cheeks, the icy coldness that seemed to frost the gray eyes to silver, and it registered subconsciously on him that passion made her beautiful.

"I've talked to Frankie about this same thing a couple of times—most of the rodeo cowboys have. I'm not saying anything I haven't told her straight out." His words were gruff and rapid. "Bullfighting is just no job for a woman," he concluded emphatically. "If you ask me, it's a suicidal job even for men."

Ruth and Wilson were now sitting back watching the two young people intently, as if the arena had narrowed and they'd become spectators.

Sara's voice was soft and dangerous. "Don't you see that you can't start dividing jobs into sexual categories? What about women vets, for instance, Mitch? Same thing, in your valuable estimation? Vetting is no job for a woman either, I suppose?"

He made a low, angry noise in his throat. He had to restrain the urge to reach across the two feet that separated them and take her by the shoulders, shake some sense into her.

Kiss her into silence?

Now, wouldn't that just confirm her impression of him as a sexist male.

Angry green eyes met disdainful gray, and the clash was almost audible. When the tension became unbearable, Sara shoved her chair back abruptly and got to her feet, turning to Ruth with a strained facsimile of a smile.

"Can I help you clear up and do these dishes?" she managed to ask.

Ruth got up as well, palpably relieved to end the tense scene. "Heavens no, Sara, there's a dishwasher in the kitchen." She slid a troubled glance at Mitch. "Why don't we all go sit on the porch where it's cool and have some more coffee?" she suggested hopefully.

Sara shook her head. "I really must get home now, I still have to stop at the clinic tonight." Impulsively she reached a hand to Ruth and grasped the woman's chilly fingers warmly in her own. "Thank you so much for having me and making such a lovely dinner."

A tiny, strained smile flitted across Ruth's mouth and then was gone. "It was such a pleasure. But I'm afraid I'm not good company these days. I'm so lonesome, but I can't seem to..." The easy tears that lurked so near the surface filled her eyes and trickled down her cheeks, and she mopped them absently away with the back of one hand in a gesture that tore at Sara's heartstrings. Wilson came up behind his wife and put a protective arm around her shoulders.

"Now, Mother, don't start in crying again," he admonished heavily, but there was male helplessness in his blustery voice.

Mitch had gotten to his feet. He didn't say anything, but when Sara finished her strained goodbyes and thank-yous and hurried across the yard, he followed her out the door. All the way to the truck, he walked stubbornly and silently beside her like an ominous shadow, his loping stride matching her own step for step.

How could this...this narrow-minded chauvinist... affect her without saying a darned word? Her heart pounded as if she were running full speed, and she could feel the pulse in her throat hammering. Her knees felt trembly.

When she reached the truck, she whirled around and faced him.

"I'm very grateful for your help with the pigs," she snapped primly. He was still frowning, and she'd never seen anyone who could frown quite that effectively.

Except maybe Wilson Carter, come to think of it. Mitch was more like his father than he probably realized.

Tilting her chin at a deliberately aggressive angle, she turned away and opened the door of the truck.

His hand suddenly closed around her upper arm, the hardness and power of his fingers evident through the thin sleeve of her T-shirt, forcing her to turn and face him.

"Sara," he said, and in his voice was a confused blending of regret and warmth, and something more, that stopped her angry movement away from his grip.

"Damn it all, I'm sorry the day ended this way." He lifted one shoulder in a rueful half shrug, still holding her arm, and she felt the urgency in his touch.

"The fact is, I always liked and respected your sister Frankie." His eyes were a clear, transparent green with flecks of gold in the warm light. Sara noted that he'd actually forgotten his hat, and his shining dark hair was alive in the dying rays of the sun, his skin as bronzed as an old copper penny, making the lightness of his eyes more arresting.

"Sara, I like you, too, even though I may not agree with all your ideas. And I'm grateful to you for staying to supper tonight." He hesitated a bit, then blurted, "You know, that story you told about the snake? I think that's the first time I've heard my mom actually laugh since I came home three months ago.'' His face tightened, and the frown reappeared. "She went into a kind of depression when Bob was killed, and we can't seem to get her out of it."

"I'm sorry about your brother, Mitch," she said softly.

He nodded. "So'm I." A wry grin came and went, and he looked beyond her, squinting off into the sunset, his voice harsh. "Sometimes I'm damned mad at brother Bob for dying and leaving me holding the bag with this ranch and all. Bob always got along with the old man a hell of a lot better than I did, and for all I know he even liked raising pigs and sheep and staying in one place. . . ."

Sara didn't understand all that he was saying, but she heard the trace of bitterness in his tone clearly enough. He was still holding her arm, and not knowing what to say, she simply stood and looked at him for long, endless moments, recording the high forehead and endearingly crooked nose, the hard, sensual mouth and strong chin.

He was such an appealing man. They'd had fun together.

Yet he'd said things at dinner that made her want to break Ruth's dinner plates over his well-shaped, thick skull.

But now his words touched her. This other Mitch was struggling with his inner self the same way she had countless times in her life, and it made her feel close to him, in a way that could only prove to be dangerous. She didn't need or want the complications of romance at this particular stage in her career, and his words made it clear that settling down was the last thing he wanted or needed.

He was a cowboy at heart, a rover. She'd do well to stay as far away from Mitch Carter as she could get.

And with total female irrationality, she found herself hoping that maybe he was about to kiss her.

The awareness between them arced for one dangerous, endless second. Then he dropped her arm as if it scalded him and took a step back.

"Anyhow, Sara, what I wanted to know was, would you maybe stop by if you're around this way and have a coffee with Mom? Just if you're in the area."

Disappointment trickled through her. He only wanted company for his mother, then. Well, she liked Ruth.

"Sure, Mitch. Thanks again for holding the pigs."

She hopped in the truck, and in the process of backing and turning, she deliberately avoided looking his way.

As she drove off down the long lane, though, she peered hungrily into the rearview mirror.

He was still standing there in the yard, cupping his hands around a match to light a cigarette, in that way that suggested a winter gale instead of a breathless midsummer twilight. He was a lonely figure, poised there in the sunset.

A cowboy, strong in going and weak in staying.

One of Gram's favorite sayings popped illogically into Sara's head as the truck hit a pothole, forcing her to pay attention to the gravel road ahead.

"Never fall in love with a man thinking you're gonna change him."

Sara snorted and determinedly kept her attention on avoiding the worst of the ruts until she turned the corner and knew Mitch was lost to view.

That would be the day when she, Sara Wingate, doctor of veterinary medicine, fell in love with a Montana cowboy who probably thought a woman's place was in the kitchen.

Barefoot, probably.

Pregnant, certainly.

Sara felt a wave of heat envelope her that had nothing to do with the weather and a whole lot to do with the biological processes involved in becoming pregnant by Mitch Carter.

That would be the day.

# Chapter Three

Mitch was slowly getting used to waking up each morning in the same place.

For the first weeks after he had left the rodeo life and come home to stay, he'd spent his groggy waking moments, as he always had to do on the rodeo circuit, trying to figure out where in hell he was, the name of the town, the location of the nearest diner for breakfast.

Now, as morning followed morning on the Carter ranch and the gentle dawn of a Montana summer brightened the window in his small cabin out behind the main house, he gradually became accustomed to stability and routine, to waking up in the same narrow bed under the same patchwork quilt he'd had as a boy.

He no longer had to repeat silently, you're on the ranch, ten miles out of Plains, Montana.

You're home.

He still didn't like it. Home didn't seem to fit how he felt at all.

There was an unchanging pattern that stifled his soul on this ranch where he'd been born and grown to young manhood.

Even as a boy, he couldn't wait to grow up and leave, and homesickness was a thing that had never troubled him in his years on the road.

Now he was a man, and he was going to have to learn to want to stay and grow old here, just the way his parents had done.

It was the hardest thing he'd ever tried to do, this taming the restlessness in his character, and some mornings he despaired. He sorely missed the excitement, the challenge, the raw emotion he thrived on during competition. It bothered him most when he was still halfway between asleep and awake, when logic still slumbered and instinct ruled his brain.

But the morning after he met Sara, these thoughts were totally absent for once.

Instead, there was the image of a tall woman with golden brown hair and soft gray eyes, hovering tantalizingly just behind his eyelids.

And the dream he'd been enjoying was about Sara, as well.

Ridiculously he felt himself blushing crimson at the vivid memory of that dream.

MITCH AND SARA HAD TESTED the pigs on Tuesday.

That Friday evening, just past seven o'clock, having showered, shaved and changed into fresh Levi's, Mitch steered his pickup into the dusty parking lot at Bitterroot Resort and wondered which of the assorted vehicles might belong to her.

Or did she bring the vet truck home with her at night? It wasn't here now, at any rate.

There was the usual collection of vehicles clustered around the sprawling log building that housed the tavern, indicative of the clientele the place attracted: customized hot rods, trucks with mag wheels, several decrepit hulks apparently held together only with baling wire, five shiny motorcycles and four saddle horses hitched to the old rail.

Bitterroot Tavern was the favorite watering hole for the rowdy young males in the area, which automatically made it the favorite hangout for the less-inhibited females.

Mitch pushed open the heavy door.

The jukebox was turned loud, playing fifties rock and roll, and the air was thick and blue with cigarette smoke. The din of voices rose and fell in waves of indecipherable sound, punctuated with pithy curses and loud cheers from a group around the bar in the corner, where a lively game of keno was in progress.

Mitch's gaze roved quickly around the room, checking and dismissing all the women.

Sara wasn't there.

It was crazy to think she would be. She wasn't the type to hang around a tavern like this one, just because her stepfather owned it.

Still, Mitch hadn't banked on feeling quite so let down. His shoulders slumped with disappointment as he maneuvered his way over to the bar.

"Evenin', Mitch," the bartender-owner greeted.

"Hello, Dave."

Dave Hoffman loomed half a head taller and fifty pounds heavier than most of his patrons, and it was typical of him that he would remember Mitch's name after the most casual of meetings, here in the noisy tavern weeks before.

"What'll it be?"

"Draft," Mitch replied.

Dave served him efficiently and then dialed the telephone on the shelf under the bar, frowning when the number obviously didn't answer.

"Damn," he muttered irritably, hanging up the receiver. He raised his voice in an effort to be heard over the din. "Any of you guys see Doc Stone's old jalopy on your way over here? Doc Stone, the old vet from Plains?"

Several people casually shook their heads, but most didn't pay any attention to Dave's query, except for one skinny young man plugging quarters into the cigarette machine.

"Doc Stone? He's gone to Spokane, hitched a ride on my cousin's plane this afternoon," he volunteered, retrieving his package and ripping off the cellophane wrapping.

Dave muttered a soft string of swear words.

"Somebody call for a vet?" Mitch asked quietly.

"My stepdaughter works for Doc Stone, and she's out on a call and needs a helping hand pretty bad. I figure the old codger's taking advantage of her. He's never around at all, anymore." Dave muttered distractedly, "Now what the hell am I going to do? I promised her I'd round up the doc and send him over."

"Sara needs help? What's the problem?"

"You know Sara?" Dave studied Mitch with narrowed blue eyes.

Mitch nodded. "She was up at our ranch the other day, blood-testing pigs. The Carter ranch?"

"Yeah, I remember. That was the day Floyd O'Malley pulled the fast one on her with his shoulder."

"Yeah, that was the day. Is Floyd out on call with her tonight?"

Dave snorted and jerked his chin over at a small table in a dark corner of the room. "He's right there, been lifting full tankards of beer with his sore arm all afternoon. He's in no shape to help with anything."

"What sort of help does Sara need, d'you figure? Where is she?" If only it wasn't pigs again, Mitch thought with a sinking feeling in his gut....

"She's out in the valley—Bill Forgie's place about fifteen miles west of Paradise. He's raising Arab horses, and one of his prize mares is having trouble foaling. Bill's away, he's driving a horse trailer down to Missoula to pick up a stallion, and Sara called about half an hour ago, said she was going to need assistance. Only her and Bill's wife out there, and she has to do an operation or something."

"I remember Bill Forgie, we were on the ball team together in high school." With the feeling he might be getting in over his head, Mitch added slowly, "I've watched plenty of foals get born, but I don't know how I'd do helping at surgery. I'm willing to drive out and give it a try, though, Dave."

"Know the old Skinner place, where the bridge crosses the river? Take the left fork in that road, go about four miles after that," Dave explained eagerly. "If you can help Sara, I'm grateful to you, Mitch. I'd go myself, but leaving this place unsupervised on a Friday night . . ."

The drive through the early twilight out to the isolated ranch was pleasant. In a short time, Mitch was steering down the long driveway. The veterinary service truck was parked next to the old frame barn, and Mitch pulled his own truck in neatly beside it and climbed slowly out, admiring the open lush fields and the clear green water in the pond not far away. Bill Forgie sure had himself a beautiful piece of property.

In a pasture below the barns four magnificent Arab horses were grazing, and Mitch paused for a moment to admire them.

He looked around appraisingly. The house and barns were obviously very old and in need of much repair, original log structures by the look of them, and the small truck parked up by the buildings looked ancient. It was obvious

Bill Forgie had put his money into stock instead of fancy trappings, Mitch noted admiringly.

The double doors to the barn were open, and he could hear subdued female voices and the gasps of a mare in terrible pain as he stepped inside.

The mare was inside a roomy box stall, and Sara was on her knees beside the trembling animal. There was no sign of the foal yet, although blood and some placental fluid were evident in the straw on the floor of the stall.

Sara was in the process of plunging a syringe into the mare's flank, and she didn't glance up. Mitch turned to the short, pretty woman standing outside the stall area.

He lifted his hat politely. "Ma'am, I'm a friend of Bill's from way back. Mitch Carter's my name. I dropped by to see if maybe I could help."

Bill's wife had strawberry-blond hair and a noticeably pregnant middle, and she gave Mitch a look of utter relief and gratitude.

"I'm Carol Forgie. Lord, you have no idea how grateful I am to see you. I'm absolutely no help to the doctor—I keep getting nauseous and I can't even bend over properly. Bill won't be back for hours and . . ."

Tears glistened in her cornflower-blue eyes.

Just then, both of them turned toward the stall as the mare's breathing changed audibly, and her painful gasping seemed to ease slightly.

Mitch moved quickly over to where Sara was kneeling, the used syringe still in her hand, and he crouched down beside her.

"Hi, Sara," he greeted softly. "Doc Stone's gone to Spokane, and Floyd's tied one on at the tavern," he related rapidly in a low voice. "I'll help if I can, just tell me what you want done."

Sweat was trickling down Sara's forehead in tiny drops, and she rubbed the back of one hand distractedly across it. Her gray eyes were troubled as she glanced at the mare's heaving body and then met Mitch's concerned eyes. There was no way to tell him how relieved she was at his arrival, how even in the midst of this emergency the sound of his voice had sent her heart racing.

She motioned at the shoulder-length polyethylene glove discarded on the straw nearby. "I've just examined the mare again—her name's Scarlett—and I'm almost certain now that the foal's dead. I got my finger in the mouth, and there's no tongue reflex, no pulse, no heartbeat." Her despair was reflected by a slight tremor in her voice, and she struggled to control it. A professional didn't reveal the depth of their emotions about a situation like this, she scolded herself. It didn't help much, however. She cared deeply, and that was that.

"Scarlett's pretty weak, and I don't want to lose her, but it seems as if the foal's hopelessly lodged inside her. I've tried and tried to reposition it, with no luck." She was thinking out loud as much as filling Mitch in on what was occurring. Her forehead creased in an unhappy frown, and she said softly, "I don't see much alternative now except to extract the foal, and I'll need your help."

It took a moment for Mitch to absorb her meaning, and when he did he gave an involuntary shudder. He'd heard once or twice of similar situations in which the fetus had to be cut up inside the mother with a wire saw and extracted piece by piece.

He swallowed hard. What was he getting himself into? How did this infernal woman manage to involve him in these damned awful situations?

He was no vet, for God's sake. What if he got sick?

He shuddered again as he caught sight of Sara's large bag of obstetrical instruments on the floor nearby. The top of the bag gaped open, and the tools inside reminded him of medieval torture devices. He suddenly felt more than a little queasy, and he sympathized with Carol Forgie.

But he was reminded forcibly that at least one of them was a total professional. Sara knew exactly what she was doing.

"I've given Scarlett an injection to relax and sedate her. With your help, Mitch, I'll have one last try at getting the foal in position for delivery before we have to..."

The unfinished sentence hung ominously between them as she quickly and thoroughly washed her hands in the bucket of water and antiseptic and then pulled a fresh polyethylene glove up over her hand and arm to the shoulder of her one-piece jumpsuit.

She'd bandaged the mare's tail earlier to keep the dirty hairs from causing infection, and now as Mitch helped clumsily, she crouched down and gently, carefully, slid fingers, hand and arm into the mare's vulva.

There was no sound in the barn now except for the mare's heavy, labored breathing and occasional grunt of pain, and Sara's panting breaths.

She was soon lying prone on the floor with Mitch doing his best to support her shoulders and brace her straining form as she tried repeatedly to reposition the incredibly long legs of the unborn foal and get them in the proper position for delivery.

"Can't...legs are...locked..." she gasped, her face fiery red with the effort and the awkward position she was forced to maintain. She shut her eyes, throwing her entire concentration on the invisible task she had undertaken.

Through her coverall, Mitch could feel the muscles in her warm, slender body straining beneath his hands. He was oblivious to Carol Forgie, hovering helplessly nearby, to the passage of time, even to the steamy and overwhelmingly pungent smells of animal excrement and imminent birth rising around them.

There was only Sara, and himself, and the mare. It seemed as if they were locked in a desperate struggle with birth and death, and sweat ran freely down into his eyes and dripped off his chin. He fumbled once for the clean handkerchief in his pocket and used it to tenderly wipe Sara's face free of sweat.

His reward was a grateful glance as she tried yet again.

This time, inch by slow inch, she worked the spindly legs out. The nearly unconscious mare gave small grunts and whinnies of pain now and then, and each time she had a contraction the foal's body would be forced down, then drawn back, often canceling the progress Sara had just made.

Finally Sara was exhausted, on the verge of admitting defeat. She twisted her head and looked up at Mitch, and her eyes were full of the agony of failure.

"No use," she whispered. His heart plummeted, and he felt Sara slump.

Suddenly the mare jerked abruptly, gave a cry and a gigantic heave, and the foal neatly slid out, knocking Sara backward in the straw and landing almost perfectly in Mitch's arms.

Carol gave an excited cry and moved closer, but her voice faded into despair as she realized the little body Mitch held was motionless, lifeless, the open eyes staring blindly.

"Oh, it's dead," she wailed, as Sara scrambled toward it.

"Massage, like this," Sara ordered feverishly, and as Mitch rubbed the wet, limp body, Sara swiftly wiped the nostrils and mouth clean and began blowing into the lungs.

Breathe, she begged silently, blowing as hard as she dared into the tiny open mouth. She blew until her own lungs protested, and she drew a quick lungful of air and blew again.

And then, unbelievably, the little animal sucked air in, once, paused, choked...then more evenly, with rhythm, he inhaled, exhaled, choked again...he was alive. He was breathing on his own.

His big eyes moved, his delicate body quivered.

"That's it, that's a smart baby," Sara crooned. She untwisted the forelegs with gentle concentration, and within a miraculous few moments, the foal struggled to his feet, reeling drunkenly on his spindly legs.

"Hot damn, he's alive," Mitch crowed exultantly. "Sara, darlin', he's alive, you got him breathing." Adrenaline coursed through his veins, the same exultant pleasure he used to feel at winning the main event at the rodeo. He felt like tossing his Stetson in the air and whooping for joy.

Sara heard his casual "darlin'," and it compounded the joy she felt. But her job wasn't finished.

"Let's get some intravenous fluids into Scarlett quick to replace the electrolytes she's lost, and then we're going to have to get her up so this guy can nurse. He desperately needs that first mother's milk. It's full of nutrients and special antibodies he can't get any other way."

Working swiftly and efficiently, soothing the mare with a stream of words and tenderly stroking hands, she soon had the drip in place.

Fifty minutes later, with Mitch helping, Scarlett rose unsteadily to her feet and Sara helped the staggering foal to find the teat and nurse. Scarlett stretched her graceful neck around to take a long, considering look at her difficult offspring. She hesitated and then finally began to lick him. The last of Sara's concerns faded.

"She's accepted him," she breathed softly. "They'll be fine now."

Tears clouded her vision, the aftermath of tension and the incredible relief of having both mare and colt survive. It was nothing short of a miracle.

Sara let the fat, salty drops roll freely down her cheeks, her heart contracting with joy and humble gratitude that she had the knowledge needed to assist in the birth and that nature had provided the necessary extra dose of luck that every vet prayed for at such times.

A dusty sunbeam was filtering through a small window high in the log wall, and as Mitch watched, its light picked out Sara's face, gray eyes shining silver and wet with tears, long, curling lashes bunched wetly on cheeks stained with dirt. Her hair, caught in its usual haphazard knot at the back of her head, was coming undone, and wispy strands curled around her ears and down her back. Straw stuck to her bloodstained coverall.

Mitch glanced bashfully at her, his own eyes suspiciously damp, and she turned her head just then and smiled at him, a watery, blazingly triumphant, ecstatic grin.

He looked into the shining glory of her face and everything in his immediate world shifted, rearranged itself. It was as if he'd been asleep all his life and suddenly awakened.

He fell in love with Sara at that exact moment in time.

CAROL, TEARY AND WONDERFULLY relieved, hurried up to the house to make coffee.

"Bill promised he'd make it home before dark, and I just can't wait to see his face when we show him the foal. I just can't wait," she chattered as she hurried away.

Sara struggled out of the filthy blue coverall, revealing well-worn jeans and a faded yellow T-shirt. She shook her head at the state of Mitch's clothing.

"If you're going to insist on being in on the vet action like this, you ought to get a coverall and keep it in your truck," she teased him, wondering momentarily why he kept looking at her in that curiously intense way.

Probably because she was an absolute disaster of a mess, she concluded, lifting a hand up to her hair, painfully aware all of a sudden of the state of her hands and arms and of the probable dirt on her face. She hurried over to the outside tap and filled a bucket to wash off the worst of the grime, acutely conscious of Mitch following close behind.

She always carried soap, towels and washcloths in the bag with her instruments, and she lathered a cloth and scrubbed vigorously at her arms, dried them hurriedly, then bent forward and applied the dripping, soapy washcloth to her face and neck, closing her eyes. They were still screwed tightly shut when she felt a warm male hand grip her wrist firmly, extract the washcloth and then gently rub it across one cheek and down her jawline.

"You missed a place right here," he said softly, and she was aware of the deep resonance of his voice and of its slight unsteadiness. She drew her breath in sharply when his callused fingers took hold of her chin as if she were a child he was tenderly washing.

There was nothing at all childish about the way his touch made her feel, however. Her breath quickened and the pulse in her throat felt as if it were hammering wildly. The places his fingers touched felt scalded.

She stood utterly still. For some obscure reason, she kept her eyes shut as he clumsily blotted her face dry, aware of how close he was to her, of his fingers still holding her chin.

There was an instant when she could smell the man-scent of him, the heady combination of clean perspiration, cigarettes and after-shave, mingling with the more intimate, sweet and faintly beery odor of his breath as he whispered questioningly, "Sara?"

Then his lips closed over hers before there was time to answer his tentative question. His hand left her chin, came slowly up to cradle the back of her head, tilted it expertly to the exact angle he needed, and she felt the brim of his hat touch her forehead as he turned his head one way, then the other, barely brushing her lips.

"Sara," he murmured, answering his own query, breathing her name as he kissed her more deliberately this time, and she thrilled at the note of wonder in his voice.

All the same, she wasn't prepared for the sensations exploding within her. His lips were testing, tasting her essence, and her secret places reacted hot and urgently. Her lips parted, and his tongue touched delicately at each corner of her mouth.

His tongue questioned.

Hers answered eagerly.

The tension of the afternoon, with its dramatic birth and successful conclusion, culminated now in heightened emotional awareness for each of them.

For Mitch, holding this woman and kissing her was like some long-forgotten dream. There was a sense of rightness about it, of heady, delicious exploration. But there was also intense and immediate need, the healthy and overwhelming hunger of a man for his woman, compounded by the fiery response her lips and mouth and body offered after those first tentative moments.

His hands slid down and around her hips, drawing her closer, and Sara felt her own arms encircle him, felt the iron-hard muscles tense and quiver as her widespread fingers traced slowly down the long line of his back from broad shoulders to narrow waist.

The feel and smell of him enveloped her senses as intensely as his mouth explored and ravaged and incited her emotions. His embrace was both knowing and yet somehow shy, endearing and yet incendiary, a mixture that sent need snaking hotly through Sarah's abdomen. She moved her head restlessly, wanting the kiss to deepen even more, and neither noticed when his hat fell off and tumbled to the straw at their feet.

Her hips were touching his, and she moved against him sinuously, urgently, intimately, unable to control the impulse. Their breath came in short gasps, and each could feel the other's heartbeat. His lips left her mouth, nibbled their way down and over her chin, and the very tip of his tongue traced a burning trail down her throat to where the pulse thundered.

The growling of a large truck's engine as it made its way slowly down the rutted driveway above the house gradually intruded on the small, heated space they'd created. Sara was the first to move, taking a shaky step backward and nearly stumbling over the forgotten bucket on the floor beside them.

Mitch steadied her, arms firm on her shoulders, and swore under his breath.

"It's Bill. His timing's gone all to hell since he played shortstop years ago," he said as lightly as he could manage, instinctively offering her time and space to deal with what had flamed between them. But his eyes were dark and heavy with unconcealed passion when they met hers.

Her skin was flushed, and she still panted as if she'd been running hard. "I don't, I mean usually...this doesn't happen this way for me...I mean, the first time I..." she stammered, and felt her face flame at the gauche statement.

But he nodded slowly, his gaze holding hers.

"For me either, Sara," he breathed fervently, and she instinctively believed him.

For a long, timeless moment, they stared at each other. Then a slow, wicked twinkle grew in the green depths of Mitch's eyes, and he lowered his tone to a lecherous growl. "Hell, woman, if that's a first effort, think what we can accomplish with some practice. Why, we can probably get real good at this," he drawled, picking up his Stetson and brushing it off, fitting it back on his dark head in one deft movement and giving her a lurid wink from under the brim.

She had to smile at his nonsense, and the smile broadened as she took in the streaks of dirt smearing his cheeks and chin. "You'd better take that hat off again and give your face a wash," Sara suggested.

"I will if you will," he said with a grin. "You've got dust from me all over your neck."

A blush she couldn't control turned her face rosy pink as she remembered in vivid detail just how that had happened, and Mitch had to stop himself from gathering her close all over again.

They were both acceptably clean when they sat down in the kitchen of the farmhouse a little later with their excited hosts.

Carol poured steaming cups of hot coffee for herself and Sara, while the men enjoyed a cold beer after they'd made another trip out to the barns to inspect the colt.

Bill was elated about the foal and obviously pleased to see Mitch again after so many years.

"I followed your career the whole time you were in rodeo, Mitch, felt proud as all get out when you won All Around Cowboy those times. Then we were over at Carol's folks' place one night and we happened to see you on TV, doing commercials, and I figured I'd be boasting about how I knew you when. Thought for sure it'd be Hollywood next stop.''

"No chance," Mitch declared fervently. "That little taste of making a film was more than enough for me. Never saw a bigger waste of people's time than that performance.''

They talked about television commercials and the process of filming for several minutes, and then Bill said awkwardly, "Terrible thing, your brother getting killed that way. We were at the funeral, Carol and I, but with your mom so broke up, we didn't want to intrude, coming over to introduce ourselves. You home for good now?''

Mitch's features seemed to tighten, and his glance fell to the beer can he was holding. His voice was low, the distinctive drawl more pronounced when he answered.

"Looks that way. After Bob died and Mom got so depressed, Pop started talking about selling the ranch and moving to Spokane or some such nonsense. They never thought much of the rodeo life I led—Mom was always scared I'd get hurt, and it got worse during those months after Bob died. She became more and more anxious, and I did some thinking and made the decision to come back and try my hand at a steady job.''

He grinned wryly, but Sara could sense the bitterness behind the words and the smile, just as she had the first night they'd met. Mitch was not entirely content with being home again.

"I always figured I'd come back someday anyhow and be a rancher," Mitch was adding with an attempt at lightness that didn't quite make the grade.

"Professional rodeo's a young man's game, forty's about the limit and I'm thirty-four already. So it just happened sooner rather than later for me, coming back here and set-tling down.'' He swigged the last of the liquid from the can.

''Truth is, Bill, I'd like to do exactly what you're doing someday, only instead of Arabs, I'd breed and train quar-ter horses for rodeo stock.''

Bill nodded eagerly. ''Raising any kind of livestock's a tough racket these days, but Carol and I dreamed of having a breeding stable from the day we got married five years ago. We're carrying a hefty mortgage on both this ranch and on our stock,'' he confided forthrightly, ''but if we can make it through these first couple years, we'll survive.''

He reached an arm over to the chair beside him where Carol sat and draped it across her shoulders. ''Not too many conveniences way out here, but we like it fine, don't we, sweetheart?''

Carol's affection for her husband was patently clear in the loving way she fondled the work-roughened hand cradling her neck and turned her head to give him a smile full of love.

''It's the best sort of life I could ever imagine,'' she said softly.

Sara felt a strange constriction in her chest, not envy, but wistful recognition of something rare and beautiful as she watched Bill and Carol Forgie. Here was a couple with a common dream and a wealth of love for each other that lit-erally shone around them like an aura.

Would she find that kind of relationship someday? Her eyes drifted down to the rounded shape of Carol's preg-nant middle under the blue gingham smock.

How wonderful it must be to carry a child for the man you loved, to create that child from shared passion, bear it, watch it grow and develop.

The memory of a recent kiss made her hotly aware of the man sitting across the table from her, and she glanced at Mitch, lounging casually back on his wooden chair.

She found him watching her intently. It made her uncomfortable because she had the uncanny feeling that he was
reading her thoughts and remembering the intensity of their
embrace just as she was doing.

He raised one eyebrow at her quizzically.

She had the strangest feeling he was asking a silent question.

## *Chapter Four*

Sara was an early riser. She made a practice of arriving at the veterinary clinic before 8:00 a.m.

It was only seven twenty-nine the next morning when she pulled up in front of the old house Doc rented as a clinic and parked on the deserted main street of the small town of Plains.

It was Saturday, which usually meant fewer calls to attend to at outlying farms and more drop-in clients with small-pet problems. It also meant Floyd wouldn't make it in until late, and when he finally did appear, he'd be nursing a monstrous Friday night hangover.

Unlocking the back door of the wood-frame building, she was greeted by a chorus of mewing as the three clinic cats converged on her demanding breakfast. Sylvester, as usual, was firmly in charge of the two females, Tinker and Agnes.

"You disgraceful bully," Sara chided him, crouching down to give each of them a rub and a comforting scratch behind their ears, holding Sylvester firmly back with a foot so the girls could share in the affection.

"I swear it's never dawned on you that you're neutered and ought to be growing fat and lazy," she murmured to the battle-scarred orange reprobate when his turn came. She had to laugh as he hissed menacingly, thinking he was intimidating the females.

"Just wait until the girls find out you're all talk and no action, buster."

Sara opened cans of cat food for them and then filled the coffee maker and set it to brew. Her eyes felt grainy from lack of sleep, but conversely, the same strange sense of exhilaration and ridiculous excitement that had kept her awake most of the night went right on bubbling inside her this morning.

No use pretending it had much to do with the safe delivery of the Forgies' foal, either, she admitted, washing out grimy mugs at the sink and wondering momentarily if Floyd ever cleaned anything up after himself. He methodically used every single mug there was in the cupboard, abandoning them anywhere in the building he happened to be when the last drop of his corrosively strong tea was drained. What in heaven's name must his apartment look like?

She rinsed the dishes with boiling water from the kettle and wondered idly if Mitch was tidy.

Why did every thought pattern she'd had in the past twelve hours revert to Mitch, resulting in a mental image of his tall frame, his unruly, soft dark hair, his green eyes?

Not to mention his kisses. Her imagination stubbornly ended up every time with her being held tightly in his arms.

Leaning her bottom against the sink, she folded her arms across her middle and took stock.

Face it, Wingate, you've allowed yourself to get all dreamy and distracted over this guy. A person would think you'd never been kissed before, the way you're mooning about. Now get your tail in gear, there's work to be done, and Mitch Carter's wasting your time.

Sara hurried into the room off the kitchen that Doc Stone had set aside as an infirmary and set about briskly cleaning out cages and feeding and watering the few patients in residence.

The job was actually Floyd's, but animals couldn't be expected to wait around until his hangover abated enough for him to finally come to work. Sara had taken over their morning care shortly after she'd started working at the clinic.

In the other room, the coffee maker belched loudly, signaling that it was ready just as Sara reached the last cage. The inhabitant was Daisy, a small pampered terrier scheduled for surgery later in the morning. Daisy was to have what her delicate lady owner referred to as "correction of a female problem."

Sara had tacked a more succinct note on the cage. Spay: No Food or Water.

Daisy whined piteously, and Sara paused to talk to the nervous little animal for a moment before going into the kitchen to pour herself her first cup of coffee.

The hot, strong liquid was both comforting and revitalizing, reminding her of that cup of coffee yesterday after the safe delivery of the foal. In an instant, she was back beside Mitch, sitting as she had the evening before in the Forgies' kitchen, drinking coffee and mostly listening as Mitch talked with Bill about hopes and dreams that Sara mentally filed away.

She must have a file going, because every detail was there in her head the instant she relaxed her guard.

Like now. She sighed, stroking Agnes, the witch-black cat that had landed in her lap the instant she sat down. She gave up the effort of shoving Mitch Carter into the corners of her mind.

Instead, she let him take over, sorting through impressions as the coffee in her cup dwindled and the street outside the clinic slowly came alive with early Saturday business.

Mitch had lost a brother he loved, his only brother. He'd reluctantly left a life-style that suited him to come back here and work with a father he obviously didn't get along with.

He hated pigs, loved horses and kept a remarkably cool head in emergencies...probably a trait he'd acquired on the rodeo circuit. Certainly every working day contained an emergency of some sort when you were a rodeo cowboy.

He'd been a hero in his field, yet despite the recognition he'd earned, Mitch was anything but egotistical.

In fact, he was endearingly bashful at times...a wry grin twisted her mouth. And boldly confident at others. At strategic moments, Mitch Carter wasn't backward at all, she remembered with a shy smile that faded abruptly.

He must have had an awful lot of practice over the years, to learn to kiss like that.

She gave herself a mental shake and shoved Agnes off her lap. Here she was, like any spinny teenager, mooning over a kiss in a barnyard.

The phone rang.

"Stone's Veterinary, can I help you?"

"My dog has a terrible case of worms, can I stop by and get something for him? You're that new lady vet, aren't you? Well, Doc Stone always used to give me..."

Back to work, Wingate.

By ten forty-five, she'd answered a dozen phone calls, seen to a puppy's sore paw and given him his shots, and was in the process of advising an eccentric old woman in a black bowler hat that her cat had a diaphragmatic hernia and needed an operation as soon as possible.

The cat's owner, Miss Emily Crenshaw, didn't take the diagnosis well at all. She promptly burst into tears.

"But I haven't any money, Doctor, only my pension, and that barely covers essentials. I can't afford an operation. How much will it cost, Doctor?"

Hurriedly reducing her own fee for the surgery, Sara named the lowest figure she could possibly quote.

Emily still looked profoundly shocked and shook her head sadly, chin quivering and tears dripping down her faded cheeks as she tenderly lifted her nondescript-looking black cat off the examining table and into her arms, shuffling toward the door.

"An operation's out of the question. She'll just have to live with the pain, won't you pet? That's far too expensive for us, isn't it, Queenie? We'll just have to get along without it. Poor old Queenie."

"But the trouble Queenie's having with her breathing will get steadily worse, Miss Crenshaw. You see, she has a tear in her diaphragm, and each time she runs or jumps at all, it enlarges. It could easily prove fatal."

But Miss Crenshaw simply shook her head hopelessly.

Feeling like a money-grubbing, unfeeling monster, Sara watched the pathetic figure clutch her precious cat to her concave bosom and heard herself saying weakly the instant before the door closed behind the cat and its owner, "Look, I'll have a talk with my boss, maybe we can work something out."

Sara knew what they'd work out. She'd do the surgery free and meticulously deduct the cost of the medications she'd used out of her own check.

Emily's tears dried up as if by magic. "Oh, you are a dear girl. When shall I bring Queenie in?"

Resignedly Sara checked her schedule.

"How about Thursday morning at eight? No food or water after six the night before."

When the old woman and the cat were gone, Sara slumped into a chair momentarily, one of her professor's words ringing in her ears.

"Some pet owners will try about anything to trick you into treating their animals free of charge. Be very careful about people who insist they can't pay for treatment. Some may be telling the truth, but an awful lot are shysters."

Surely Emily Crenshaw wouldn't try anything like that. The woman looked penniless. Still, Sara's only major problem with her job had nothing to do with the animals she treated; it was this matter of dealing with their human owners that daunted her. And the poor, pathetic old ones like Miss Crenshaw usually ended up costing her money instead of earning it for her.

Floyd still hadn't turned up by eleven thirty, and neither had Doc Stone. Sara couldn't put off the surgery on Daisy any longer. The dog's owner was planning to take her pet home later that afternoon, and Sara knew there'd be an ugly scene if the operation hadn't been done when the woman arrived.

There'd been a lull in patients for the past half hour, and Sara took advantage of it to prepare the surgery and then sedate the little dog, hoping each moment that Floyd would finally make an appearance.

She'd already begun the operation when her assistant stuck his head in the door of the surgery, eyes as red as the blood she was mopping from the neat incision in Daisy's abdomen. Floyd had an air of importance about him that Sara knew from past experience was simply an act designed to deflect her anger away from its rightful object.

"Mornin', Dr. Sara. Sorry I'm late in, but . . ."

Sara didn't wait for the implausible and imaginative excuse she knew Floyd would come up with.

"I've put the answering machine on the phone—take it off, will you, Floyd?" she interrupted. "And I also have a note on the front door that says back in half an hour, take that down as well. I can't very well do this and monitor the waiting room by myself," she said pointedly. "Do you have any idea what time Doc Stone might be coming in today?" Sara couldn't control the trace of annoyance in her tone.

The senior vet was supposed to have an agreement with her about Saturdays. Sara had offered in the beginning to work from eight until one, and then the older man would take over, leaving her with a precious free afternoon.

Except that in the six weeks she'd been working for him, Doc Stone had appeared to relieve her exactly once.

"Ahhh, me head's not on straight just yet." Floyd was the very essence of abject apology. "Doc said yesterday to tell you he was going out to the horse auction in the valley so he wouldn't be able to come in until late today. It slipped me mind entirely."

Floyd shut the door hastily behind him when she glared at him, and Sara returned her attention to the inert body of the animal on the table, deftly stitching up the incision she'd made and forcing herself not to think about Doc Stone or Floyd at the moment.

Daisy would be just fine in a day or so.

Sara felt pride at a job well done as she tenderly carried the small, limp form back to its cage in the infirmary. She made the dog comfortable before she allowed herself to dwell on Floyd, Doc Stone and the difficult situation she'd landed in by taking this job. It was a subject she'd studiously avoided facing for several weeks.

Stripping off her gloves and the protective green operating smock, she washed in the antiquated bathroom and wandered back into her tiny office, mulling it all over.

The thing was, she'd desperately wanted the job only months before and had been humbly grateful when the acerbic little vet hired her.

She loved the work and the surroundings. It was the people she worked with that she found unreliable at best, irresponsible at worst.

It hadn't taken her a week to figure out that being Doc Stone's assistant actually meant assuming almost full responsibility for his busy rural veterinary practice. As soon as he'd realized she was fully competent—two days after he'd begrudgingly hired her, it seemed to Sara—the wily old vet had all but disappeared, leaving her to run the entire business nearly alone, while paying her the meager salary of an assistant.

But that wasn't the worst of it. Over the past weeks, she'd begun to suspect that it was a blessing her boss didn't do more of the actual vet work. Doc Stone was making mistakes, serious errors in judgment that troubled Sara.

The first indication had been a puzzling emergency call Sara made to a ranch that raised feedlot cattle.

Doc had visited the ranch the day before and used a relatively new drug while medicating the animals' feed. Sara was called because several of the animals were unsteady on their feet and had stopped eating.

Meticulous checking on Sara's part revealed that the cattle were suffering from a drug overdose. Doc had gotten the new drug dosage wrong—fortunately not enough to kill the animals or leave residue in the meat. But for several horrible days, Sara wasn't entirely certain of that.

Because she was able to correct the dosage almost immediately, there was no lasting harm done. The farmer didn't ask exactly what the problem had been; he seemed relieved that she was able to correct it and of course Sara didn't volunteer the fact that Doc had caused it.

He was a respected practitioner in the area. She didn't want to publicly embarrass him.

But then she'd realized that Doc was using old syringes and needles routinely, a practice guaranteed sooner or later to result in contamination of one animal by another.

She'd tried to talk with him about both problems.

He'd been angry and defensive.

"I've been a vet in this area longer than you've lived, young lady," he'd snapped, and his totally bald head had seemed to glow with rage. "No female fresh out of college can tell me how to do my job."

"But what if..."

He was much shorter than Sara, but he'd seemed to tower over her as his raspy voice put her in her place.

"So I make mistakes. Do you think you never will? Does all this fancy new training they give you insure you'll never do anything wrong?"

He was adept at avoiding issues, at making her feel he'd done her a huge favor by hiring her at all, which was probably an honest reflection of how he felt. He'd made it plain from the beginning he'd prefer a male vet, that he was hiring her only because he felt grateful for things Dave Hoffman, her stepfather, had done for him in the past.

Well, she consoled herself, if worse came to worst, she could always leave Plains and find another job somewhere, regardless of how much she was beginning to love this isolated corner of northwestern Montana, or how much she enjoyed being able to be with Mom and Gram...and Dave. Her new stepfather was fast becoming one of her favorite people.

And now, to add to the complications, had Mitch Carter become a factor as well in her desire to stay here? There was no denying the powerful attraction she sensed growing between them.

In a burst of honesty, she admitted that the last thing she wanted at the moment was to pull up stakes and leave Plains.

Which left her right back at the beginning, meekly allowing herself to be bullied by her employer.

It was almost a relief to be interrupted by Floyd, who was sticking his head around the door and screwing his florid features into a sympathetic grimace.

"George Dolinger's on the phone, roarin' like a bull." Floyd snickered at his own wit before adding, "George is always roarin'. He says his prize mare's just been bred by somebody's runaway stallion. He wants her aborted immediately."

Dolinger owned one of the largest ranches in the area. Sara had met him only once and thought him a cantankerous little man.

She sighed and picked up the phone, determined to be both cheerful and businesslike.

"Good morning, Mr. Dolinger...."

A stream of curses made her hold the phone away from her ear.

"... and you can tell Stone I've no intention of allowing some young female still wet behind the ears to mess around with that mare. Now get him out here on the double, you hear me?"

Sara drew a deep breath and tried to curb her rising temper.

"Unfortunately Dr. Stone is not here at the moment, and I'm not certain when he'll be in," she said as calmly as she could.

"What's that supposed to mean?" The man sounded on the verge of a coronary. "I want this animal aborted immediately, and I want Doc Stone to do the job. Is that perfectly clear? So I suggest you send Floyd to find him and give him the message, you hear me?''

"But I've just told you . . .''

Bang. Dial tone. Sara glanced at the receiver, and she was trembling with rage when she finally put it down.

It didn't take much imagination to figure out which particular veterinary procedure she'd delight in performing on Mr. George Dolinger. The man was utterly impossible and rude to boot.

The office door swung open abruptly, and Sara snapped, "Floyd, if that horrible man calls back, you can tell him..."

Sara stopped abruptly in midsentence. Mitch stood in the doorway, grinning at her, brown Stetson tilted firmly down over his forehead, powerful body clad as usual in fresh denims and cotton shirt. His boots showed signs of careful polishing.

"Afternoon, Doc." He ambled casually into the room and turned an old wooden chair around so he could straddle it. He rested his arms on its back and studied her calmly until she felt uncomfortably self-conscious.

"Trusty old Floyd told me to just come straight in and to pass on the message that he's on his way out for lunch." Mitch's voice held a note of sarcasm.

Floyd was a slippery, smooth-talking, lazy rascal, in his estimation. "The guy wouldn't be much help if an ax murderer walked in here straight off the street, would he?" He raised a questioning eyebrow at her, adding, "I figured maybe that's what you and I could do."

"Murder someone with an ax? Boy, have I got just the person in mind." Suddenly the whole day seemed much brighter, and Sara shoved her hair back from her forehead and returned his smile with a dazzling one of her own. To blazes with George Dolinger.

"I was thinking more of lunch, but if you'd like me to murder the man you were swearing about when I came in, maybe we ought to tend to him first."

Sara thought of all the calls needing to be answered, the farm visits that meant driving from one emergency call to another around the countryside if Doc didn't show up.

The least she was entitled to was a lunch break.

It wasn't hard to make up her mind. She got hurriedly to her feet, and before the phone could start ringing again, she switched on the machine.

"Quick," she instructed, going over to the door and peering out to make sure the coast was clear and no one had come into the waiting room during the past few moments. "First, we lock the front door and put the Out to Lunch sign up. Then we sneak out the back way, preferably in disguise."

"Gotcha." Mitch had the sign on the front door before Sara had finished running a quick brush through her hair and hastily adding some pink lipstick. She was absurdly glad she'd worn a pair of quite decent blue cotton pants that morning with a gaily striped knit shirt instead of her usual uniform of T-shirt and blue jeans. There was only one little stain on her knee and hardly any animal hair at all on her shirt.

She looked really presentable, considering the mess she could end up in around here.

"How did you happen to...I mean...what are you doing in town?" she began, but he'd settled his hat firmly on his head and grabbed her hand.

"Silence, woman, till we make our getaway."

He tugged her out the back door, making a great pretense of checking in both directions before he hustled her through the back gate and down the grassy path, and then up the sidewalk to the main street before he answered her question.

"How did I escape from Carter's work farm before sundown, you mean? Well, the tractor had a flat. I'm getting it fixed."

It wasn't the entire truth, and the old man would have a fit when he found out Mitch had chosen a sunny day in June to fix a slow leak they'd lived with for heaven knows how long.

Mitch couldn't have cared less. For the first time in months, he was exactly where he wanted to be. He was walking down a sleepy street in his hometown with a beautiful woman by his side, and he was content.

Hustling along beside him, her fingers still firmly captured in his calloused hand, Sara nodded sagely and teased, "A flat tire, huh? Of course, Mr. Carter, we repair tractor flats all the time at the clinic. How silly of me. Where is the poor injured thing, anyway?"

He shot her a narrow-eyed glance and said deliberately, "Truth is, I wanted to see you, Sara. Somewhere outside of a barn or a pigpen and without an audience."

His forthright declaration shut her up for the entire time it took them to reach the café.

Floyd was cozily jammed into a booth with three of his drinking cronies. He looked comically surprised when Sara paused beside his booth and said in a friendly but firm tone, "I hate to rush you, Floyd, but you're due back at work in ten minutes."

Before he could answer, Sara sailed past and Mitch carefully took a table on the other side of the small café, as far from Floyd as they could get.

"You like steak?" he demanded, removing his hat and ruffling his hair so it stood enchantingly on end above his forehead. Sara had the urge to reach over and smooth it down for him.

"Yes, umm, sure, but I was thinking more of an egg salad sandwich, it's only noon."

The redheaded waitress, who'd been sitting drinking coffee with two friends, got up and wandered nonchalantly toward them.

"We'll have sirloin steak with baked potatoes and all the trimmings, and ice cream on apple pie for dessert. Coffee now," Mitch ordered firmly and rapidly. The waitress smiled warmly at Mitch, her eyes assessing his body and face in minute detail.

"Sure thing, honey," she cooed at him, setting out place mats and glasses of water, cutlery, catsup and steak sauce.

"Mitch, I'm not sure I want all that food," Sara protested weakly. "Besides, I ought to get back to the clinic before too long."

"Surely Doc Stone gives you a lunch hour?" Mitch queried.

"Doc Stone doesn't come around enough to give me my paycheck, never mind time off for lunch," Sara blurted.

Mitch's eyes narrowed. "I wondered if something like that was going on. The other night, Dave Hoffman said he figured the old man was taking advantage of you."

The waitress appeared, pouring them mugs of coffee, making sure there was cream and sugar. The woman also made sure, Sara noticed with amusement, that her breast brushed against Mitch's shoulder whenever she bent over.

He didn't even appear to notice. "The old codger should just retire and be done with it, let somebody else take over and do a proper job."

Sara had to agree. She'd fantasized often enough about buying the practice outright and running it her own way, but that meant coming up with a fair amount of cash. She still owed her sister, Frankie, and Dave as well for their generous contributions toward her education.

Much as she'd love it, it was out of the question.

"I couldn't afford to buy the practice anyway, so I guess I'll just have to put up with things the way they are," she commented.

"Is that what you eventually want from your life, Sara? To own a vet practice of your own?"

All of a sudden, she felt as if she were walking on eggs. She met the level green-eyed gaze and said evenly, "Of course I want that, among other things. That's nearly everyone's dream when they graduate as a vet, to have a practice of their own. It just takes time to be able to afford it, that's all."

"You said, among other things. What other things do you want, exactly?"

The color rose in her cheeks. Mitch Carter was disturbingly forthright, and he was paying close attention to what she said.

"Oh, a husband, a home, a whole pack of kids, dogs, horses, chickens, geese, a cow and a couple of goats for starters," she listed jokingly.

His forehead creased in a frown, his clear green eyes steady on hers, and he wasn't smiling.

"Don't you think that being a full-time vet and being somebody's wife and somebody else's mother might be a tough way to go?"

She shrugged impatiently. "Of course it wouldn't be easy...."

Sara broke off as the waitress set rather wilted salads in front of each of them, fussing unnecessarily with Mitch's.

When the woman had moved reluctantly off, Sara swiftly turned the conversation so that the focus was on him.

"How about you, Mitch? You said yesterday you wanted your own stud farm. Do you really figure you could settle and be happy living that sort of quiet life after the rodeo years?"

His gaze was faintly mocking. "Well, it wouldn't be easy," he parroted smoothly. "Because I'd also want a wife and a passel of kids, dogs, chickens, goats . . . but no pigs. Not one damned porker is ever gonna set foot on any spread of mine," he assured her with a determined twinkle in his eye.

Sara laughed, but she realized he hadn't actually answered her question at all—any more than she'd answered his.

The distant future was an area best left alone for the moment, she decided prudently.

"I've been thinking a lot about your mom, Mitch," she said instead. "I'm going to drop by and see her like I promised, but don't you think it might be good for her to get out more, maybe get a job of some kind? My mom always says that it was having to get out and earn a living for my sister and me that kept her sane after my dad was killed."

The idea had crossed Mitch's mind. There were times when he felt strongly that his mother needed to get out of the house before she drove both him and the old man around the bend worrying about her, before her depression deepened and she was lost to them. A shiver ran down his spine. It was a problem that nagged at him constantly and made him feel helpless.

"It wouldn't be a bad idea, but she'd never do it. Mom's never worked outside the house, she hasn't any training or anything. And Pop would hyperventilate."

Until recently Mitch would have scoffed at the idea of his mother getting a job. She'd been the ideal mother and wife in his opinion, always there for her family, taking care of them, happily making them the focus of her existence.

But she definitely wasn't happy anymore. Something needed changing in her life, and perhaps this golden-haired woman with the glorious smile was on the right track with this idea of a job.

They tangled over some of her opinionated ideas, but still, Sara was a woman he felt comfortable talking with, even about sensitive things like this problem with his mother. Sara cared; it was obvious in her tone, and that caring was evident as well in her way with animals.

His salad bowl was whisked efficiently away, and a steaming platter was slapped down in front of him and then another in front of Sara.

A basket of rolls followed, and a saucer of butter patties. More coffee and more cream.

A different sauce for the steak.

Mitch thoughtfully studied the huge piece of meat, the generous servings of potatoes and carrots and peas. He remembered the ten or twelve pancakes and the three eggs he'd consumed at breakfast that morning and wondered uncertainly if he could do justice to the mound of food in front of him.

Ordering a full-scale meal had seemed one certain way to keep Sara from dashing back to the clinic quickly, but for some reason, being around her curbed his usually ravenous appetite.

He raised his head and found Sara studying her plate as well, but there was pure, unadulterated hunger in the look she was giving the steaming food.

She glanced up and met his eyes a bit sheepishly. "I'm absolutely starving," she confided suddenly. "I had a piece of toast at six-thirty and then just coffee. This looks fantastic."

She began to eat with unself-conscious appetite, and Mitch suddenly felt elated.

There was something wonderful about feeding your hungry woman.

# *Chapter Five*

It was after eight that evening when Sara got home to Bitterroot. She parked the vet truck among the other vehicles in the gravel lot and wearily climbed out, wondering if she even had the energy to make it as far as her tiny log cabin under the pines.

What she wanted more than anything in the world was a steaming hot shower, followed by a leisurely swim in the large pool of naturally warm mineral water that formed the central core of the resort. The muscles in her arms and legs ached with the aftermath of wrestling with animal patients, but as always, it was the strain of dealing with humans that had exhausted her most.

The pool was deserted tonight, and Sara felt ridiculously grateful. Loud voices and bursts of laughter came from the direction of the bar, however, and she stayed away from the lighted windows.

She wasn't up to bantering with anyone, and the rowdy cowboys who sometimes filled the pool as well as the saloon with their raucous shouts and horseplay simply wouldn't understand her reticence.

"Sara?"

The commanding tone came from an open window on the second floor of the rambling main building, and Sara tilted

her head back and smiled up at the figure braced against the
sill.

"Hi, Gram."

Adeline Jeffers took careful stock of her granddaughter,
noting the weary slump of the young shoulders and the less
than buoyant way Sara moved across the cedar planking
that surrounded the pool.

"You eaten any supper yet, girl?" she demanded.

Sara shook her head. "Nope, but I had a huge steak for
lunch, so..."

Gram snorted dismissively. "That's history by now. It's
going on nine at night. A body needs good wholesome food
every five hours in order to keep going properly, especially
when you work so hard. You go wash up, I'll be down in the
kitchen."

The curtain fell back over the window, and Sara didn't
bother making any protest. There wasn't the least bit of use
arguing with Gram, and besides, it was wonderful to have
someone fussing over her.

Still, she cast a wistful eye at the softly bubbling water of
the pool and decided her swim would have to wait until late
tonight, or even early tomorrow morning.

Well, no matter. Tomorrow was Sunday, and with any
luck there'd be time for things like swimming and lying
around.

Maybe. Sick animals were no respecters of Sundays, Sara
reminded herself wearily.

Gram had a hot bowl of homemade vegetable soup and a
thick chicken salad sandwich ready when Sara appeared in
the lodge kitchen half an hour later, clean and damp and
feeling marginally better after a good long scrubbing in her
tiny shower.

There was a cheery yellow place mat set for her at the old round kitchen table, and a tall glass of milk accompanied the food.

"Sit yourself down, girl, and eat." Gram folded her own long, spare frame into a chair across from Sara and poured herself a large mugful of the strong tea she loved. She watched with hawklike attention as Sara dutifully attacked the food, discovering how hungry she was with the first bite. "Mmm, this tastes so good, Gram."

Adeline's changeable gray-green eyes twinkled with spirited humor, and she nodded with satisfaction and waited until the food was gone before demanding, "What kept you out so long on a Saturday, Sara? I thought that old fraud you work for was supposed to take over Saturday afternoons."

Adeline loved hearing about the varied crises in her granddaughter's work, and she was certain that just by listening, she'd learned enough to do a little animal doctoring herself if the need should arise. She refilled her mug and sat avidly forward in her chair, wrinkled cheeks glowing pink, snowy white hair screwed back tight in a bun, knees spread wide as if she might have to leap up at any moment.

"Doc Stone didn't turn up, and I had to go out on an emergency call to a farmer I've met once before and thoroughly detest." Sara shuddered at the recollection.

"Apparently one of his cows spent three days calving. He didn't bother calling us, whined something about knowing it would all turn out okay. Well, the calf was born two days ago, and then the poor cow came down with milk fever. She was already paralyzed by the time her owner called the office this afternoon."

"Did you ever." Gram was a wonderful listener. She fixed Sara with her attentive, green-eyed stare and shook her head in commiseration. "Do a man like that good to be pregnant himself and in labor for three days." She made a disgusted clucking noise with her tongue and waited for Sara to continue.

Sara deliberately included lots of detail when she was telling Gram about these episodes, and she was careful to include technical stuff, which she knew fascinated her inquisitive relation.

"Parturient paresis—that's the technical name for milk fever—isn't hard to treat, you just return the serum calcium level to normal with an injection in the jugular vein, and the results are really spectacular."

Gram nodded as if she knew that all along.

"This poor animal looked nearly dead when I started, and within half an hour she was up on her feet again. But Gram, the awful part was the mess that cow was lying in. You wouldn't believe the stench and filth in the barn. This farmer, Myron Schulty is his name, is too lazy to keep his barns clean, and the poor animals are up to their fetlocks in manure."

Gram grimaced at the vivid image and shook her head with disgust. "What's wrong with people like that? Dead lazy, and probably thinks the world owes him a living, besides. To let a cow suffer for three days and then finally call you on a Saturday afternoon? This Myron Schulty needs a good dressin' down, I'd say."

Gram's narrowed eyes and grim expression silently said that she'd be delighted to get her hands on Mr. Schulty and give him what for.

"I'm just glad he didn't wait till three in the morning, as he usually does." Sara shuddered. "People should have to pass some kind of test before they're allowed to own animals. The poor things are totally at the mercy of their owners."

Gram nodded in understanding. "I've always thought the same thing exactly about having children. Some people just aren't fit to raise young uns, and they ought to have to take out a license afore they're allowed to get pregnant."

Gram's theories made perfect sense, even though most of them would cause rioting in the streets if they were put into effect.

"I met a couple who are going to make great parents," Sara confided on a more cheerful note, going on to tell Gram all the details about the Forgies and their beautiful ranch, realizing only when she was well into the story of the birth of the Forgies' foal that she was going to have to mention Mitch.

"...So just when I figured for sure it was dead, the foal came popping out like a stuck cork, right into... umm...actually, Mitch Carter had stopped by, and he was helping me, and right away, I started trying to get the little thing to breathe...."

Sara should have known better. Gram had an uncanny built-in detector that signaled when either of her granddaughters was trying to lead her away from what she sensed was a key issue.

"That was the same Carter boy who invited you for supper with his family the other night, wasn't it?"

Sara had to smile at Mitch being called a boy.

"Yes, Gram. And I had lunch with him in town today, as well." Might as well get all the facts out up front, because Gram would discover them anyway. J. Edgar Hoover had missed out on a good thing, not hiring Gram.

"He the one ordered you the steak?"

Sara nodded, hoping her cheeks weren't really as warm-looking as they felt.

"Must be a good sensible boy, this Mitch, getting some nourishment down you for a change. Ask him home for a meal, why don't you. It'd be a treat to have a hungry young man to cook for besides Dave. Goodness knows you and your mam don't eat enough to make it worth dirtying pots."

In another minute, Gram would be phoning Mitch herself and inviting him over so she could put him through a major inspection, Sara suspected uneasily.

"Actually, I wanted to talk to you about Mrs. Carter, Gram. Ruth, her name is, and . . ." Sara quickly related the tragic story of Bob Carter's death, and of how it had affected Mitch's mother.

"I wondered if maybe you and Mom would come along some afternoon and we'll go out and visit her. She needs people around. I think she's alone out there too much."

Gram's eyes were soft with compassion, but her voice was full of firm conviction. "I always said, best thing for a sore heart is busy hands. See if that old tyrant of a boss of yours will condescend to working Thursday afternoon and letting you off. He owes you for today anyhow, and we'll take a drive out. Poor woman, nothing worse than losing a child. I never had to go through that, thank the Lord." Gram got up in one dynamic motion, poured herself fresh hot tea and plunked a plate of sugar cookies in front of Sara.

"Eat, girl, get some meat on those bones of yours. And," she went on without missing a beat, "now tell me more about this Mitch Carter you're sweet on. He ever been married?"

An hour later, feeling full of food and dazedly empty of secrets, Sara walked toward her cabin, a rueful smile playing across her features.

Being away at school had obviously dulled her wits. She and Frankie had perfected a few methods over the years for steering Gram on detours around their romances . . . but Sara hadn't managed at all well tonight. Gram now knew just about as much about Mitch as Sara did, with the exception of how it felt to be kissed by him.

And Gram probably could reconstruct even that without any problems at all.

THE SOUND OF A JAY loudly scolding woke Sara the next morning. It was half past eight, and the sun was filling her window with golden warmth. Pulling on jogging shorts, a top and her well-worn runners, she ran through the summer woods for half an hour, loving the feeling of leisure and freedom, the good sensation that loping along brought to her muscles.

After a shower, she slid into her bikini and dove into the bubbling mineral pool for the swim she'd promised herself the night before, and she'd just climbed out when her mother's voice called from the lodge.

"Morning, dear." The sun glinted off of Jennie's golden-brown hair. Sara had inherited that hair, but her mother was much smaller and more rounded than Sara, dainty and full-figured, feminine and youthful this morning in her violet cotton sundress.

How many times during her growing-up years had Sara wished fervently that she'd inherited Jennie's full-breasted, curvaceous figure instead of the tall, muscular shape she'd gotten instead?

Sara toweled off that rangy body, realizing that somewhere along the way she'd come to terms with herself, learned to appreciate her own personal build.

Certainly Mitch seemed to like the way she was put together.

The thought came automatically, the way thoughts of Mitch had a habit of doing.

"Breakfast in fifteen minutes, Sara. Gram's made sourdough pancakes," Jennie announced, and Sara waved an arm at her mother and sprinted to her cabin for still another shower and a vigorous shampoo to rinse the mineral water from her hair.

Gram was at her creative best this morning. When Sara hurried in a few moments later, there was a golden stack of fluffy cakes waiting on the table in the dining room, with pots of butter, pure maple syrup and sizzling platters of eggs, sausage and bacon, plus plenty of juice and coffee.

Sara looked at the smiling faces seated around the table and felt a thrill of pure pleasure at being with her family after years of living in school dorms or sharing tiny cramped rooms with strangers.

"Come sit here," her stepfather boomed, indicating a chair beside him, and Sara slid into it, thinking with a pang that the only thing that could possibly make the scene even better would be having her sister Frankie here, occupying a chair across from her and sharing a delighted wink now and then over one of Gram's more outrageous statements.

As if her mother had read her mind, Jennie said at that very moment, "I really wish Frankie would come home for a visit, I'm lonesome for her. She hasn't seen Bitterroot yet or had a chance to really get to know you, Dave."

Jennie's gaze went fondly to her husband, and Dave met it with open adoration in his eyes. He was a big man, well over six foot three, powerfully muscular. Hard work had kept him from gaining excess weight. His thick black hair was threaded generously with silver, and there were deeply grooved smile lines around his sparkling brown eyes.

How great it was for her mother to have found love and companionship with this man after so many years of being alone and struggling to raise her daughters, Sara mused. And Dave was one of the kindest, most generous stepfathers a woman could have. Her final year at school had been easier than all the rest, simply because Dave had insisted on sending her a generous check every month. That had allowed her to put all her energies into studying, instead of exhausting herself juggling the numerous part-time jobs she'd usually taken to support herself.

"I tried to phone Frankie the other night, but I had to leave a message with an answering service. I hope she calls back today while I'm home," Sara remarked to her mother. She'd wanted to touch base with her sister, but mostly she'd wanted to hear what Frankie had to say about Mitch Carter, Sara admitted to herself a trifle guiltily.

Frankie kept an apartment in Coeur d'Alene, Idaho, as home base, but in the summer months when rodeo season was at its peak, she was on the go, traveling from one rodeo to the next.

"What was all that hollerin' and cussin' I heard from downstairs just after midnight?" Gram sat down beside Sara and raised a questioning eyebrow at Dave.

"Oh, just a couple of the young guys from the saloon got in an argument. I had to help them out the door," Dave explained with admirable understatement.

Jennie and Gram exchanged a telling glance, and Dave forked up a huge bite of breakfast, chewed and swallowed before he went on, "I know, you've both been telling me that it's past time we made a few changes here at Bitterroot, and I agree. I sure don't want to spend my life wrestling young bucks half my age out of the tavern every Friday and Saturday night. Trouble is, at the moment the saloon earns us a fair chunk of the money that keeps this place operating, so we've got to be cautious about making drastic changes."

"Wasn't Bitterroot once a famous spa, Dave? Mom told me some of its history, and I remember she said it attracted people from all over the world at one time. Didn't your grandfather build the whole thing himself?"

Dave nodded, and Sara listened closely as he filled in details for her.

Jennie had explained that the sprawling hundred-acre holding that comprised Bitterroot had been in the Hoffman family for years, consisting of ninety acres of timbered wilderness and ten acres of half-cleared, half-developed land surrounding the sturdy, spacious two-story log building. The main floor consisted of the tavern, several bathrooms, the huge old-fashioned kitchen with wrap-around enclosed porches, plus the combined living-dining room where they now sat, and there were bedrooms upstairs.

Outside were seven rustic little cabins scattered across the property, arranged more or less in a wide circle around the large central pool of naturally warm mineral water that formed the central core of the area.

"Grampa Hoffman was a surveyor for the railroad in the late 1800s," Dave explained, settling back in his chair and lighting a pipe to enjoy with his coffee. They'd all consumed so much food no one felt like moving.

"He heard about the mineral springs from an old Indian. He came to have a look and fell in love with the place. The sparkling water flowed constantly, just as it still does, maintaining a steady eighty-six-degree temperature. Anyway, he right away saw the commercial potential of such a natural phenomenon, and he bought the land, dug out the original water hole and cemented in the swimming pool. He put up all the buildings and even built much of the furniture, and then he wrote letters to people he knew, craftily inviting them to come and spend a holiday, free of charge. He installed bathtubs in each of the upstairs bedrooms here, so the modest Victorian ladies could enjoy the mineral water in absolute privacy. He'd ingeniously and practically piped the hot water to each of the buildings for both heating and plumbing purposes.''

Dave drew deeply on his pipe and expelled a cloud of fragrant smoke. "He was smart enough to hire the best cook he could find—prob'ly not as good as you, Adeline, but good enough so everybody who came raved about the food.''

Gram looked pleased as anything with the compliment, and Sara decided that Dave had inherited a great deal of his own grandfather's cleverness.

She looked around with new interest at the room they were sitting in. Like all the other rooms in the central lodge, its high-beamed log ceilings and handmade furniture supplied an authentic rustic charm.

For years, Bitterroot enjoyed a popularity that made Dave's grandfather a wealthy man. But ironically, that wealth turned his only son into a ne'er-do-well, an irresponsible playboy who had no interest whatsoever in the prosperous resort where visitors from all over came to bathe and relax.

"When Grampa Hoffman died and my father took over," Dave admitted with rueful candor, "he quickly leased the place out, moved to Seattle and lived off the money. Without supervision and with the ever-dwindling profits going to pay his drinking and gambling debts, Bitterroot soon disintegrated."

By the time the property passed to him, Dave had had to work day and night, fixing roofs and drains and modernizing, generally making the place livable once more. But apart from the saloon trade, Bitterroot did little business.

The tavern had become a wide-open, rip-snorting boozing center for the rowdy young cowboys and die-hard drinkers in the area, which successfully discouraged any family trade that might have resulted from renting the cabins.

"The first thing we ought to do," Adeline announced firmly, "is start serving good home-cooked food. A lot of the men who drink in the tavern would buy a plate of dinner if it were offered," she insisted, "and with a square meal under their belts, they'd have lots less room for booze."

Jennie nodded agreement, looking around the large room thoughtfully. She and Gram had already put up crisp white curtains on all the windows, and flowering plants in bright pots or wicker holders created splashes of color against the weathered old log walls.

"This used to be a public dining room," she mused. "It wouldn't take much to turn it into one again. All the tables and chairs are stacked out in a shed. D'you think people would start coming if we started a restaurant? What d'you think, Sara?"

"There's nowhere young couples can go around here and have an evening out, with dinner and maybe dancing, unless they drive for hours and want to spend a fortune," Sara said after a moment's contemplation, thinking of Bill and Carol Forgie, or maybe herself and Mitch.

"It might take a while to catch on, but I think a restaurant would be a great idea. I'll bet people from farther away would start coming again for weekends, bringing their kids for a swim in the hot springs, if you got a reputation for good food, did some advertising."

"That kitchen needs work, if we're gonna start cooking for more than six or eight people," Gram said practically. "The stove is older than I am and way more cantankerous and that's goin' some. But the place is plenty roomy, and the walk-in cooler works fine...."

For over an hour, excitement grew as ideas and plans evolved. The necessary changes would be expensive, but they didn't all have to be done at once. Gram and Jennie would start serving meals on a small scale at first and gauge the rest from the response.

"We'll have a limited menu, maybe a choice of two main dishes, and that way it won't get too complicated," Jennie was planning.

Gram snorted. "The heck with any choice. That's what's the matter with eating places today. A body gets worn-out just readin' the dern menu, figurin' out what in tarnation he wants. We'll serve the kind of meals people used to eat back when I was a girl, good hearty dishes with plenty of home-made bread and greens, maybe give 'em a choice for dessert of pie or cake or pudding, if they need to make choices."

Jennie and Adeline got into a heavy discussion about recipes at that point, and Dave was busily making calculations on several paper napkins. Sara got up quietly and began clearing the table.

She was in the kitchen, putting dishes in the old enamel sink and covering them with hot soapy water when the telephone rang.

Drying her hands on a towel, she picked up the receiver, resigned to the fact that it would be some veterinary emergency that would use up the rest of her Sunday.

"Sara?"

The deep male voice was unmistakable. It was Mitch, and her heartbeat suddenly picked up speed. They went on for several minutes about what a nice day it was, and then Mitch cleared his throat and said nonchalantly, "I have to ride out to the west pasture this afternoon and check on some calves. I wondered if you'd care to come along? I'll drive in and pick you up."

"I'd like that, but why don't I just drive out there and meet you? It'd be quicker that way." It would also get her away from the telephone fast and the chance of an emergency that could ruin their plans.

Mitch agreed, and Sara hurried in to tell her family where she was going.

"Why don't you bring that young man home with you for supper tonight?" Gram was determined to check Mitch out, Sara knew.

"I'll ask him, Gram. See you later."

She was wearing fresh, faded jeans and a scoop-necked red T-shirt with short sleeves. She hurriedly pulled a brush through her curly hair, deciding to leave it loose on her neck. A touch of lipstick and mascara, and she hurried out to her car, a decidedly decrepit old Chevy.

The drive out to the Carter ranch passed quickly, and when she drove into the yard, she could see Mitch, a saddled horse on either side of him, walking up from the barns.

Sara pulled to a stop and swallowed hard, eyeing the animals Mitch was leading toward her.

When he'd suggested a ride, she'd assumed he meant in a truck.

She knew the name and location of every single muscle and bone, every organ and sinew in a horse, and she loved working with the animals. She just didn't enjoy getting up on their backs.

In fact, she'd only been on a horse twice in her entire life, and neither occasion was memorable.

Mitch, with a crooked smile that forced an answering smile from Sara, wrapped the reins around a post and came striding over to open the car door.

The first thing he said was, "Where're your hat and boots?"

Sara remembered the oversize gum boots in the trunk, considered them for all of a second and discarded the idea.

"I, umm, actually, I don't have any real riding boots, Mitch. Won't my sandals do?"

He studied the leather soles and the assorted stylish straps on her bare feet, pushed his hat back and slowly shook his head.

"Nope," he said shortly.

Might as well get the whole truth out at once, Sara decided. Maybe, she thought hopefully, he'd decide they'd better take the truck after all.

"I don't own a cowboy hat, either," she announced.

"No problem," he announced cheerfully. "I think Ma's got boots and a hat you can borrow." He reached out and took her arm, tugging her out of the car. "C'mon," he urged, laugh lines crinkling around his green eyes as he looked at her and caught the wary look she was giving the horses. "Ma's been making us a lunch. We'll just get you outfitted and be on our way. You do know how to ride, don't you, Sara?"

She gave him a haughty look.

"Well, do you?" he insisted, one thick eyebrow tilted inquiringly, and she felt a giggle bubbling up as she looked him straight in the eye and said "Me? Know how to ride? Absolutely . . . not."

"But you're a vet, you learned all about horses."

Sara shrugged, spreading her hands as if to say, so what?

"Nobody thought of teaching us how to ride them. Frankie tried once but she gave it up as a hopeless job."

Mitch tilted his head back and started to laugh, and she laughed with him. The old dog came out of the shed and started to bark, and one of the horses whinnied.

They were still laughing as they went in the kitchen door, and Ruth looked up from wrapping sandwiches and had to smile at them.

HALF AN HOUR LATER, Sara was on the back of a big, gentle gelding named Steamboat, doing her best to steer the animal in the general direction of Mitch and his horse, a good fifty yards ahead of her.

She was feeling out of her element in general and a very long way from the ground in particular. She had Ruth's well-worn brown Stetson on her head and a pair of Wilson's worn cowboy boots on her feet because Ruth's had been too small.

Sara felt wicked pleasure at wearing Wilson's boots. All sorts of smart comments occurred to her about having no problem filling his shoes, none of which she'd probably ever get a chance to use on Mitch's father. But it was nice to have a few things in reserve, she mused, doing her best to stay upright in the saddle.

Mitch had patiently unsaddled the sprightly filly he'd originally outfitted for Sara and saddled Steamboat, with the laconic comment that old Steamboat moved slowly, easily and had never shown the slightest sign of temperament.

Or speed, for that matter.

In fact, Mitch said with a straight face, Steamboat had a tendency to go to sleep while being ridden.

That suited Sara just fine. If she was fated to break her neck, she'd just as soon not do it falling from the back of a horse, thank you.

"Hurry up, you two," Mitch called over his shoulder, and Steamboat imperceptibly increased his measured gait politely to catch up to the other horse, making Sara feel even more insecure.

She tightened her hold on the reins and Steamboat obligingly went back into slow motion. Another ten minutes went by and now Mitch was several hundred yards ahead, reining his horse in constantly just to keep her in sight.

"Kick him in the ribs, Doc. Get him to move or this is going to take us all week," Mitch was hollering impatiently, and Sara gave Steamboat the gentlest of nudges with the heels of Wilson's boots.

Maybe, Sara thought later, the complacent horse actually had fallen sound asleep and her halfhearted kick had given him a nasty start, because without any warning at all, Steamboat went into high gear.

He accelerated from an amble to a gallop without any in-between, and Sara promptly dropped the reins and grabbed the saddle horn. In her alarm, she must have brought her boots hard into Steamboat's sides, and that unnerved the poor gelding enough to spur him into even greater effort.

With absolutely no grace or dignity, Sara clutched whatever parts of the horse she could and screamed bloody murder, passing an astounded Mitch at what amounted to a full gallop.

Her hat blew off, and she felt herself begin the inevitable slide that was going to take her down to the ground, now rushing past Steamboat's hooves at an alarming rate.

# Chapter Six

Sara was aware that poor Steamboat was actually making a
desperate effort to keep her in the saddle; each time she
lurched to the side, Steamboat would correct to the other
side, obviously trying his embarrassed best to stop Sara
from falling off.

After the first moment of utter astonishment, Mitch and
his horse moved like a well-oiled unit, with all the technique of countless rodeo rescues at their command.

Mitch effortlessly drew abreast of Steamboat's neck until the horses were nearly touching. With one long arm, he
then scooped Sara off of Steamboat's back and onto his lap,
holding her firmly against him.

And Sara could feel him laughing even before she looped
her arms gratefully around him and hung on as Misty
slowed and then stopped.

Steamboat stopped nearby as well, gave them a disgusted
look and then calmly dipped his head and took a mouthful
of grass.

"What the..." Mitch could hardly talk for laughing.
"What the hell did you do to him? I've never seen that horse
anything but comatose, and all of a sudden, he's going past
me like the favorite at the Kentucky Derby."

Sara didn't think it was quite that funny. "You said to kick him, so I did," she explained in an aggrieved tone. "But not very hard."

She was becoming more aware every minute of being held extremely close to Mitch's warm body, of his arms cradling her against him.

He didn't make the slightest effort to release her, even though Misty was standing stock-still by now. Sara was sprawled off balance across Mitch and the horse, but his arms made her feel totally secure.

"I, umm, I lost your mother's hat back there," she managed to say in a shaky voice.

"We'll find it, don't worry." The laughter was fading from his voice, replaced with a husky intensity that made Sara's heart pound.

Her head was cradled snugly in the curve of his arm and chest. Her legs dangled down Misty's side, one hip pressed against Mitch. Her arm was snaked around his torso, her fingers touching the hard muscles on his back, and his long, blue-jeaned leg was under both of hers.

Tension grew between them, and she struggled to sit up straighter.

"Don't move," he begged softly. "Stay close to me for a minute, Doc."

He tipped his head, and his eyes traced the line of her soft lips for a long, breathless moment. The intense green seemed to grow smoky and opaque. He moved his hand up, cupping her head with his fingers, lowering his mouth slowly until his lips closed over hers. His hat got in the way, and he nudged it off, letting it fall in the soft grass where Misty was grazing.

He kissed her as if they had all the time in the world. He explored her mouth leisurely with lips and tongue, inviting her to follow the path he set. The movements of the horse beneath them made him clasp her even tighter in his embrace, and when Sara answered his kiss with passion of her own, she felt his breathing quicken, his body grow tense against her.

Sara was aware of the strong, hot sunlight creating a scarlet blur inside her closed eyelids, of the slight breeze that ruffled Mitch's hair so that it tickled softly on her forehead. She felt encompassed by the rock-hard strength and security of his arms and his clean-smelling body, but most of all, she was aware of his lips on hers, of the way her body ached to be even closer to him.

Misty made an impatient, sudden movement, and they drew reluctantly apart, their breathing equally labored.

"The back of a horse isn't the ideal spot for this, is it?" he said raggedly as she squirmed, aware all of a sudden of the way the saddle was digging into her buttock.

She sat up straighter, raised an eyebrow and smiled at him. "Oh, I don't know. It feels pretty romantic to me, this getting rescued from the back of a bronco by a handsome cowboy."

The joking banter bridged the intensity of the moment, allowing them both time to still the emotions raging within them. After a moment, Mitch helped her slide down from Misty's back.

He retrieved first his hat and then her horse. Soon, with a few valuable pointers, Sara was once again on Steamboat, Stetson firmly pulled down toward her nose in a parody of the way Mitch wore his.

This time, she nudged Steamboat into a gentle trot, and by the time they reached the rambling upper meadow with its grove of willows clustered around a rushing stream, Sara felt that although she wasn't quite Olympic riding material yet, at least she felt more at home on Steamboat than she would have thought possible a few hours earlier.

Steamboat ambled over near the water, turned his head back and gave Sara a pained look that obviously indicated it might be nice if she got off and let a poor horse have a drink in peace. She slid to the ground, feeling as if her legs had turned to jelly.

"Feel like a sandwich?"

Mitch had dismounted as well, pulling from his saddle-bag the carefully packaged bags of lunch Ruth had prepared and handing them to Sara.

They ate sitting on the grass beside the creek, sharing the thermos of iced tea.

Swallowing the last of a cheese-and-tomato sandwich prepared with Ruth's homemade bread, Sara sighed deeply.

"This is the first time since I started working for Doc Stone that I've managed to lose the feeling that the phone is about to ring any minute and I'll have to leave," she said. "This was such a good idea, Mitch."

He was a few feet away, sitting with his back against a stump, unwrapping the third package of sandwiches. He glanced over at her, humor sparkling in his eyes.

"For a while there, I had my doubts about it," he teased. "I figure Steamboat did, too, but with some practice, that horse'll make a cowpoke out of you yet."

She wrinkled her nose at his teasing, and he studied her, sitting with her long legs folded under her and her shining hair wild and ruffled by the breeze. In spite of the hat, her nose was sunburned and a few freckles had sprouted.

Tenderness welled inside of him.

"I feel such a fool, not knowing how to ride," she said.

"Truth is, Sara," he admitted gruffly, "you're so good at your job, you sort of scare a guy. It was a relief to find out there're some things you can't do."

She had a way of looking at him, straight on, with none of the coyness some women affected, no false denials or phony modesty.

"I imagine you're just as good at your job as I am at mine." She settled herself more comfortably. "Tell me what it's like, being a rancher, Mitch. I see the problems ranchers have with their stock, but I don't actually have much idea how you spend your days."

He gave her a long, unfathomable glance and then looked away from her, squinting out across the meadow to where, in the far distance, a small herd of cattle grazed.

Rancher, she'd labeled him, and as always, it stuck in his throat.

Well, wasn't that what he was?

Some deep rebellion inside of him still wanted to deny it. He still never thought of himself as a rancher.

If he were asked what he was, he'd automatically say rodeo rider, wouldn't he?

How did a man make the transition, how did a man learn to live with the fact that he was sentenced to one sort of life when his body and soul still wanted to do something else? And increasingly often, he felt trapped.

It made him angry, deep in his gut, that sense of unrest, and the anger made him ashamed. After all, he wasn't a kid anymore, longing for excitement and travel. He'd had that, and he ought to be content now with this new life that fate had arranged for him.

Trouble was, he wasn't. Content.

His glance went back to Sara, sitting motionless, watching him with those thoughtful gray eyes and waiting patiently for him to get around to answering her.

Knowing her was making it a little easier, and also a little harder, maybe. The feelings she stirred in him weren't the temporary ones he was used to feeling for women he'd met on the circuit.

Sara was permanence, a house and kids and deep roots in one place.

All the things he wasn't sure yet that he wanted.

Except that he knew he wanted Sara.

He reached in the breast pocket of his shirt and drew out the package of cigarettes he kept there, noting how crumpled they were and remembering how she'd felt, helpless in his arms, crushed tight against his chest.

His body surged at the memory, and he quickly shifted to a different position, expertly shaking one cigarette from the pack and extracting it smoothly with his lips.

He found a match and lit it with a thumbnail, automatically cupping a hand around the blaze, drawing the smoke into his lungs and savoring it before he expelled it in a cloud the breeze drew up over their heads and away.

"Describe the life of a rancher. Well, let's see."

His gaze went back to the cattle, and he began awkwardly trying to tell her what ranching was like, drawing scanty word pictures for her, unaccustomed to describing things instead of simply doing them.

"Ranchers used to be cattlemen, plain and simple," he began slowly. "That's changed now, because the market for beef has dropped, so ranchers like my father have to get into other stock, like those damned pigs, or maybe sheep."

Sara reached over to fill his cup with more iced tea, and he thought how soft her skin had felt to his lips back there on the trail.

"Ranching's one big gamble, I guess," he went on. "A rancher's entirely his own boss, and whether he makes it or not depends a lot on how well he knows his job. It's not a thing a man learns in any school, it's something you pick up by living the life, something a man teaches his sons over years and years. Pop used to put Bob and me on the saddle in front of him and take us out on cattle drives when we could barely walk."

Funny, he'd forgotten Wilson doing that until right now. It was hard to remember the old man being anything but cantankerous, the way he was mostly... but there had been a time when Mitch had been a boy that he figured his father was the next thing to God.

"But you didn't really want to be a rancher, did you?" Sara asked quietly. "I remember you saying that your brother liked it, not you."

Mitch took another long drag on his cigarette and shrugged.

"Guess a man can't always spend his whole life doing just what he wants to do. Like Pop keeps saying, rodeo isn't a lifelong profession, anyway. So sooner or later, I'd have had to come back here. A man has to work at something, and I'm not trained for brain surgery."

Her quick smile came and went.

"Would you have come back, Mitch? Or would you have bought a small place of your own and started a stud farm, maybe?"

She'd been listening when he spouted off to Bill Forgie, he remembered. And obviously, she'd filed away everything he'd said. It comforted and annoyed him both, that she understood how he felt and what his dreams were. He wasn't used to sharing his thoughts with anyone.

He shrugged noncommittally. "Might still do that someday. Not right now, of course. It takes all my time to keep up with the work around here. Today, for example. This is fun, having you with me, but I'd have had to ride up here whether you came along or not, whether or not it's Sunday. Branding season's coming up, and it's important to know how many yearlings we've got, where they are, and what shape they're in before we start rounding them up.''

"So you have to know all the places they might be on your land,'' she surmised, and Mitch smiled wryly.

"Not just where they are, but how much water there is, where it is, how long the vegetation in an area will sustain a cow, what other animals are around, maybe endangering your cattle. For instance—'' he gestured with the hand holding his cigarette ''—there's a pack of coyotes hanging around here, you can see their signs all over the place. They won't bother anything but a newborn or an animal that's really sick, but a timber wolf would. A good rancher keeps a close eye on wildlife sign.''

Sara questioned, and he patiently answered, describing the particular work each season brought for the rancher, the routine of fencing, haying, seeding, planting and harvest, along with the constant work the stock created.

"It doesn't sound as if you get much more time off than I manage to,'' she sighed at last, and Mitch shook his head.

"Nope, probably not. You got old Doc Stone to answer to, and I've got Pop.'' He shook his head. "Ask me, one of 'em's about as bad as the other.''

"You don't get along too well with your father?'' Sara ventured.

Mitch frowned and shook his head. "The old man's set in his ways, and I don't always think his methods of doing things are any better than mine. We end up having a few words now and then.''

That was the understatement of the year. Down and out shouting fits described the situation better, Mitch admitted to himself. The old man just had a way of worming under his skin, no matter what good intentions Mitch had each morning.

"Maybe anger's just his way of dealing with your brother's death," Sara suggested hesitantly. "I've heard my mom say that after my dad was killed in the mines, she was angry inside for a long time."

Mitch hadn't thought about it that way. Maybe Sara was right, but it didn't make Wilson any easier to be around, whatever the reason for his bad temper. And Mitch had no intention, either, of spending this precious afternoon with Sara analyzing his father.

He reached out and grabbed her hands and tugged her to her feet. "C'mon, let's take a walk along the creek."

Willows grew on either side of the rushing stream, and birds seemed to be everywhere, swooping and calling to one another. The wide Montana sky above them was cloudless, piercingly blue, and the air smelled freshly washed.

Mitch clasped Sara's hand in his own, leading the way down a faint trail that wandered carelessly along the water's edge.

"Bob and I used to come down here fishing when we were kids," Mitch reminisced. "We hardly ever caught anything, but Mom always packed us a big lunch, and it felt like a holiday somehow."

"It feels that way today, too," Sara said softly. "Like a holiday."

He slid an arm around her shoulders, nestling her against his side, feeling desire and contentment combine in a heady confusion of feeling.

He wanted her, the most simple, direct way a man could want a woman, but there was much more to it than that. It amazed him that for the first time in his life, sexual desire was something he was willing to postpone temporarily.

He wanted to know so much more about her than just how her body felt when his possessed it, although that urge was almost overwhelming; he desired her fiercely. But first, he wanted to understand the person inside that body, get to know the many different faces of Sara.

For the first time, he was greedy not about sex, but about something much less tangible. He wanted to capture the essence of her mind, find out how and why she thought and felt as she did, learn the patterns of her habits and strengths, get to know the endearing fabric of her weaknesses.

And he didn't have a clue how to start. Seduction was one thing; getting her to confide in him was quite another.

"Too bad I didn't bring some fishing gear today, we could have tried our luck," he finally commented after several silent moments. He peered down into the stream. "Did you and Frankie ever go fishing when you were kids?"

Sara shook her head. "Growing up in a female household doesn't do much for your fishing skills," she said with a wry laugh. "We learned to sew, and Gram taught us how to cook, but we're not great outdoors. Although I do remember once when Mom decided to take us camping, and we ended up scared out of our wits because Frankie was sure she heard a bear. We spent the night in the car with all the doors locked."

They traded stories of their childhood and growing-up years as they ambled contentedly along the winding path. An hour passed and felt like several minutes. At last the position of the sun overhead alerted Mitch to the work he had to do, and reluctantly, he turned them back in the direction of the horses.

They mounted, and for another hour rode in what seemed a haphazard fashion over the surrounding meadows, locating cows with calves that had become separated from the main herds and gently urging them back with the group. Sara was becoming more familiar with riding and controlling her mount, and although she wasn't a great help to Mitch, she felt she didn't hold him back too badly either.

"Want a drink before we start back to the ranch?" Mitch called at last, and Sara gratefully climbed off Steamboat in a spot where the stream widened and poplars formed a shady grove.

She knelt and scooped water into the cup Mitch unearthed from the lunch pack and drank, then filled it again and reached up to hand it to him.

He watched her kneeling at his feet, naturally graceful, with her shining, tangled hair spilling out from under the soft-brimmed hat and her snug jeans outlining her curving thighs and buttocks, and all the tamped desire that had been building during the past hours seemed suddenly to ignite in a burning knot of fire in his body.

Instead of taking the cup she proffered, he pulled her to her feet, heedlessly spilling the water in the process. But neither of them noticed, because suddenly there was an electricity between them, a keen awareness that had smoldered just under the surface all day.

She came up slowly, already within the circle of his arms, and before she had time to wonder what would come next, his lips were on hers.

There wasn't any exploration this time or any holding back. The kiss was deep and drugging, conveying immediately the passionate wanting Mitch could no longer control, and with lips and open mouth and pillaging tongue, he conveyed that need.

Sara's lips were warm and eager under his. The restraint he'd practiced disappeared entirely as the sweetness of her mouth and the feel of her body against him roused every primitive urge.

Her hat fell off, and without interrupting the kiss, he reached up an impatient hand and sent his own hat spinning after hers.

She arched against him and he kissed her throat, the hollow under her jaw, the soft pulsing center at the base of her neck.

"Mitch...oh, Mitch," she breathed as his lips traveled back up her face, capturing her lips once again, and desire spilled like hot liquid through him.

His hands cupped her breasts, and he felt the nipples harden. He groaned and wrapped his arms around her, molding her hips tightly against him, and his arms slid around her shoulders and under her knees.

The next moment, she was lying full-length in the soft grass, and Mitch was beside her, holding her, pressing the entire length of his body against her in delicious rhythmic movements that matched the quickening thrusts of his tongue as he kissed her.

"Mitch...Mitch, stop."

Her words finally penetrated the surging wave of desire he was riding. With an effort that seemed superhuman, he rolled away from her, panting hard, staring up into the blue heavens and waiting for the fire to die enough so he could think, or talk.

Finally he rolled his head in the grass, facing her, and her gray troubled eyes met his.

"I want you, Mitch," she said forthrightly. "I'm not teasing or playing games here." She struggled to a sitting position, and after a moment, he did, too.

"It's just that making love is an awfully big commitment as far as I'm concerned. A two-way commitment. And I'm not sure I'm ready, or have enough time in my days for that right now."

She paused and drew her knees up, resting her arms on them, head down. "I'm not sure you do, either," she finished softly. She sounded miserable, and Mitch reached out a hand and circled her wrist.

"Sara, it's okay. If you need time, that's fine with me." He caught her chin in his fingers and forced her to look at him, adding deliberately, "I know what you're saying about commitment." He swallowed, because the rest of what he had to tell her was difficult for him to put into words. "Sara, this thing between us. I want you to know that it's not just . . ." He searched for a word, and the only one he could think of sounded biblical and dramatic, but he used it, anyway. "It's not just lust with me. This scares the living hell out of me," he finally blurted in a rush, "but I think I'm falling in love with you. I'm telling you because I can't have you believing I'm just some fast-talking cowboy out to make it with you."

She sat motionless, staring at him. His fingers went from her chin to her hair, smoothing the tumbled curls tenderly, picking out bits of twigs and grass.

Finally she nodded the slightest bit, and her words came out in a rush. "Mitch, I know. I know what you're saying, because I think the same thing is happening to me."

Her words sent joy surging through him, and he realized that he'd been holding his breath, waiting to see what she'd say.

"So what do you think we should do about it?" His voice was concerned and puzzled, and she reached a hand out and touched his jaw gently.

"Maybe just leave it alone for a while and see if it grows?" she suggested, and it felt as if the responsibility for the whole thing wasn't his alone anymore; they could share the decisions that had to be made.

She was wise, this Sara. Time was exactly what he needed to come to terms with his life. By saying no, she was saying yes to a future with him while refusing to rush into something that might endanger that future.

She knew he needed time, and he was thankful for it.

THEY RODE HOME in the dizzying brightness of afternoon heat, not saying much, but soaking in the sounds of the horses' hooves, the creaking of the leather saddles, the smells of the open range and the ripening hay.

It was the same country they'd ridden across earlier that day, and yet to each of them, it felt strange and exceedingly new, like the vista that stretched between them back there by the stream.

Love made everything look different somehow.

Mitch was coming to Bitterroot for supper, but he had to take his own truck so he'd have a way home again.

Ruth and Wilson were out when Sara and Mitch arrived at the Carter ranch house, so Sara helped Mitch unpack the picnic things.

She'd forgotten to tell Ruth about the visit Adeline had planned for Thursday, so she scribbled a note and left it on the table, thanking Ruth for the hat as well and adding a teasing line to Wilson about the boots.

"See you in an hour, Mitch?"

Instead of answering, he gripped her shoulders, drew her into his arms for a quick kiss on the lips and another on the tip of her nose.

"Drive carefully," he growled.

Sara did, and with every other mile a new obstacle to loving Mitch rose to haunt her, and with every in-between mile, a correspondingly delightful memory of the time they'd spent together made her lips curl upward into a smile.

ORGANIZED CHAOS GREETED HER at Bitterroot.

Adeline and Jennie weren't women who allowed grass to grow under their heels once they'd come to a decision, and they'd started immediately turning the large dining room into an area where the public could come for dinner.

With Dave's help, they'd unearthed the heavy old dining tables and chairs, and there were now six tables scattered in the heavy-beamed dining room where that morning there'd been only one. They'd done inventory on dishes and cooking utensils and had careful lists of everything needed to update the kitchen and outfit the dining room.

They'd wanted to move an old sideboard of Jennie's out of a bedroom and into the dining room to use as a serving center, but the piece proved much too heavy for them, even with Dave's help.

"How come you haven't got a billboard out on the highway advertising this place yet?" Sara teased, marveling at how much they'd accomplished in one day.

"Write that down, Jennie," Gram instructed, busily running a duster over the tables. "A big sign out on the road would be a derned good idea. Phew, where does the dust come from?"

"I sure hope you two have some plans for food for tonight in the middle of all this," Sara went on. "Because I did as you said, Gram, and invited Mitch over. He'll be here soon. I'm going over to the cabin to have a shower and then I'll help with supper."

"No need to hurry," Gram said serenely. "There's a big roasting chicken in the oven, and I'm making biscuits. Jennie, you can whip up that special chocolate cake of yours for dessert. Did you young folks have a nice day, Sara?"

Nice wasn't exactly the words she'd have chosen to describe a day two people admitted to each other that they were falling in love and didn't know what to do about it.

Nice didn't even begin to cover it, but she sure wasn't about to tell Gram that.

"We had a wonderful time, we rode horses. I'll tell you all about it later."

"Maybe we can feed your young man and then talk him into helping us move that pesky old sideboard," Gram was plotting as Sara hurried out the door.

She made her way past the pool and under the trees to her cabin.

Standing under the shower for the third time that day, all Sara could hear was a deep voice saying, "I think I'm falling in love with you, I think I'm falling..."

Those words and the vivid recollection of Mitch's arms and kisses suddenly made Sara smile wryly.

Cold showers weren't a bad idea at all, the way that man made her feel.

# Chapter Seven

Gram was in fine form during supper, and Sara alternated between laughing at some of the things her outspoken relative came out with and feeling guilty for putting Mitch through what amounted to an offbeat inquisition.

Gram was simply curious. She wanted to know everything about everybody, and a bit more than everything about anyone who was interested in her granddaughters.

Bringing a male friend home for a meal had always been the true test of a relationship during Sara's growing-up years. If the guy got through dinner with Gram and still asked her out again, he was made of the right stuff.

The thing was, Gram never asked only the usual sort of questions, like what a person did or what their plans were for the future. She got around to them eventually, by sort of slipping them in between questions not so ordinary.

"Here, have two more of these biscuits, Mitchell. No need to hold back on the grub, there's plenty more in the kitchen. You believe in dreams, young man?" she began shortly after they'd sat down at one of the tables.

Here we go, Sara thought, looking across the table at her mother. Jennie rolled her eyes in helpless sympathy. Mitch was beside Gram, which Sara knew was anything but accidental.

"Dreams?" Mitch looked startled, as well he might. He paused in the act of buttering the biscuits.

"I don't really think I dream all that much," he replied, automatically glancing Sara's way. Lately his dreams had centered mostly around her and were x-rated. He certainly wasn't going to admit that at the dinner table with her relatives around.

Gram snorted. "Hogwash. Everybody dreams; all night, every night. If you concentrate on remembering and learn to figure 'em out, dreams can be a sort of road map for living. Now, surely you can remember a dream or two for me, and I'll tell you what I figure they mean. I'm good at it, had a whole lot of years' practice." She laid down her fork and waited expectantly.

Dave was seated at the head of the table, and he sent Mitch a look full of sympathy. "Might as well cough up a nightmare or two, Mitch," he suggested. "She's gone through all of ours."

Mitch glanced again at Sara, and she winked at him, one long-lashed eye closing slowly and opening in a silent signal to beware.

A twinkle came into his eyes. "Well," he began slowly, "I do have this one dream pretty often, about meeting a wise and beautiful woman who interprets my dreams and tells me my future. Trouble is, I never can remember what it is she says," he teased gently.

Gram made a noise in her throat and looked at Mitch over the top of her glasses. "You wouldn't be putting me on, now would you, Mitchell?" she inquired in a steely tone.

"Yes, ma'am, I sure would be," he said fervently, and everyone laughed, Gram included. There was nothing she liked as well as being beaten at her own game.

"So you were a rodeo rider. Sara says you know our Frankie. How do you feel about children?" Gram demanded a short while later, passing Mitch a blue bowl heaped with mashed potatoes.

"Mother, for heaven's sakes," Jennie objected. "Mitch is here for dinner, not an interview. And how do you get from Frankie to kids, anyway?"

"Simple," Gram declared shortly. "Frankie was married to a rodeo man, and they never had any children. I just wondered how Mitchell feels about a family. Maybe this contraception business is general amongst rodeo people."

Sara groaned loudly, but Mitch didn't seem to mind at all.

"I don't know much about kids," he confessed. "I've got three small nieces I never had a chance to get to know. They've gone back to Seattle now with my sister-in-law, after my brother died. I never got around to having any kids of my own."

"Never been married, then?" Gram inquired blandly, and Sara rolled her eyes ceilingward. "Mind you, marriage don't cut much ice these days, lots of people having babies without getting married. How you feel about that, son?"

"I figure a kid deserves two parents if he can get them," Mitch said thoughtfully. "And no, ma'am, I've never been married. How about you?" he asked, turning the tables on Gram neatly.

Gram didn't bat an eye. "Only married once, and it was great while it lasted. But he wasn't a family man, Jennie's father. Charming, but he had a bit of the wanderlust in him, always moving on somewhere new. I got fed up with it, so we divorced when Jennie was just a baby. He died out in Australia, years ago. Funny, isn't it? Neither my daughter nor my granddaughters had the benefit of two parents while they were growing up."

There was regret in Gram's tone, and silence fell around the table for several moments, until Mitch bridged it.

"I had a friend from Australia, a bronc rider named Tim. I always wanted to take a trip over there someday," Mitch volunteered, and Dave said that he'd always dreamed of that, as well.

Mitch entertained them then with some strange tales Tim had told him about Australia and its animals, and for the next half hour, the dining room was filled with stories and laughter.

By the time Sara's mother served huge wedges of chocolate cake thick with chocolate icing, Sara had relaxed completely.

Mitch was obviously able to handle Gram with one hand tied behind his back.

Inevitably, just as she was about to start on her cake, the phone rang, and it was Doc Stone.

A dog, an expensive purebred shepherd, had been hit by a car on the street in town. The poor animal was badly injured, needing extensive surgery. Doc and the owner were waiting at the clinic for Sara to come and assist with the operation because, Doc reported blandly, Floyd O'Malley was not at home.

Dead drunk, Sara interpreted silently, cursing the unreliable assistant. The last thing she felt like doing this Sunday night was going to work, but there was no choice.

Hurrying back into the dining room, she swiftly outlined the situation. Mitch got immediately to his feet.

"I'll drive you," he offered, but Sara shook her head.

"I have no idea how long this will take, so I'd best have my own vehicle," she decided regretfully. It would have been nice to have had a little longer to spend with Mitch.

"Sit down and have another piece of cake, Mitchell," Gram ordered, adding, "Best keep your strength up, because we were hoping we could get you to help us move some furniture around. Right, Jennie?"

"Better have two more pieces," Dave instructed. "That damned thing they want moved must weigh five hundred pounds, and if I know these two, that's only the beginning."

Mitch caught Sara's eye as she hurried away, returning the wink she'd given him earlier.

"If there's enough furniture to move, I may still be around when you get back," he said.

THE OPERATION TOOK much longer than Sara expected, mostly because Doc turned every bit of the procedure into a major production, checking and rechecking the wounds, the dog's condition, the transfusion devices, and generally hindering Sara.

She'd realized shortly after she arrived that the old veterinarian was unsure of the operation, and she ended up doing the major part of it without making it obvious. Doc breathed down her neck during the entire procedure, his hands trembling badly, uttering under his breath in a manner she found irritatingly distracting.

Sara wished fervently that he'd just go home and let her do the work by herself. It surely wouldn't be as difficult to manage alone as it was putting up with the older veterinarian's fussing and bungling.

But the dog's owner, a retired army captain named Major Whitmore who lived in solitary splendor in one of the largest old houses in Plains, had been adamant that Doc Stone perform the operation on his beloved Angus, obviously not wanting to trust his precious pet to Sara's less-experienced ministrations.

They finally finished the procedure just past midnight, and Doc left, muttering that he would phone the major and give him a report on Angus. The dog had come through the operation well, and the prognosis was excellent.

Still, Sara was afraid to leave the clinic until she was certain the beautiful shepherd was coming out of the anesthesia and resting comfortably, and it was long past 2:00 a.m. before the dog was stable enough to satisfy her.

Finally she drove home and collapsed into bed, making sure the alarm was set for six-thirty in the morning.

Clinic hours started at eight on Mondays. Sara was supposed to open and Floyd was due at nine, with Doc taking over at noon.

Well, she concluded as she checked her alarm, there wasn't much hope that either Doc or Floyd would appear anywhere near on time, so she'd better make sure for Angus's sake that she was there.

Her final thought before she tumbled into bed was of Mitch, laughing uncontrollably as she thundered past him on Steamboat earlier that day, of the way his green eyes danced and his white teeth contrasted with his tanned skin, and of how his rough chin felt scraping across her cheek.

BY TWO THE NEXT AFTERNOON, Sara was ready to fall asleep standing up. She also was having trouble walking; riding Steamboat had made various parts of her anatomy so sore she felt like moaning each time she sat down.

Not that there'd been much chance to sit that morning.

The clinic had been busier than usual, and just as she'd thought, neither Doc nor Floyd appeared when they were supposed to.

Floyd had wandered in at ten-thirty full of the usual set of excuses about stomach problems, and Doc Stone had made a brief appearance an hour ago, fussing around the infirmary over Angus and then disappearing again, supposedly for only a few moments in order to pick something up at the post office. There'd been no sign of him since.

There were a number of farm visits to be made that afternoon, and Sara would be late before she even began. All at once, she'd had enough.

She was darned well going to track Doc down and give him an ultimatum, she decided angrily. Stomping down the hallway on her way to the door, she heard a strange choking sound from the infirmary.

"Angus?" she called, hurrying over to the cage where the big dog was lying. The sound came again, accompanied by a whimper, and then there was ominous silence. Sara ran over to the cage, her heart thumping fearfully.

Angus was lying as she'd left him, all his intravenous tubes intact, but she could tell at a glance that he was dead. Sara stared down at the dog in disbelief. She'd checked him at half-hour intervals all morning, and he'd seemed to be recovering slowly but steadily.

"Floyd," she screamed, and the rusty-haired assistant hurried into the room behind her. Sara did her best to make her voice sound as normal as possible.

"Floyd, did you administer anything to this animal in the last little while?" she demanded.

"Not me. Doc gave him a shot when he was here awhile before. Doc said Angus was restless and in pain. He said he gave him a tranquilizer," Floyd said defensively. He took a step closer to Angus. "Ahh, the puir thing's gone," he announced sadly. "The major's going to be beside himself," he added unnecessarily. "He spent a bundle on that dog, 'twas his pride and joy."

Sara waited until Floyd left the room. Then she closed the door and walked over to the waste bin.

The empty drug vial was right on top, and the moment Sara saw it, she knew what had happened. Doc had confused two medications with similar-sounding names. One would have simply tranquilized Angus and helped him rest easier.

The other, the vial she held in her hand, was for totally different circumstances and undoubtedly had been the cause of Angus's death.

Sara sank into the wooden chair in the corner, and tears began to trickle down her cheeks, sad tears for the unnecessary death of a helpless animal, tears of utter frustration and rage against the circumstances of the death.

Well, tears wouldn't solve a thing. She blew her nose hard and tried to take rational stock of the situation.

Major Whitmore would have to be told his dog was dead. It was no good waiting an indeterminate time for her superior to appear and take on the responsibility; she had to make the call as soon as possible.

Professional discretion forbade telling the major the whole truth about what had happened.

Sara delayed the phone call another fifteen minutes while she sent Floyd out to find Doc, which she realized was an absolute waste of time when Floyd came puffing in shortly afterward.

"Doc's gone out to the Mason farm. Jerry in the post office said Larry Mason was in there when Doc came in and asked him to come out with him and have a look at a colt Larry's thinking of buying. Guess he won't be back for a couple of hours."

Resignedly Sara picked up the phone and dialed Major Whitmore.

Instead of being heartbroken, the major reacted with anger, which quickly turned to barely controlled rage.

"Angus is dead? Dead, you say? I find that absolutely intolerable, do you hear me? Intolerable. Bad show. How can my dog be dead, tell me that, when Dr. Stone himself assured me last night and again this morning that my dog was coming along fine, and now you tell me he's dead. Was Dr. Stone there when he died?" The major's loud tones grew even louder, echoing through the receiver.

Sara moved the instrument farther away from her ear.

"No, he wasn't," she said as evenly as she could. "I came in right afterward, though, and if anything could have been done, I would..."

"I find this hard to understand, how my dog could be doing well just hours ago and suddenly die like this. With a so-called veterinary doctor in the room with him?" The major snorted, and Sara held on to her temper with difficulty.

"Angus was badly injured. With extensive surgery such as he had..."

"But the surgery was successful, Dr. Stone assured me of that."

Sara screwed her eyes tight shut. This was always terrible, telling an owner that a pet had died. But in this particular case, she felt even worse than usual, because she knew in her heart that Angus needn't have died.

Her stomach felt nauseous, making her swallow hard and wish fervently that the conversation would end soon.

"All I can say is how sorry I am." Her voice stuck in her throat.

The phone clanged as the major hung up in Sara's ear.

She was shaking. Hastily making for the bathroom, she sloshed cold water over her face and tidied her hair, all the while going over the choices she had to make about her job.

She'd been going along, avoiding a showdown, but the dog's death proved to her that she couldn't tolerate the situation any longer.

When her boss appeared much later, Sara was prepared.

"Well, Sara, beautiful day, isn't it?" Doc's rather sallow face wore a bright smile and he seemed in high spirits for once. "Sorry to be a trifle late, I had to make a call...."

"Could I see you in the office, Doctor?"

Sara turned her back and hurried into the small room, waiting for him to follow her and then shutting the door firmly behind them as Floyd suddenly appeared in the outer office, curiosity evident in every line of his body.

"What is it, Sara? There are patients waiting, my dear. We really don't have time...."

Reminding her of the patients he ought to have been tending to for over the past two hours was the final straw. Outraged, Sara glared at the plump little man in front of her.

"The dog we operated on last night died," she reported icily. "I'm quite certain his death was a result of that injection you gave him when you raced in here just past noon today, Doctor." She drew the broken vial out of her trouser pocket and held it out, her fingers trembling slightly as she underlined the drug's name with a fingernail. "As you can see, this isn't the thing to give an animal just recovering from anesthesia."

Doc's face paled slightly as he reached for the vial with one hand, fumbling for the glasses he wore on a gold chain around his neck.

He perched the spectacles on his nose and studied the vial for several long moments, head tipped back, bringing the tube close and then holding it far away and squinting at the label.

Finally he laid the container carefully on the desk, and with a heavy sigh he moved around and sank into the desk chair, folding his arms across his chest and staring noncommittally up at Sara.

"Well, my dear? What is it you have to say to me?"

The time had come for a showdown, and Sara wanted to sound totally in control, but she was sure her voice wouldn't behave.

She was right.

It quivered with the force of her emotion as she began, "I know I got this job mostly because you and my stepfather are old friends, Dr. Stone, but I think by now I've proved I can do my job, in spite of the fact that both you and Floyd don't respect the agreement we had about working hours or time off. You're both taking advantage of me."

The older man didn't so much as blink at her. He sat absolutely silent, watching her with that disconcerting stare that revealed nothing about what he might be feeling or thinking.

Sara cleared her throat. "I've gone along without saying anything, because I love the work, and also because, of course, I need the job. However..." This was the part that was the hardest, and the thing that needed saying the most.

Sara was pretty certain that in a few minutes, she'd be without a job or even a recommendation that would help her to find another, but there was nothing for it except to be honest now that she'd gone this far. In her mind's eye, she saw Angus, dead in the other room.

"You've made two serious errors in your treatments within the last month that I know of, as well as being careless about infection with those syringes. Because I'm the new vet around here, people are quick to blame me for these mistakes instead of you," Sara blurted.

"There isn't much I can do about what people say," she continued, "but when animals die needlessly, the way the shepherd just did, I can't morally sit by and watch it happen, either."

She swallowed hard. "You gave me a chance when you hired me. I feel I owe you a chance as well, so I won't say anything about this latest accident today. But if something like this happens again, I have to tell you that I'll report it to the Board of Veterinary Surgeons.''

Doc Stone didn't blink an eye. "Is that all, Sara?" he demanded frostily.

His attitude, his total lack of response or regret over what he'd done to Angus jarred her and made her even angrier than she had been, taking away any trace of nerves and leaving her cold and empty inside. She'd undoubtedly lost her job, anyway, so she might as well say everything she had to say.

"No, it isn't all," she replied evenly. "I think you ought to be aware that Floyd's drinking is affecting his work to such a degree that he's barely useful around here. He's late for work constantly and can't be relied on. For the sake of the next vet you hire, something ought to be done.''

There. She'd made a job of it that time, all right.

Her heart was pounding so hard she could hardly breathe, and her stomach churned, but somewhere inside she felt more at peace with herself than she'd felt for weeks.

She waited fatalistically for Doc to fire her.

He sat in exactly the same position, without changing expression, for several moments. Then he raised his eyebrows questioningly and said dryly, "Well? Am I to assume that's everything you have to say, young woman?"

Unable to utter another word, she simply nodded. And waited.

"I'll have a word with Floyd. You mustn't be too hard on him, there are circumstances . . ."

Doc's voice died away without finishing the sentence, and still Sara waited.

"Well." Doc unfolded his arms and put his palms on the desk with something like a sigh. "I suppose I should call the major and give him the news about his dog."

"I already did," Sara said. "He wasn't exactly friendly. I simply said that the operation had been extensive, and there were no guarantees with injuries of that sort."

"I'll have a word with him myself later today. Now we ought to see to the patients who are waiting, don't you think?" He got up slowly. "Are there calls to make?"

Dumbfounded, she nodded.

"Very well then, off you go and take care of them." He slipped his glasses off his nose. "I'll try to keep more regular hours from now on," he said gruffly. "You're off Saturday afternoon, aren't you? And Sunday?"

He knew very well what days she was supposed to have off.

"I worked all last Saturday, so I'd like this Thursday afternoon off instead, please," she heard herself saying firmly, and he simply nodded.

Sara walked out of the office in a daze, catching sight of Floyd's wide backside scurrying into the other room as she opened the door.

Undoubtedly he'd had his ear pressed to the keyhole and had heard every single word she'd said about him.

Well, eavesdroppers never heard anything good about themselves, Gram always maintained.

Sara gathered the things she'd need for the afternoon calls and made her way out to the truck as if she were a robot.

Sliding behind the wheel, she sat staring out without seeing a thing.

Had the scene in there actually happened or had she only dreamed it? She'd imagined it over and over in her mind, with her boss furious and hollering at her, and not a thing accomplished except the loss of her job.

Instead, Doc had sat quietly and seemed to listen, not even reacting when she told him her decision about reporting him.

She reached down and turned the key in the ignition.

Actually she probably hadn't accomplished one single thing except to get all of it off her chest. She'd bet money that Doc and Floyd would go right on doing their disappearing acts.

And would Doc go right on endangering the lives of his patients?

If he did, would she have the courage to do what she'd threatened, and report him?

Nothing ever was easy. She'd overcome one major hurdle, only to find herself with a whole new set of problems to worry over.

But at least she still had a job, which was amazing.

She checked the call list and figured out in her mind what roads she had to follow to get to the right farm. Flipping through the list of calls, she cursed under her breath. They were going to take her all afternoon and evening, even if everything went perfectly, which it never did.

Oh, well. Being a vet kept her so busy that at least she didn't have time to worry herself into a nervous breakdown.

She pulled up in front of a pay phone. Best call home right now and let them know she wouldn't make it home for supper.

Five minutes later, Sara climbed back into the truck, feeling worse than she had before she made the call.

Mitch had left word with Jennie that he'd drop in at Bitterroot after supper tonight, supposedly to help Dave with the installation of the wiring for the new electric range Jennie and Gram had ordered this morning, but Sara guessed that he'd been hoping she'd be there as well.

She wouldn't get to see him.

She slammed the truck door unnecessarily hard and scowled at a stray dog wagging its scrawny tail at her from the sidewalk.

Damn it all, anyway. Being a vet kept her so busy she didn't even have time for falling in love properly.

TUESDAY AND WEDNESDAY were exceptionally hectic, but they were also pleasantly surprising to Sara.

Both mornings, Floyd actually arrived at work on time, without a visible hangover. And Doc appeared promptly to take over the office on Tuesday so she could do calls and then was on time to do them himself on Wednesday.

Sara got to the office early on Thursday. She unlocked the door, and Tinker and Agnes immediately wound themselves around her ankles in an ecstasy of welcome.

"What have you girls done with old Sylvester?" Sara asked, bending to give each cat a personal greeting. The feisty old neutered tom was nowhere to be seen, even though Sara called him several times and filled the food dishes, which usually brought him on the double.

"Have you ladies locked Sylvester up somewhere to teach him manners?" Sara teased as the dainty females began to eat, politely sharing with each other this morning. There was none of the usual hissing and bullying that would have taken place if the domineering male had been present.

"Well, he'll turn up soon enough and make your lives miserable again," Sara assured them, plugging in the coffee and checking the morning's list of appointments.

Scheduled for surgery first thing was Emily Crenshaw's cat, Queenie. Sara had discussed the situation with Doc the day before.

"The cat has to have a diaphragmatic hernia repaired, and the owner is destitute, so as long as you agree, I'll do the surgery free of charge and take the cost of medication out of my salary," she explained.

"Crenshaw is the woman's name? Emily Crenshaw?" Doc Stone inquired, and Sara nodded.

"Do you know her?"

"Yup." Doc's expression, as usual, revealed nothing.

"I felt sorry for her. She adores that cat, and she's so darned poor," Sara said, hoping that Doc would open up about Miss Crenshaw, but he didn't say another word.

"It's okay about the operation, then?" Sara persisted, and Doc peered up at her over his glasses.

"Certainly," he said dryly. "If you want to donate your time and part of your salary to Emily Crenshaw's cat, that's entirely up to you, my dear."

Something in his tone made Sara uneasy, and she'd spent a few moments wondering if perhaps she'd made a mistake about the woman's financial situation.

But Sara's assessment of Emily Crenshaw as destitute was reconfirmed when she arrived with Queenie clutched in her arms shortly before 8:00 a.m. that Thursday.

The woman wore the same black bowler hat and threadbare black coat she had worn the week before, and this time Sara took careful note of every detail.

Emily's purse was green plastic, with one strap mended with tape. The stockings on her veined legs were full of runs, and Emily had a pair of decrepit-looking running shoes on her narrow feet.

She simply had no money, that was clear.

Sara gently took Queenie from Emily's arms.

"C'mon, Queenie, there's a good cat."

Sara no sooner had her arms around the animal than Queenie turned from a laconic, placid bundle into a ferocious, hissing maniac. Sara had scratches up and down her arms and across one cheek by the time she finally managed to contain the feline inside a cage in the infirmary.

"She'll have to stay here overnight," Sara told Emily after the cat was safely stowed away. "You can come and pick her up in the morning." She eyed the animal warily. "Has she been this bad-tempered for long?"

The cat had struggled last week when Sara examined her, but today she was absolutely ferocious.

"Poor Queenie," Emily was moaning, wiping her eyes with a tissue from the box on Sara's desk. "She's never been away from me overnight, that's what's wrong. She senses I'm leaving her. She sleeps right beside me, has a special pillow all her own, you know."

Sara dabbed with antiseptic at the deep scratch on her arm and winced, trying her best to dredge up the proper amount of sympathetic comfort for Emily and not feel animosity for Queenie.

"We'll take good care of her, and of course she'll be quite groggy, so she won't be too upset at being away from you," Sara assured the pathetic woman, walking with her to the door.

When Emily finally left and Sara began preparing for the operation on the cat, she was grateful that Floyd again arrived on time to help.

They had all they could do to hold the cat down long enough to administer the anesthetic. Queenie was like a wild thing, crouching and attacking, biting and hissing and refusing to be petted or gentled. Floyd used a canvas restraint to protect Sara and himself, but Queenie managed to inflict damage despite it.

"That's a nasty bit of business, that unfortunate animal," Floyd pronounced darkly, holding a bit of gauze to his thumb. Queenie had bitten a hunk out of him before she finally succumbed to the drug that put her to sleep so Sara could get on with the operation.

"At least a hernia isn't too difficult to repair," Sara foolishly declared. "It won't take long at all."

Two and a half hours later, she wished fervently that she'd never laid eyes on Queenie. Everything that could have gone wrong with a supposedly straightforward procedure had, and at one point Sara had been certain she was going to lose the cat from hemorrhage.

Several of Queenie's vital organs were protruding through the large tear in her diaphragm. There were adhesions to deal with, and each stage of the operation took twice as long as it ought to have.

After what seemed an eternity, Queenie was once again in the infirmary, stable and sleeping peacefully, and Sara could hurriedly turn her attention to the other appointments for the morning, apologizing to disgruntled people who'd been waiting for a long time.

Doc was only a little late, arriving before she was finished with the morning's work.

"That hernia operation delayed everything," she apologized, and he seemed to hide a grin as he turned toward his office.

She'd have to phone Jennie and Adeline and tell them she couldn't make it for the trip out to visit Ruth this afternoon.

Her heart sank. She'd been looking forward to an afternoon away from animals and their problems, an afternoon of old-fashioned woman talk ... with maybe a chance to spend a few minutes with Mitch thrown in as a bonus.

"I couldn't believe how many problems that cat gave me," she admitted to Doc. "If the woman were paying for it, I'd charge her double and a half."

"Happens sometimes, always at the most inconvenient moment," he said laconically, adding, "You're off this afternoon, anyway. I'll take over from here. Floyd can phone and postpone the nonemergency farm calls. We'll do them first thing tomorrow morning."

Feeling like a kid let out of school, Sara drove as fast as she dared back to Bitterroot. She'd shower quickly and put on a dress for a change, that nice midnight-blue cotton that Jennie had picked out for her weeks ago and that she'd never worn...and maybe pin her hair up in a high and complicated bun at the back and put a bit of makeup on. She grinned at herself in the truck mirror.

After all, it was time Mitch saw her in something other than blue jeans and work clothes.

Trouble was, to get herself done up she was facing what she'd always labeled Too Much Fuss About Nothing.

And for once in her life, she was looking forward to the effort.

# Harlequin's

## Best Ever "Get Acquainted" Offer

*Look what we'd give to hear from you*

**6 FREE GIFTS 6**

Return This Sticker
and Get 6 Gifts—FREE
Compliments of Harlequin

**GET ALL YOU ARE
ENTITLED TO—AFFIX STICKER
TO RETURN CARD—MAIL TODAY**

# *Look what we've got for you:*

. . . A FREE digital clock/calendar
. . . plus a sampler set of 4 terrific Harlequin American Romance® novels, specially selected by our editors.

. . . PLUS a surprise mystery gift that will delight you.

All this just for trying our Reader Service!

If you wish to continue in the Harlequin Reader Service®, you'll get 4 new Harlequin American Romance® novels every month—before they're available in stores. That's SNEAK PREVIEWS with 9% off the cover price on any books you keep (just $2.49★ each)—and FREE home delivery besides!

## Plus There's More!

With your monthly book shipments, you'll also get our newsletter, packed with news of your favorite authors and upcoming books—FREE! And as a valued reader, we'll be sending you additional free gifts from time to time—as a token of our appreciation.

THERE IS NO CATCH. You're not required to buy a single book, ever. You may cancel Reader Service privileges anytime, if you want. All you have to do is write "cancel" on your statement or simply return your shipment of books to us at our cost. The free gifts are yours anyway. It's a super sweet deal if ever there was one. Try us and see!

★Terms and prices subject to change without notice.

# Get 4 FREE full-length Harlequin American Romance® novels.

*Plus* this lovely lucite clock/calendar

*Plus* a surprise free gift

▼ PLUS LOTS MORE! MAIL THIS CARD TODAY ▼

## Harlequin's Best-Ever "Get Acquainted" Offer

**Yes,** I'll try the Harlequin Reader Service® under the terms outlined on the opposite page. Send me 4 free Harlequin American Romance® novels, a free digital clock/calendar and a free mystery gift.

154 CIH NBH7

PLACE STICKER FOR 6 FREE GIFTS HERE

NAME _____

ADDRESS _____ APT. _____

CITY _____

STATE _____ ZIP CODE _____

PRINTED IN U.S.A.

*Don't forget...*

. . . Return this card today and receive 4 free books, free digital clock/calendar and free mystery gift.

. . . You will receive books before they're available in stores and at a discount off the cover prices.

. . . No obligation to buy. You can cancel at any time by writing "cancel" on your statement or returning a shipment to us at our cost.

If offer card is missing, write to: Harlequin Reader Service,
901 Fuhrmann Blvd., P.O. Box 1867, Buffalo, N.Y. 14269-1867

# BUSINESS REPLY CARD

First Class    Permit No. 717    Buffalo, NY

Postage will be paid by addressee

*Harlequin Reader Service®*

901 Fuhrmann Blvd.
P.O. Box 1867
Buffalo, NY  14240-9952

No Postage
Necessary
If Mailed
In The
United States

# *Chapter Eight*

By eight o'clock that evening, Sara was slumped in a battered deck chair beside the pool at Bitterroot letting the water drip from her body and her skin dry in the warm evening air. She'd forged up and down the pool until she was exhausted.

The saloon was quieter tonight than usual, which was why she'd chanced putting on her bathing suit and taking a swim.

With any luck, no eager cowboy would wander out and notice her and decide she really needed company. As a precaution, she'd positioned herself so that her chair back shielded her from the doorway that led to the saloon across the courtyard.

She shook her sopping hair out of her eyes and wondered idly if any trace of the careful makeup she'd applied that afternoon still lingered after forty minutes spent churning up and down the swimming pool.

Probably not.

Wasted effort, getting all dressed up and fixing her hair that way.

Mitch had been conspicuously absent all afternoon. Ruth had finally mentioned that Wilson and Mitch were miles away, helping a neighbor with haying.

So much for putting on a dress, Sara thought with a wry grin. At least her mother and grandmother had been pleased for once with the way she looked, although Gram hadn't been fooled for a second as to the real reason for Sara's finery.

But all she'd said was, "You clean up real pretty, child." And then she'd winked knowingly.

Sara heard the sharp clip of boots on the cedar decking behind her, and her heart sank.

Damn. She was going to have to deal with one of the cowboys from the saloon after all, which would probably mean getting up and retreating to her cabin fairly quickly, depending on how much the guy had had to drink.

The footsteps came right up behind her chair and stopped.

"I hear the visit with Mom went really well," Mitch said quietly. "I thought about you the whole damn time I was slaving on the tractor out in those fields today, Doc."

He came around and sat down easily in the other deck chair, looking freshly showered, wearing clean denims and an open-necked light green shirt that matched his eyes . . . and, of course, his Stetson was tilted jauntily over his forehead.

Sara sat straighter in the chair, wishing she'd at least worn her newer bikini. The old red one she had on was faded to a tired, streaked pink, and the elastic was none too good in the bottoms.

"We had a super visit," she assured him, with just the slightest trace of a catch in her voice. "I think it did your mom a world of good."

It felt absolutely wonderful to have him sitting there, grinning his crooked grin at her while his eyes quietly made a sweep up and down her almost naked body and then narrowed.

"Hi, beautiful," he said, in quite a different tone than before, deep and meaningful. "I wish I'd brought my swimsuit, the water looks great."

But it wasn't the water he was looking at, and his gaze made Sara much warmer than she'd felt moments before.

"Dave probably has a spare set you could borrow..." she began, but Mitch shook his head.

"I'll bring my suit next time. Tonight I want to spend a quiet hour or two just talking with you, if that's possible," he explained, glancing over at the saloon, where voices and music from the jukebox were spilling out into the early July twilight. "Are we likely to have a chance for that, sitting out here? And what's the probability factor for an emergency call from the clinic tonight?"

He wasn't being sarcastic at all, Sara realized, just practical. After all, evening calls for her from the clinic were commonplace, and the night she'd asked him for dinner, she'd ended up working.

"Want to go for a walk?" she suggested impulsively. "That'll get us away from both the saloon crowd and the phone. There are lovely trails all through those woods back there, and it won't be dark for at least another hour or two."

He nodded emphatically, and she jumped to her feet, giving the sagging bikini a necessary hoist and bringing an appreciative look from Mitch that made her blush.

"C'mon, I'll put some clothes on. My cabin's this way."

They strolled across the yard, and the sounds from the saloon grew fainter as they threaded their way through the tall old pines to where her tiny cedar cabin was, half-hidden among the trees.

It had a small front porch nestled under the roof overhang, and Sara had brought an old rocking chair from the lodge so that she could sit outside in the evening, watching night fall, listening to the birds...and swatting mosquitoes.

They climbed the three wooden steps and Sara opened the heavy door.

The log cabin was a single large room, sparsely furnished, with a couch that doubled as a bed, a chest of drawers, a small wood-burning heater in one corner, and a table with several chairs. Sara had a coffeepot and a hot plate but no kitchen. There was a bathroom lean-to added on at the back of the structure; when Dave's grandfather had first built the cabins, outdoor plumbing was the rule of the day, so Dave had added the bathrooms at a later date.

Mitch looked around curiously, paying close attention to the framed certificate Sara had hung proudly on the wall declaring her a Doctor of Veterinary Medicine. There was a framed photo of her graduating class on the bureau, and he spent several minutes picking her out of the group.

"Ever miss your college days?" he inquired.

"Not for a moment," she assured him. "Those years were hard because there was never enough money, so I felt as if I were running from class to work without enough hours for sleep. It's wonderful now, getting a paycheck every month, being able to live by myself and still be close to my family."

"This cabin is a lot like mine at the ranch," he told her. "Mom wanted me to stay in my old bedroom in the house, but it made me feel as if I were smothering, living in the house again with Mom and Pop. So I fixed up what used to be the hired man's quarters, a little cabin out behind the garage, and I like it fine."

"It's like having the best of both worlds, isn't it?" Sara pulled clothing out of the closet, underwear out of a drawer, and headed for the bathroom.

"I'll be ready in a minute," she promised, hurrying in and shutting the door, then stripping off the bikini. She groaned when she took a quick glance in the mirror. There wasn't a single trace left of the carefully arranged hairdo or the subtle makeup job she'd managed earlier in the day.

Her face shone from the long swim in the mineral pool, and her hair was hanging in ropes down her back and drying into a stiff, impossible frizz at the front.

Hurriedly she turned on the shower and rinsed her head, rubbing it with a towel and tying the entire unruly mass of hair back with an elastic at her neck.

She donned denim shorts and a patterned blouse, splashed on cologne as an afterthought and opened the door.

Mitch was out on the porch, rocking leisurely to and fro in the chair. He turned and smiled when she came out.

"You look nice," he assured her, and she smiled warmly at him, wondering if a time would ever come when her grooming would coincide with their meeting.

"What'd you do to yourself?" He touched the scratch on her cheek gently and then traced the other scratch marks on her arms as well.

"Oh, there's this miserable cat I had to do an operation on...."

Sara explained about Queenie, and Mitch laughed as she outlined how the cat had attacked both her and Floyd.

They wandered slowly along the trails where Sara usually jogged. The heat of the afternoon still lingered in the air, even in the depths of the forest, and the birds sounded sleepy as they sang their evening songs.

"I saw a deer jump across this path the other morning," she confided. "It's thrilling to still see wild animals in their natural habitat. In many places, the wild things are disappearing."

Mitch had her hand clasped in his, fingers fitting between fingers. "Montana still has a lot of wild game. In fact, Pop was saying the other day that there's a small herd of wild horses up in a canyon in the hills above the ranch. Of course, there used to be huge herds of wild horses ranging all around here, but there aren't many left now. The town of Plains actually used to be named Wild Horse Plains.''

Sara swung their hands back and forth between their bodies.

"I'd love to see a wild horse," she said eagerly. "It would be something to tell your grandchildren someday."

Mitch hadn't been thinking too much about grandchildren, but it sounded like a fine idea.

"Why don't I saddle up a couple of horses on the weekend, and we can ride up to the canyon and maybe get a look at them?"

"That would be fun." Sara grinned mischievously up at him. "Steamboat for me again, right?"

"Unless you think he's too spirited for you," Mitch said seriously, and Sara used her free hand to give him a poke on the arm.

"I had your mom and mine laughing this afternoon about old Steamboat running off with me," she said.

"Did you tell them how I saved you, just like one of those heroes in an old movie?"

Her cheeks grew pink. "I only told them some of it. There were parts of that rescue that were x-rated."

"Let's see," he said thoughtfully. "Were those the parts that went something like this?"

He pulled on her hand, turning her neatly into his arms.

His kiss was full of the hunger she roused in him. They stood for uncounted minutes, lost in the wonder of lips and tongue and hands, bodies straining together.

When they reluctantly drew apart, an owl was hooting overhead and the first faint glimmers from a half-moon shone down through the tall pines.

"We'd better go back. Gram's liable to send out a search party if I'm gone too long."

On the way, Sara chatted to him about the afternoon she and her relatives had spent with his mother.

"They got along famously, and your mom served such a big afternoon tea I couldn't eat supper. She actually had several recipes for squares and things that Gram doesn't have. And your mom and mine talked about grieving, too, which I think was good."

"They must have also talked a lot about this restaurant at Bitterroot your mom and Gram are planning," Mitch remarked offhandedly, "because Mom went on and on about it at supper time. Said she's coming over early next week to see all the changes they've made."

Sara was thoughtfully quiet, wondering if she ought to tell Mitch exactly how the conversation about the restaurant had developed.

"We could sure use another good cook a couple days a week over there, once we get properly set up," Jennie had said halfway through the conversation, and Gram had agreed heartily, adding, "I don't suppose you'd be interested, Ruth? Be the best thing in the world for you right now, getting out with people, having a job to go to."

"Work was the only thing that kept me sane when my first husband was killed," Jennie added. "It would be the best thing you could do for yourself, Ruth."

Sara, sitting quietly back with a sandwich and a cup of tea, watched Ruth's face and wondered suspiciously if her mother and Gram had had this idea cooked up long before today's visit.

There was surprise first on Ruth's face, then an expression of longing and regret.

"Oh, I don't think I could. I've never worked except at home, you know," she said shyly.

Gram snorted. "Hogwash. Anybody who cooks for threshing crews like you have could do the job at Bitterroot with one arm tied."

Ruth's face flushed with pleasure. "Do you think so, really?" she'd asked wistfully.

That was why Ruth was coming over, so that she could look things over and decide if she wanted the job. Sara thought of Wilson and wondered what his reaction would be to the idea. Obviously Ruth hadn't mentioned it yet to him or to Mitch.

Well, it was her decision, her secret for the moment if that's how she wanted it. Sara didn't say anything more to Mitch about it, and soon they were back at her cabin.

"I'd best be getting home," he said reluctantly. "Pop's a firm believer in starting the day at 5:00 a.m."

Sara chuckled. "He and Gram must've gone to the same school. She figures anything after eight in the morning is afternoon."

One last, long, tantalizing embrace, and Mitch settled his hat back on his head and turned down the path.

"Want to go see those wild horses Saturday or Sunday?" he inquired.

"Sunday," she decided. "Late afternoon." Maybe there wouldn't be any emergency calls this Sunday. Maybe if there were she could get them taken care of early.

And maybe she was being an incurable optimist to think she could get away at all.

"Good," Mitch said. "Then we can use Saturday night to go to the dance in the hall at Plains."

Sara vaguely remembered seeing posters advertising the event. "That would be nice, as long as I don't have to work," she said tentatively.

"It's not until eight in the evening," he said reasonably enough. "You'll be done by then, won't you?"

She hesitated. If past Saturdays were anything to go by...

"I sure hope so," she said guardedly, and Mitch seemed to take that as a positive answer.

"It's a date. See you then."

She watched him walking away, admiring his loose-limbed cowboy's stride, until at last the deepening evening turned his form into an indistinguishable mass against the darker background of the trees. Then, slowly, she went inside, turning on the small lamp on the bureau and catching sight of herself in the round mirror above it.

Her shiny, makeup-free face was somber, her eyes worried, and she stared at her reflection.

A dance on Saturday, a ride on Sunday.

In Gram's old-fashioned lingo, Mitch was courting her with a vengeance.

She'd told him forthrightly that she was falling in love with him, and she was... more intensely each time she was with him.

Already her job had interfered with their time together. It was ridiculous to think that it wouldn't go on doing so; having a vet practice in a small community and keeping regular hours were diametrically opposed.

So what was there to do about the inevitable conflict?

Give up her job?

It wasn't even a consideration.

Give up Mitch?

Just as unthinkable.

She'd simply have to bungle along, juggling work and romance as best she could, hoping Mitch would understand when one thing conflicted with the other.

FRIDAY BEGAN WITH Emily Crenshaw waiting for Sara on the steps of the clinic at just past seven in the morning.

"I've been here over twenty minutes already," the little woman announced with more than a trace of irritation in her high-pitched voice. "I thought there was someone here all the time. I'm shocked you leave the poor animals all alone for hours and hours. Does this mean that my poor Queenie has been alone all night, no doubt in pain and with no one to take care of her?"

Sara stepped past the woman and fitted the key into the lock.

"One of us always does a late-night check if we think it's necessary, Miss Crenshaw. I looked in on Queenie yesterday afternoon, and she was recovering nicely."

Fat lie that was. The abominable feline had pretended to be pathetically groggy and totally docile—until Sara opened the cage door and reached in to check her incision.

The cat went berserk at that point, hissing and spitting, and Sara narrowly escaped a bite just like the one Floyd was nursing.

Queenie was one bad-tempered cat, and Sara looked forward to giving the animal back to its owner as fast as possible.

The clinic's female cats, Agnes and Tinker, were voicing their impatience for breakfast and half tripping the two women as Sara led the way into the infirmary.

She opened the door, became immediately aware of sounds that shouldn't be occurring and came to a halt so quickly that Miss Crenshaw bumped into her and then peered under Sara's arm to see what was going on.

"Ohhhhh . . . Queenie, my poor darling Queenie . . ."

Miss Crenshaw's wail fitted right in with the howling, hissing and spitting erupting from the cage where Queenie was being kept.

Sylvester, back from wherever he'd been for the past week, had climbed on top of Queenie's cage, and, with both front paws batting feverishly, he was doing his best to subdue the hissing female demon inside, cursing and spitting at her, tail waving madly from side to side.

Queenie, the stitches across her shaved midsection raw and angry-looking, was lying on her back, ears laid back as far as they'd go, murderous intent in her eyes and voice as she sought to grab Sylvester's paws as they swiped within inches of her belly.

The noise seemed much greater than two cats could make between them, and Emily Crenshaw's immediate wails of anguish and outrage filled any momentary seconds of quiet there might have been.

She darted past Sara like an avenging demon and, plastic handbag flying in Sylvester's direction, went to Queenie's rescue.

"Shoo, you bad animal, get, get, go on . . ."

Sylvester saw her coming and beat a hasty retreat, leaping down and scurrying out the front in a clever zigzag pattern that got him safely past the virago with the handbag.

Miss Crenshaw promptly turned the force of her wrath onto Sara, brandishing her purse as if she might wallop Sara with it.

"What kind of place is this," she shrieked, "allowing a vicious animal like that to terrorize poor Queenie after what she's just been through? I have half a mind to report you, young lady! This is a disgrace. Queenie is the gentlest of cats, and that ugly . . ."

She went on and on the entire time it took Sara to prudently don a pair of canvas gloves and gingerly open the cage door to find out whether any real harm had been done to Miss Crenshaw's cat.

Sara did her best to ignore it, checking the patient and dodging teeth and claws in the process.

"There's absolutely no harm done, Miss Crenshaw," Sara finally announced. "Queenie's incision is healing nicely."

Too bad her disposition wasn't as well.

Gingerly Sara lifted the cat out and placed the animal into the arms of her owner.

"Sorry about all that, but Queenie's fine, and that's really all that matters, isn't..."

Miss Crenshaw clasped her cat to her flat bosom and gathered verbal steam. Gone was the meek, pathetic little woman Sara had felt sorry for; in her place was a vicious, nagging little troublemaker threatening, of all things, a lawsuit against the clinic.

"I have friends, you know, people in positions of authority who wouldn't hesitate to take the stand..."

It took fifteen exhausting minutes to patiently edge Miss Crenshaw and her ill-mannered cat to the door and half shove her through, still yattering. Sara had managed to hold her temper, but only barely.

She promptly locked the door and shakily went about making a pot of coffee, double strength.

Sylvester was sitting in the middle of the kitchen counter, happily lapping up milk from an overturned pitcher.

"Traitor," Sara accused, lifting him down none too gently. "Troublemaker."

These days she definitely knew she ought to have taken computer science and forgotten all about vetting.

MITCH PULLED A CIGARETTE out of the package in his shirt pocket and lit it as his father opened the thermos and poured them each a cup of lemonade. It was hot, and they'd been fixing fences all morning under the cloudless sky. The break was more than welcome.

Mitch slumped down against the shady side of the pickup, drawing the smoke in and breathing it out, enjoying the peacefulness of the surroundings, the smell of open country. Even the old man was in good spirits today, not finding one thing yet to complain about.

It might be just the right time to discuss what Mitch had been planning.

"I'm gonna have Misty bred," he announced abruptly, handing his cup back for a refill.

"Good idea. She's a fine mare." Wilson sat down heavily in the shade from the truck. "Hank Shorten has a pretty good-looking stallion over at Buffalo Ranch," he said helpfully, filling the cups to the brim and handing Mitch his.

"I'm taking her to a place outside of Missoula where they breed top rodeo stock," Mitch announced.

Wilson paused, cup halfway to his mouth, and gave his son a disbelieving look from under the brim of his hat.

"What kind of stupidity is that?" he demanded. "Taking time off to transport a mare to be bred when there're perfectly good stallions right around here. Pack of nonsense, I say." He snorted. "Damn fool waste of time. And money, too. Bet they soak you a bundle for stud fees on a deal like that."

"Yeah, it's expensive," Mitch admitted reluctantly. "But it's the route to go if you want top-quality colts," he insisted, recognizing the growing irritation in Wilson's voice and thinking he should probably just shut up about the whole thing.

But damn it, this was important to him. Wilson had to know sooner or later, anyway. Might as well make it sooner.

"I've been talking to Bill Forgie. He's starting a breeding stable for Arabs, and that's what I want to do eventually, Pop, only mine will be quarter horses for rodeo stock. There's good money in it once you get started and develop a name for yourself."

Wilson snorted. "Why the hell can't you just settle down and work the ranch? I never saw anybody as restless as you are, always after some dream or another. Starting a breeding stable'll cost you a bundle, maybe cost you the ranch in the long run when you end up pouring all your time and energy and money into horseflesh. We've got a good balance now, with the hogs, sheep and the cattle. Hell, Mitch, I haven't worked my whole damn life just to watch you fritter away a good ordinary living I've spent my lifetime building up."

Mitch felt his temper escalating.

"I'm not suggesting going to the bank and mortgaging the damn ranch, Pop. I'm not buying a dozen horses right away or asking you for anything. I'm trying to tell you about an idea of mine."

"You were always full of flighty ideas, all right."

Mitch threw the cigarette away violently and lurched to his feet, glaring at his father.

"You want me to be Bob, don't you, Pop? You can't forgive me for not being the son who did everything right, who was your fair-haired boy." Mitch felt the angry blood pumping through his veins, the words forming on his lips faster than he could spit them out.

"Well, I'm not him, old man. I cared for my brother, but I never wanted to be what he was. Thing is, you're stuck with me now, with having to deal with me instead of him.

You may not like it, but you're stuck with it, because brother Bob is dead."

The last words were spoken with quiet intensity, and too late, Mitch caught sight of his father's face, shielded from sight before now by the brim of his hat.

Wilson's rugged features had turned sickly pale under the ruddy tan, and there were deep lines around his eyes, knifing down from nose to mouth. There was agony in his eyes, and Mitch felt a stab of remorse.

"Look, Pop..." he began to apologize, but Wilson held up a hand, like a cop stopping traffic.

"Shut up," he ordered viciously. "You've said enough. Although you're right about one thing at least, I do miss your brother, damned right I do."

Wilson turned on his heel and stalked off across the open field, steadily walking away from Mitch until his figure became small and foreshortened in the shimmer of the sun.

Where the hell was he going? Mitch wondered anxiously, staring helplessly after him. There wasn't a damn thing out there except grass and a couple of trees.

After a few moments he began to berate himself for his outburst, yet feeling ridiculously wounded by what his father had just admitted.

Mitch knew he wasn't the type of man Bob had been.

He'd never wanted to be. Why couldn't Wilson just accept him the way he was?

The old man was enough to drive a guy nuts. And that was no excuse for the things Mitch had said. But the words must have been festering inside.

Not knowing what else to do, Mitch gathered up the tools and began tightening the sagging barbed wire, working furiously.

It was forty minutes before Wilson came back.

Silently the older man picked up his own tools and went to work with Mitch.

The only words exchanged for the rest of the day were ones absolutely necessary about the job.

Several times that afternoon, Mitch wondered why he hadn't said to hell with the Carter ranch and gone on with his own career last spring instead of coming home.

Home. That was a laugh. Home was supposed to be somewhere you wanted to be.

Well, he wasn't wearing a ball and chain. Why the hell didn't he just get on a bus?

After all, the rodeo life was still out there; he could pick up right where he'd left off.

By the time he and Wilson drove home silently for supper, Mitch was sorely tempted to do just that.

There were several things stopping him.

One was his mother. He didn't think he could just walk off and leave his mother the way she was.

The other was Sara.

SARA MANAGED TO FINISH her last farm visit of the day by seven-fifteen Saturday evening, and she did it by skipping lunch and dinner. During the course of the afternoon, she gobbled two apples and several raisin cookies a farmer's wife had given her. When the last call was finished, she exceeded the speed limit every mile of the way home. Then she showered, dressed and swiped on lipstick and eyeliner in record time.

She was trembling slightly from both hunger and exertion by the time Mitch tapped on her cabin door, but damn it all, she was ready.

And it all seemed worth it when she opened the door and his eyes widened as he looked her up and down. Then he whistled, a soft, appreciative wolf whistle that thrilled her.

She was wearing a soft blue cotton sundress, with a nearly bare top and straps that crossed in the back, and high-heeled sandals. She'd left her hair loose and wild, curling around her head and shoulders.

"You look real pretty."

"So do you," she replied, taking in his Western-cut, steel-gray suit, the high gleam on his boots, the new-looking deep gray Stetson on his head.

They stood smiling foolishly at each other.

"Well, lovely lady, let's go dancing."

He gathered her close to his side, and they were already halfway down the path when the phone in the cabin began to ring persistently.

Sara hesitated, and Mitch groaned.

With an immense effort of will, she ignored the summons and went on walking beside Mitch, and he let out a deep sigh of relief and gratitude.

"It's probably nothing, anyway," she assured him and herself, and he agreed heartily.

She didn't tell him that if it were a real emergency, the answering service had the number of the hall where the dance was being held.

As Mitch put his hands around her waist and hoisted her up into the cab of the freshly washed and shining half-ton, Sara sent up a hurried prayer to heaven, asking that the animals in the area get through this one evening without any calamities befalling them.

So she could, too.

## Chapter Nine

Music and laughter greeted Sara and Mitch as they walked into the small hall in Plains where the dance was being held. A country band was on the stage, belting out a Western tune, and couples crowded the dance floor.

There was a cozy, intimate atmosphere in the old building, probably because almost everyone knew everyone else; at least a dozen people had greeted them by the time they found seats at one of the small card tables scattered on the periphery of the dance floor.

"Care for some punch?" Mitch asked as soon as they were settled. "Strictly nonalcoholic—this place isn't licensed."

Before Sara could answer, Bill Forgie appeared at Mitch's elbow with Carol beside him.

"Saw you two come in, mind if we join you? The band is taking a break."

"Only if you come with me and do battle for glasses of that bilious-looking red stuff," Mitch assured Bill with a welcoming grin and an affectionate thump on his friend's shoulder.

Carol sat down across the table from Sara.

"Ooops," she exclaimed comically as she pulled her chair still farther out—her pregnant tummy kept her from sitting anywhere near the table.

"I've still got weeks to go, and I can't figure out how I can get much bigger than this, can you?" she asked, wrinkling her nose at the mound underneath her gaily patterned maternity dress. "The doctor assures me this is only one little baby, but I have moments when I wonder."

"You're absolutely glowing," Sara complimented the pretty blonde. "You're a walking advertisement for the pregnant state."

"That's because I'm boiling hot all the time. The glow is actually good old sweat," Carol said with a laugh. "And I no longer walk, I just sort of lurch along and hope everyone steers clear."

The men returned, and soon, the four of them were sipping fruit punch and catching up on anecdotes about the foal Sara and Mitch had delivered.

"You two sound like doting relatives," Bill teased when they insisted on knowing every detail about Scarlett and her baby.

Mitch caught Sara's eye and they laughed. The birth of the foal was special to them, a milestone in their relationship.

The lights dimmed and the music started again, a romantic waltz.

Mitch stood up, taking Sara's hand and leading her onto the dance floor. His arm held her tight to him, and with confident grace he swooped her into the rhythm.

"You're good at this," she remarked, loving the sensation of being in his arms, of having him guide them expertly among the other couples.

"I've had lots of practice. There's always a dance after a rodeo," he explained. "A guy eventually learns his right foot from his left," he added lightly.

Sara was quiet, feeling a ridiculous pang of jealousy for those times when he must have held other women just this same way at countless other dances.

As if he'd read her mind, he drew her still closer into his arms and dipped his head until she could feel the heat of his breath in her ear.

"Tonight's special, though. You're special to me, Sara. You're the most beautiful woman in this room, you know that? I'm gonna dance every single dance with you, and afterward, I know this place where the moon's twice as big as anywhere else. I'm gonna take you there and hold you and kiss you . . ."

He was wonderfully romantic. His words drew heated pictures in her mind. With a sigh of blissful contentment, she felt his cheek press hers, his large, callused hand move slowly, sensuously, across the naked skin of her back, sending delicious waves of feeling trickling down her spine. His hand dropped to her waist, tugging gently until she was molded against him, thigh pressed to thigh, her breasts crushed against his chest. In a deep baritone, he hummed in her ear, low enough so that only she could hear.

Sara closed her eyes and floated. There were only the two of them, lost in a magic dreamworld as one romantic song came to an end and with hardly a pause, another began.

It was near the end of the third song that Sara felt a tap on her shoulder.

She opened her eyes, and Mitch paused between one step and another. A portly matron who'd been taking tickets at the door when they came in stood beside them.

"There's a phone call for you, miss," the woman said apologetically. "You are the new vet over at Doc Stone's, aren't you?"

Sara's heart plummeted. She glanced up, and Mitch's eyes were shuttered and unreadable. He raised an eyebrow questioningly at her.

"Sorry, I'll have to see what it's about," she whispered to him, and, feeling suddenly bereft, she moved out of his arms to follow the woman to a small back room where the phone lay off the hook, ominously waiting.

"Dr. Wingate here, can I help you?"

"This is George Dolinger, and a stallion of mine's been ripped to shreds by barbed wire."

Sara felt like groaning out loud. This was Doc Stone's affair, really. George Dolinger was totally obnoxious. She remembered the last call she'd had from him and the outright rudeness he'd displayed. Why should she have to deal with Dolinger tonight of all nights?

"I called Doc at home, and he absolutely insisted I get you instead, young woman. Now I suggest you get out here right away, because this animal's bleeding heavily and none of us can do a damn thing with him. He's rampaging around here, near broke my groom's leg a minute ago."

She was overwhelmingly tempted to say she wouldn't come. Certainly after the last verbal battle with this man, she was under no obligation to answer an emergency call when she wasn't even on duty.

A mental vision of a hysterical, wounded animal rose up in her mind's eye.

"I'll be there in half an hour."

"You know the way?" Dolinger demanded, and Sara listened as he gave crisp directions.

She hung up the phone and drew in a deep, dejected breath. Now all she had to do was break the news to Mitch that as far as dancing was concerned, the evening was over.

THE RANCH WAS BRIGHTLY LIT when she drove hurriedly down the long, winding driveway barely forty minutes later. Dolinger had turned on all the powerful yard lights, and Sara followed the graveled track right down past the palatial house to the stables.

She'd barely had a chance to turn off the motor when Dolinger himself appeared at her open side window.

"Took you long enough," was his snarled greeting, and Sara counted to three before she swung the door open, taking a perverse delight in making him jump back quickly so he didn't get hit.

Mitch had been wonderfully good about the whole thing. He'd been obviously disappointed, but he'd taken her to the office so she could pick up the truck, kissing her with hungry ferocity for a long moment before he let her go.

"You go on back to the dance," she'd insisted, hoping with every jealous fiber of her being that he wouldn't do any such thing.

"No, it's no fun without you there. I'm gonna head over to Bitterroot, see if Dave needs a hand in the bar," Mitch said.

Sara felt ridiculously pleased.

She'd hastily changed into jeans and a shirt, grateful that she also kept a battered pair of runners in with her emergency gear.

The last thing she needed tonight, she reflected now, would be to have to appear in front of this critical little man wearing a sundress and high-heeled sandals, looking totally unsuited for the job at hand.

She felt nervous and edgy enough without that.

"Help me with this equipment," she all but barked at Dolinger as she swiftly assembled the things she thought she'd need from the rear of the truck, shoving several heavy cases unceremoniously at him and struggling into a coverall.

She zipped it as she hurried through the stable door, stopping short for an instant at the scene that greeted her.

A beautiful dun-colored stallion was being held, with grave difficulty, by three men. The tall animal was rolling its eyes in terror and bellowing with pain, repeatedly trying to rear back and break loose from the ropes holding him. His legs and underbelly were smeared with frightening quantities of blood, and long, angry gashes ran from his hindquarters around to his sides. He was already having difficulty putting his weight on his hind legs.

Sara swallowed hard. With lacerations like these, it was touch and go as to whether the animal would regain full use of his limbs.

"What's his name?" she inquired loudly. The horse was making so much noise it was difficult to hear anything.

"Sergeant," one of the men bellowed.

"Try and get him into a loose box," she hollered at the men. "And make sure there's plenty of light."

"Where's hot water and soap?" she demanded of Dolinger, who was standing to one side of her and cursing in a steady, vicious stream as he eyed the damage to his horse.

He probably saw poor Sergeant simply as so many dollars and cents down the drain, Sara thought with disgust. She doubted that he was feeling sorry for the animal's pain or sympathizing with his fear.

Dolinger jerked a thumb over his shoulder, and Sara went into the well-equipped bathroom and scrubbed as quickly as she could.

"You'll have to hold him as still as you can while I inject this sedative," she instructed, preparing a syringe.

For several frustrating moments, it seemed impossible that the horse would be still for even the few seconds required for Sara to insert the needle into the jugular, but at last, there was an opportunity and she seized it.

As the stallion gradually quietened under the effect of the powerful sedative, Sara rapidly taped an intravenous catheter in place and checked his heartbeat.

It was strong.

"Poor old Sergeant," Sara crooned, watching him closely.

In a very few moments, Sergeant was obviously wobbly. He assumed a wide-base stance, swaying slightly from side to side with his head down. The time had come to administer the barbiturate through the catheter.

Sara injected the drug slowly. Sergeant drew in a deep, heavy breath.

"Support him as much as you can," she instructed as the heavy animal began to topple.

In another moment, Sergeant was peacefully asleep on the clean bed of straw, and Sara was on her knees beside him.

She opened her case and laid out the instruments she would need and then carefully examined every jagged wound, suturing blood vessels where necessary, meticulously cleansing the ugly lacerations before she began to stitch them up.

For the next three hours she was unaware of anything outside of the brightly lit circle enclosing her and her unconscious patient.

The wounds were anything but easy to repair. Jagged-edged and frighteningly deep in places, they required minute care and delicate stitching, and with several, Sara felt despair threaten to overcome her as her first attempts to stretch the animal's skin to cover the wound failed.

When at last all the edges of tough hide were sutured neatly in place, she became aware of knife-sharp pains in her shoulders and arms and a crick in her neck from hunching in one position for so long. Her chest and stomach felt tight and sore with tension.

She also became more aware of her audience. Dimly she'd known that the three men who'd held Sergeant earlier were all hunched against the stable wall, obviously paying close attention to everything she was doing.

Now there was admiration and approval in their expressions as they smiled and nodded at her.

"Good job, Doc. Hell of a mess the poor old thing got himself in."

More surprising, Dolinger was also present, sitting apart from the others, hunched like an evil little gnome on a stool in the far corner.

"Mr. Dolinger, Sergeant will have to have a cast on that back leg, long enough to allow the worst of the wounds there to heal."

Dolinger didn't fool around, Sara gave him grudging credit for that. He soon had the men scurrying around at her instruction, and soon the leg was in a firm cast.

By the time it was accomplished to both Sara's and Dolinger's satisfaction, another hour and a half were gone and Sara felt as if she were going to pass out from weariness and hunger.

"Can you guarantee my stallion will be entirely fit after this, miss?" the ranch owner demanded in an aggressive tone, and Sara met his dour gaze and shook her head.

"I can't promise anything. One of those cuts nicked a tendon, which is why I've put the cast on. I've done my very best, but you must know by now there aren't any guarantees in this business," she said, her voice every bit as cold and hard as his had been all evening.

A glance at her watch told her that midnight had come and gone, and thinking back, she remembered that she hadn't really had much to eat since breakfast, which now seemed more than a decade ago. As she stood up, she was feeling decidedly light-headed.

Sergeant was showing faint signs of recovering. Sara decided she'd like to stick around for at least another hour and make absolutely certain that the horse was safely out of the anesthetic before she headed home.

"Do you think I could have a glass of milk?" she asked Dolinger, wondering what sort of scathing lecture a request like that might bring, but unable to go on without something in her stomach.

"You hungry?" he barked, and she said firmly, "Yes, as a matter of fact I am. I didn't have dinner."

"C'mon."

Feeling like a stray dog that had been told to heel, Sara reluctantly fell into step behind him. He barged out of the stable, with stern commands to the grooms to keep a close eye on Sergeant, and marched briskly across the yard and up the winding walk to the back door of the house.

Sara noticed that the doorway had a ramp leading up to it.

Dolinger opened the door quietly, motioning her into a mudroom with low sinks and a potter's wheel in one corner, and from there into a huge, brightly lit, cheerful yellow kitchen.

He gestured silently to a bathroom off to one side, and Sara gratefully went in and shut the door.

She filled the sink with hot water and scrubbed her face, arms and hands and finished off with a cold rinse that managed to take away some of the weird buzzing in her head.

Drying off, she went back into the kitchen to find George Dolinger, sleeves rolled above the elbow, efficiently breaking eggs and frying bacon in a large iron frying pan on the range, nodding silently while a delicate redheaded woman in a wheelchair talked cheerfully to him from a spot by the table where she was making and buttering toast.

Sara wondered if she were hallucinating. The whole cozy domestic scene was far removed from what she thought of as typical behavior for Dolinger. But there he was, mouth still firmly turned down at the corners, flipping eggs in the frying pan.

"Hi," the woman said pleasantly, rescuing two slices of golden toast and popping two more into the machine.

"I heard you come in, and I can't resist a midnight feast, so I got up and came out to join you. I'm Judy Dolinger, and of course I know who you are. Sara, isn't it? Dr. Sara Wingate."

Sara went quickly across the room and extended her hand in greeting.

"I'm pleased to meet you, Mrs. Dolinger."

"It's Judy, because I intend to call you Sara. Right?"

Her smile was engagingly wide, and her startling red hair was as wild as Sara's own. Judy had deeply set brown eyes, soft and very beautiful. They were her best feature, because her face was narrow and her nose rather pointed. But the warmth shining from those wonderful eyes made Sara feel immediately welcome and at home—a feeling she'd never dreamed of having anywhere around George Dolinger.

Judy's slight body was wrapped in a deep blue velour robe, and as she maneuvered easily in her wheelchair from cupboard to table setting out catsup, strawberry jam and cups, Sara had the impression that whatever the reason for Judy's disability, it wasn't recent. The woman was totally at ease in her wheelchair, an ease that obviously came from long experience.

"George was telling me you did a magnificent job on poor Sergeant just now," Judy said.

Sara was stricken dumb. George Dolinger, miserable George Dolinger, had actually said something nice like that?

Words failed her, but Judy carried right on, urging Sara to a seat beside her at the table, whisking the generously filled plates over from the range, asking whether Sara wanted cream and sugar or catsup for her eggs.

The food was ambrosia to Sara, and she had to stop herself from gobbling. George wasn't eating; he filled a huge mug with coffee for himself and sat drinking it, but Judy companionably had an egg and a slice of toast, directing comments and questions at both Sara and George as she nibbled at the food.

Sara was flabbergasted at the difference in George's whole demeanor when he talked to Judy. His voice was gentle, and the nastiness that Sara had come to associate with his every word and expression was totally absent.

Dolinger became a different person around his wife, just like Jekyll and Hyde, Sara couldn't help thinking. And how had these two absolutely different people ended up together in the first place?

Curiosity finally overcame her. She forked up the last morsel of bacon and golden egg yolk and asked, "Did you grow up around here, Judy?"

Red hair bobbed as Judy nodded.

"I was born not ten miles from here, on a small farm back in the hills. I guess Floyd's never mentioned it to you, but he's my brother."

Sara couldn't keep the amazement from her voice.

"Floyd, from the clinic? Floyd O'Malley?"

"Yup, the very same," Judy said lightly. "He's twelve years older than me. He's worked for Doc ever since—" she glanced quickly over at her husband, and Sara had the feeling the rest of the sentence wasn't at all what Judy had been about to say "—ever since we were first married, hasn't he, George?"

Dolinger nodded curtly and got up from the table.

"I'm going out to check on Sergeant, and if he's doing well, I'll tell the grooms to go to bed," he announced abruptly. Sara made a move to get up as well, but Judy held out a restraining hand.

"Sit still for ten more minutes and finish your coffee," she insisted. "George can call you if there's anything seriously the matter, can't you, George?"

Sara watched Dolinger meekly agree, even though she felt he didn't want to. She had the feeling he agreed with most of Judy's wishes.

When the door shut behind him, Judy was thoughtfully quiet for a while, and then she said in a rush, "George doesn't want me to mention it, but Floyd's drinking too much again, isn't he, Sara?"

She waved a hand and then added quickly, "Sorry, that's hardly the way to phrase a question like that to someone you've only just met. Anyhow, I know he is, and I know it probably causes you problems and I feel badly about it. If there's ever any real trouble with Floyd, I'd appreciate knowing. Doc's always been really good about it, but I understand you've taken over most of the work lately on account of Doc's eyes, isn't that true?"

Sara felt that things were moving too quickly for her to absorb. Her weary brain seemed unable to comprehend all this new and startling information. "Doc Stone has a problem with his eyes?"

Judy clapped a hand over her mouth. "Darn, I talk too much; it's because I don't get out enough. I swamp people with words when they come and blurt out stuff I probably shouldn't. Floyd told me. I figured you'd have to know, working with Doc the way you do. But of course Doc's pretty closemouthed. Anyway, Floyd said that Doc seems to be losing a large portion of his vision. He's been to different doctors, but there doesn't seem much any of them can do. It's a terrible shame, isn't it?"

Sara felt shocked and saddened, and also absolutely horrified when she realized that many of the problems and mistakes her boss had been making were probably due to his failing eyesight. And to think she'd been blaming it all on carelessness when actually the old man couldn't see.

Remorse made her cringe as she remembered threatening to report him. She felt absolutely terrible.

Judy was watching her closely, and now she said hesitantly, "I probably shouldn't have said anything, Sara, but darn it all, it's better if people know exactly what a person's problem is, don't you think so?"

Sara nodded, and Judy went on, "Men are so darned stubborn that way, they can't ever talk about what's really bothering them. With me, of course, it's obvious I'm disabled, this wheelchair and all, but with this problem Doc has, unless you know what's wrong..."

"Yes, I see exactly what you mean," Sara agreed faintly. "I can't tell you how grateful I am that you told me."

Judy's eyes suddenly sparkled with tears. "I love Doc Stone, he's been absolutely wonderful to Floyd over the years. He hired him the spring after my accident, and Floyd's been there ever since."

Judy didn't appear to mind talking about her disability at all. Sara dared to ask, "What happened to you, Judy?"

The other woman shrugged offhandedly. "Oh, I fell off a horse. We were fooling around, Floyd and I, racing a couple of horses we had no right to be on because my mother was only boarding them for someone. Floyd's horse happened to bump mine, and I fell off and fractured several of my vertebrae."

Judy frowned and added sadly, "Floyd was home for the holidays from his first year at vet school, and after this happened to me, he refused to go back. It was so stupid of him, but he felt responsible. Dad was dead, and our mom was older and not well, so we weren't very well off. Floyd spent the money intended for his education on my medical bills, and until Doc Stone hired him he was working in the sawmill. The job Doc gave him meant he could work with animals again."

"And Dol..." Sara flushed and started again. "Your husband. How did you meet him?"

"George? Oh, he'd been our neighbor for years. He was quite a bit older than me, more Floyd's age, and at first when he wanted to marry me, I refused point-blank." Judy's mobile face was mischievous now. "I figured he was just sorry for me, and who needs that? But he kept right on asking and bringing me flowers and perfume and things, and after a couple of years, when he never stopped asking, I guess I just wore down," she admitted with a wry grin. "Marrying George was right for me, he's a wonderful husband," she added earnestly. "Even though Floyd and George don't get along all that well, my marriage was the best thing I could have done."

Sara was rapidly reassessing many of her ideas and feelings about people she thought she knew.

She happened to glance up at the wall clock and was shocked to find it past 2:00 a.m.

"Look at the time! I've got to go check on Sergeant and get on home." She met Judy's lovely gaze and said haltingly, "It's been great meeting you. Maybe I can drop in again when I'm out this way?"

Judy's wide, delighted smile flashed. "I'd love that," she declared fervently. "I promise next time I won't talk your ear off about family problems, either. I'll show you my pottery instead. George's built me a kiln out back of the toolshed, and I'm experimenting with different glazing."

Sara hurried down to the barns. Dolinger was just coming out, but he turned back and accompanied her as she went over to Sergeant.

The huge stallion was up, and the cast was holding nicely.

"As long as he stays pretty quiet, he should be well on the road to recovery in a week or so," Sara said. "I'll keep a close eye on him."

She deliberately met Dolinger's eye and said sincerely, "I very much enjoyed meeting your wife. Thank you for introducing me and for the delicious meal as well."

She had to smile inwardly at the nonplussed expression on his face. He didn't seem to have the faintest idea how to deal with a sincere compliment.

"Yeah, well, we'll see how Sergeant comes out of this," he finally replied gruffly, and Sara had to smile to herself.

The man was anything but a jovial sort, but at least Sara knew now that there was a heart beating somewhere inside him.

Wasn't love the most remarkable thing, when it could take a man like Dolinger and actually turn him into a nice guy?

For limited periods of time, of course. But one couldn't expect miracles, after all.

WEARILY, SHE DROVE HOME and collapsed into bed, smiling like a fool and clutching the note she'd found hanging by a nail on her door.

> Sara
> Have disconnected all phone lines to Bitterroot. Feel this is the only way to insure your company for longer than an hour. Sleep well, my pretty lady. Will pick you up at 2:00 p.m. tomorrow, no excuses accepted.
>
> xxxxxxx M.
>
> P.S. Adeline showed me your baby pictures, loved the one of you on the furry rug. I like your hairdo better now, but your outfit back then was great. M.

Obviously the picture was the infamous one of Sara at six months, bald as a balloon, with not a stitch on.

Trust Gram.

BY TWO ON SUNDAY, Sara was ready to believe that Mitch actually had done something to the phones, because by some miracle, there wasn't one single emergency call for her.

She'd slept in, had time for a long leisurely breakfast with the family and actually managed a discreet makeup job after her shower before Mitch arrived, riding Misty and leading Steamboat, snatching a kiss as he held the horse for her to mount.

Soon they were following a rough trail that seemed to lead straight up the mountain, and Sara was proud of the familiar way she felt with Steamboat. Today she actually imagined that she was in control of the animal, instead of the other way around.

"How did the stallion make out last night?" Mitch wanted to know as they plodded comfortably along a more level patch of trail. Sara told him the details of the repair job she'd had to do.

She'd found herself thinking a great deal about the things Judy had revealed last night.

"Did you know Floyd had a sister married to George Dolinger?" she asked Mitch curiously, and he nodded. "Yeah, she was quite a bit older than me, but I seem to remember lots of gossip when they were married. She's in a wheelchair, isn't she?"

Sara described Judy for him and told him what the woman had said about her injury and how it had affected Floyd. Mitch listened carefully.

"I probably heard all about it at one time, but being away from here for so long, I'd forgotten," he commented when she was finished. "Dolinger must care a lot for her. It can't be easy, having a wife in a wheelchair. And it sounds as if old Floyd's never forgiven himself for that accident."

"It's so stupid of Floyd to waste his life over something that happened a long time ago. Judy certainly doesn't feel he's responsible at all for what happened. She's happy, and Dolinger knows he's darned lucky to have her."

Sara added wryly, "Dolinger's not the nicest person I've ever met, except when she's around. She brings out a good streak in him."

Mitch mused silently that probably Sara did the same for him. Around her, he felt more at peace with himself than he did on his own, and the restlessness inside of him eased, somewhat.

He still felt rotten over quarreling with his father and saying the things he had. He must have a mean streak a mile deep to throw up his brother's death to the old man. And yet part of him still stubbornly felt that Wilson deserved being told how things were.

Steamboat was falling behind Misty on the trail, and Mitch reined in to give the lazy gelding a chance to catch up.

Sara looked lovely today, lithe and slim in her faded jeans and strapless ribbed sun top. She had a pink-checked shirt over it, hanging loose and unbuttoned, and the soft, tawny skin of her neck and shoulders glowed. She'd found a loosely woven straw hat somewhere, and the afternoon sun made intriguing patterns through it, sunshine and shade across her nose and cheeks.

"Did you and Dave have any problems in the bar last night?" she asked as they drew abreast again.

Mitch shook his head. "It was fairly quiet. Apparently your mom and gramma offered a huge spaghetti dinner around seven, and all the rowdies paid six bucks and ate until they nearly burst. So they didn't have a lot of empty room for beer after that. They tried but then finally gave up and sort of rolled on home."

Sara laughed. "Well, Dave's beer sales might drop, but it'll be worth it if the noise and the fights stop, as well."

"Dave's a great guy," Mitch remarked. "He's easy to talk to, and he doesn't keep handing out good advice like so many older men do. You've got a fine family, Sara."

Sara beamed at him, pleased that he liked her stepfather and the others.

"I hope my sister Frankie comes for a visit soon." She'd tried to call Frankie several times, but her vagabond sister was off on the rodeo circuit and couldn't be reached. "She'll probably phone some evening from Wyoming or Calgary, just to let us know she's alive and well."

"That's exactly what I used to do," Mitch said, and a feeling of nostalgia coursed through him all over again. Would he ever get over missing his life as a rodeo cowboy?

The path grew steeper and the trees thinned out as they climbed, and for a while there was only the creaking of the saddles and the noise of birds and crickets in the hot afternoon.

Then they crested the mountain's top and dropped into a rugged valley bisected by a tumbling stream. The valley narrowed until its rocky sides were only half a mile apart, and the nearby sound of a waterfall thundered just ahead.

"Wild Horse Canyon," Mitch announced, leading the way through thick pines and snarling underbrush into a green clearing.

Sara's breath caught with wonder. The waterfall was just above them, gushing over a precipice, making prisms and catching rainbows of light in the late-afternoon sunshine, dropping down until it formed a pool that shimmered at their feet. The glade was ringed with huge pine trees, and moss covered the earth where the horses paused.

Mitch swung out of his saddle and reached up to steady Sara as she dismounted, hands spanning her waist and lingering, holding her when her knees buckled a bit after the long ride.

"They say the wild horses come to this pool for water in the evening and then graze along the banks. We'll choose a spot and set up camp back among the trees, downwind so they won't get spooked."

It was a magic place, Sara decided as they shared the thick roast beef sandwiches and huge oatmeal cookies Gram had packed for them. There was an aura about the surroundings, a feeling that this was either the first or last unspoiled place in the world. Other people must have come here from time to time, but there was no trace of them.

No wonder the wild horses felt safe here.

The sun hung heavily over the crest of the mountain and finally dipped behind its peak. They'd unsaddled the horses earlier, led them down to drink and tied them loosely some distance away to graze. Mitch folded the saddle blankets under the plaid quilt they'd spread for their picnic. The saddles made ideal backrests, and they slouched comfortably side by side, chatting about anything that came to mind.

Mitch had taken his hat off, and hers. Now he slid an arm around Sara's shoulders, and his hand stroked gently up and down her arm, a slow, mesmerizing rhythm that sent shivers through every nerve ending. She felt lethargic, half asleep and yet highly conscious of the man beside her.

Silence fell between them as the sun's warmth lingered in the stillness of evening. A charged intentness seemed to fill the tiny glade where they lay, and she knew the exact moment when Mitch would turn slowly toward her, leaning on an elbow and gazing down into her face.

"Your eyes absorb the color of the sky, do you know that, Doc?" he said, and then he dipped his head to bring his lips down to meet hers.

His free hand glided across her midriff, and with the drugging delight of his kiss came the tentative touch of his fingers on her breast, cupping its fullness, and, as the kiss lengthened, deepened, she felt her nipple swell and strain against his palm as desire throbbed and grew between them.

He kissed her again and again, luxuriously, as if there were all the time in the world, touching the tip of his tongue to hers, running his hand lightly, tantalizingly, over every inch of her throat and breast, tormenting her until her breasts ached for more of his touch.

At last, Sara moaned and rolled away from the saddles toward him, onto her side so her body pressed his full-length, and she kissed him, abandoning control, allowing her lips to tell him how she wanted him, allowing her body to surge and undulate against the hardness of him.

She trusted him.

She loved him.

It was time now for what had seemed too soon before.

Till now, Mitch had held back, questioning, allowing her to make the decisions. Her lips, her body, gave the positive answer he craved.

"Sara," he breathed hoarsely. "Sara, honey, I want you so much." And then the words, low and passionate, that sent joy cascading through her.

"I love you, darlin' Sara."

He rolled onto his back, pulling her on top of him, legs tangling with hers until every inch of her was pressing deliciously down against him, but it was agony as well because the clothing they wore was suddenly intolerable.

She was still kissing him, long, deep kisses, endearingly clumsy.

"I'm not as good at this as you are at dancing," she teased once breathlessly. "But I'm sure I'll catch on."

"Sara," he finally gasped, running his trembling fingers through her thick, wild hair and holding her still for a moment.

She looked down at him, straight into green eyes clouded with passion, eyes that were asking her a final question.

She smiled wickedly and leaned down, tracing the scar on his right cheek with the very tip of her hot tongue as her body moved sinuously, answering the unspoken query the best way she knew how.

Between one breath and the next he rolled effortlessly so now she was under him. He balanced above her, his powerful thighs holding her captive one on each side of her hips, and he swiftly stripped off her blouse, tugged the elasticized top off over her head, and she felt the warm evening air drying the mist of perspiration between her naked breasts.

He stopped then, motionless, gazing down at her, at the tiny band of white that marked where her bikini top had been.

The milky softness of that skin contrasted erotically with the bronzed, satiny expanse above and below it, making the deep rose of her swollen nipples more evident.

His body surged dangerously, and his eyes closed tight for a moment in a struggle for control.

"You make me feel like a teenage greenhorn," he whispered.

Sara felt shy heat rising over her bare breasts and up into her cheeks as he looked at her, and he deliberately unsnapped his own shirt in one impatient movement, tossing it heedlessly aside.

Her breath caught at the muscular beauty of his chest and broad shoulders. A thick mat of dark curls spread neatly downward, and he must have worked in the sun with his shirt off, because the deep tan of his face and arms extended smoothly straight down to where his low-slung jeans rested on narrow hips.

"Mitch, you're beautiful," she breathed, and now it was his turn to be bashful.

She brought her hands up and ran her palms over him, shivering at the tactile delight of springy hair and smooth male skin, loving the shudder that coursed through him as her fingers explored, gliding across flat nipples that grew hard as pebbles when she touched them, venturing under his arms and into the nest of soft hair in each armpit, sliding around and touching the clean, long muscles of his back.

"That feels wonderful, having you touch me like that," he whispered deep in his throat. "Let me touch you, too."

He bent forward then and teased her aching nipples with the tip of his tongue, and when she gasped and linked her hands behind his head to urge him closer, he drew each in turn deeply into his mouth, tugging at them with a rhythm that her hips learned and echoed.

Sara felt thick heat gathering inside of her, centering and pulsing, needing to be ignited by him.

He was outlined against the wide blue sky and the tops of the tall trees, and they were alone in this world they'd created. The sound of the waterfall combined with the pounding of her heart, and she could see the pulse at the base of his throat throbbing wildly.

"Mitch?" she questioned, husky and pleading.

But he held himself still.

"Sara. Sara, first, can you tell me that you love me?"

There was a tender, boyish need for assurance in his husky plea, and there was naked desire in the magnificent clear green eyes that looked down into hers; not only hunger for her body, but for the verbal assurance of her love.

He touched her soul. He was both tough and shy, fearless and yet so vulnerable.

"Of course I love you," she said matter-of-factly. "As long as I live, I'll love you," she told him without even having to think, and a deep inner voice rejoiced in the truth of it.

His breath shuddered out in a sigh, and then his hands were busy with belts and denim, and she felt her jeans slither down her hips and legs as he quickly undressed first her and then himself, tugging off boots and socks and Levi's and tossing them into a heap at the side of the blanket.

They were naked together, skin against heated skin, and it was the most intoxicating feeling Sara had ever experienced.

His trembling hands reached under her, cupping her bottom, and she was aware of warmth, and wetness, as he lifted her hips.

In a long, slow movement that filled her with ecstasy, he sheathed his body with hers.

# Chapter Ten

It was Misty's low whinny that alerted Mitch to the arrival of the wild horses.

The world had been slow to right itself, and he and Sara were lying tumbled together, deliciously languorous with the aftermath of loving. The canopy of sky had turned from deep blue to a breathtaking shade of old rose and was now darkening to purple.

"Look, love. Over there."

Mitch's whisper was barely audible to Sara, and he lifted a corner of the blanket to wrap around her as she struggled to her knees and stared in the direction he pointed.

Five horses and a small colt were poised nervously on the edge of the woods opposite: four mares, rough and shaggy creatures, led by a small black stallion that tilted his nose to the wind and pawed the air restlessly, sniffing and blowing, unable to scent anything unusual yet certain with some sixth sense that things were different.

The sound of the waterfall muffled Misty's low whinny, and Steamboat paid absolutely no attention to the newcomers, engrossed as he was in munching the tender grass.

Sara and Mitch were motionless, fascinated and awed by the spectacle.

Sara was unaware that she was holding her breath, until at last she released it in a long sigh of wonder as the black stallion decided it was safe after all and warily led his harem down to the water to drink.

Mitch's arm tightened around Sara. Inexplicably she felt a knot in her chest and tears forming in her eyes as she watched the small group of horses.

They were anything but glamorous, undersized and dusty-looking, scrawny and underfed...but they were undeniably wild things, perhaps the last of an era.

There was an air of defiance and bravado about the little stallion, a totally macho feeling that he would defend his mares to the death if the need arose.

And perhaps it was fanciful, but Sara also thought the mares joined forces in their care of the colt, nosing him back if he strayed too far from the group, anxiously trailing like a pack of cautious aunts when he trotted curiously along the bank.

Suddenly Misty reared and gave a high, sharp whinny that made Sara jump, and in an instant, the black stallion was using his sharp hooves cruelly to drive his mares into the woods and away. He reared and swore in their direction, wild eyes rolling so the whites shone in the twilight.

Between one of Misty's calls and the next the wild horses were gone without a trace, and Sara felt her body trembling beneath the blanket Mitch had wrapped around her. Tears rolled down her cheeks, and she turned wordlessly to Mitch and rested her cheek on his bare chest.

"Sara?"

Her name seemed to reverberate through the muscles beneath her face, and she nodded tremulously.

"It's okay, I don't know why they make me cry. I guess because they were vulnerable somehow. I'm fine now. Why was there only that one little colt, Mitch? Wouldn't you think there'd be more foals than just that one?''

He paused before he answered, and she knew instinctively that he needed time to control his own emotions, that he'd felt the beauty and the tragedy of the horses just as she had.

"There probably were more. That's the only one that's survived, I suppose," he finally said gruffly. "At one time, there were hundreds of these herds, but there's not much room for them now in our modern world. They're a dying breed, Sara."

It was a fact, and she understood it with her mind, but her emotions weren't as accepting. Tears flowed freely, and she sniffed and apologized again, feeling foolishly sentimental.

But Mitch wasn't paying any attention to her tears.

"Sara," he said urgently, "will you marry me? Soon, maybe in the fall?"

They were kneeling facing each other, both naked, and he absentmindedly wiped her cheeks with his thumb, drying the tears that shone there.

"Will you?" he repeated insistently, thick eyebrows knotted in a frown. He tugged the blanket higher, trying to make it reach up around her shoulders.

"I know this is quick, but I can't see much point in waiting. We're right for each other, and back there—" he jerked his head over his shoulder, indicating the general direction of Bitterroot "—well, you're always busy. I haven't a hope in hell of seeing you alone long enough to court you properly. And after loving you like this, well..." He shrugged, and a smile came and went on his wide mouth. "I don't want to spend many more nights of my life without you, and I doubt that Adeline's gonna let me sneak in and out of your cabin."

There was brave humor in his words, but Sara recognized uncertainty in his eyes when he looked at her.

"Besides all that, I love you," he added. "I've never loved anyone before the way I love you, Doc."

She felt overwhelmed, confused. Excited and touched.

Her brain told her there were issues they ought to discuss thoroughly before they got into this talk about marriage, but her heart asked reasonably what difference talk would make, anyway? The issues wouldn't go away.

She loved him, too, with an intensity that frightened her.

And she felt exactly as he did. She didn't want to waste any more nights in her life without him beside her.

"If you even try sneaking into my cabin, I guarantee Gram will be after you with a loaded shotgun," she said shakily. "So I guess you're right; we'd better get married."

He didn't say a word. He simply took her into his arms with a ferocity that knocked the breath out of her.

And within a short time, lying with him as the sky darkened overhead, her breath was gone for quite a different reason, as he loved her with all the passionate intensity any woman could desire of a lover.

IT WAS FAR TOO LATE when they finally got back to Bitterroot for them to tell anyone their news...and anyway, Mitch insisted Sara keep their engagement a secret until he gave her a ring.

There was a delightful, old-fashioned streak in this man, and Sara adored it.

He knew just the ring he wanted for her, he declared mysteriously.

He'd be back no later than tomorrow evening to put it on her finger, he promised as he kissed her good-night in front of her cabin.

Then they'd tell the whole damned town, together, he declared.

They'd put a notice in the paper and have it announced from the pulpit of the church on Sunday, and maybe even hire a skywriter to proclaim it across the heavens.

He wanted every single person in Plains to know that Sara was his woman.

Sara agreed meekly, although she had a feeling it might be smart to just up and elope and skip the whole engagement part.

Mitch had never seen Adeline and Jennie in action when they felt there was a good reason to celebrate.

And as for publicizing the event . . . well, he'd soon realize it wasn't necessary to do anything except tell her relatives.

They'd do the rest, and then some.

SARA THOUGHT SHE WOULDN'T be able to sleep a wink that night, but her eyes closed the moment she hit the pillow.

She was up the next morning before anyone was stirring at Bitterroot, and she wolfed down a bowl of cereal and crept furtively out to the truck before even Gram made it down to the kitchen.

Sara felt guilty about avoiding the old woman, but she knew that Gram would take one look at the silly grin Sara couldn't seem to wipe off her face and know for certain something was up.

And Sara had never been able to keep anything from Gram for very long when that lady decided she wanted to know about it. So avoidance was by far the better part of valor this morning.

Sara breezed through the morning clinic, sunnily dispensing pills and advice, giving shots and taking temperatures, answering phone calls and feeling all the while as if she were savoring a delicious secret, one that filled her with such joy she could barely contain it.

She and Mitch were going to be married, and she was happier than she could ever remember being.

Floyd arrived at ten-thirty, bleary-eyed and totally amazed when Sara gave him a wide smile and said not a word about how late he was.

"I met your sister Judy the other day," she told him cheerfully instead of hollering about the time. "You should have told me she was George Dolinger's wife. I had no idea you were related to him."

It was unusual to have the rusty-haired assistant fumble for words, but he did now.

"I, ehh, I wanted to mention it that time he phoned here, but it's not easy, admitting to having a vile-tempered man like George as a brother-in-law. And, of course, I knew what you felt about him, you said so plain enough," he finally stammered. "Mind, he's the best husband possible for my sister, and for that I'm eternally grateful."

"Your sister's a lovely woman, I enjoyed meeting her."

Floyd's bloodshot eyes grew tender. "Judy's the finest there is."

Doc Stone came in just before noon.

Sara had thought a great deal about what Judy Dolinger had confided about Doc's eyesight. Knowing there was a physical reason for the problems he'd been having made Sara feel bad about her recent threats to report him, but the more she thought about it, the more annoyed she felt with the old doctor for not confiding in her himself. It could have saved a great deal of misunderstanding.

And now she was uncertain what to do, whether to tell him straight out that she knew or go on with the pretense he'd encouraged.

"Good morning," Sara greeted him now, but he barely nodded as he marched past her and into his office, shutting the door firmly behind him.

*If he wasn't a difficult, ornery, cantankerous man,* she thought irritably.

Well, Sara concluded, she wasn't going to let Doc's bad temper affect her. Nothing could quell her good spirits today.

She went back to work, sending Floyd out for a sandwich so she could finish necessary paperwork during her lunch hour...and also steal a few precious moments to dream of Mitch and wonder just what he was doing at that particular moment.

"Sara," Doc Stone suddenly bellowed from the adjoining room, bringing her out of her romantic reverie and making her spill some of her coffee on her fresh smock.

"Come in here, don't hover that way," he ordered imperially when she stood in the doorway. "And shut the door."

She gritted her teeth and did as he asked then sat down in the old wooden armchair across from his desk, wondering what was coming now.

"I've been doing some thinking," he announced abruptly. "And I've decided to sell the practice."

Sara's heart thumped and her brain quickly assimilated what Doc was telling her.

If another, younger vet took over, he'd probably try to run the practice by himself, especially if finances were a problem.

That's what Sara would do.

So there went her job. She'd have to look for a position somewhere else. Which meant moving, and how could she and Mitch possibly run a romance or a marriage, for that matter, with her living miles away from Plains? Mitch couldn't move. It was bad enough now, trying to be together.

All the happiness bubbling inside of her began to trickle away.

"You were absolutely right, young woman, when you laced into me last week about the mistakes I've made," Doc was going on. "The fact is, I have some damned thing wrong with my eyes; I can't see the way I used to. I suppose by ignoring it I thought it'd go away." Doc snorted. "No fool like an old one, and all that."

"I didn't know, I had no idea you were... when I said those things, I'm terribly sorry," Sara stammered, feeling awful for the old man. "I mean, someone told me this weekend about your... I would never have said what I did if..."

"Hogwash," Doc bellowed. "It needed to be said; never apologize for telling the truth, young woman. And for heaven's sake, will you spare me your pity, that's the very reason I didn't tell anybody in the first place. Who the hell wants a bunch of teary-eyed females feeling sorry for him, tell me that?" He beetled his brows ferociously at her. "Now, what sort of arrangements would suit you best, financially, for the purchase of the practice?"

It took a minute for his words to make sense.

"You mean me, buy this... but I couldn't, I don't have..."

"Of course, you don't," Doc snorted in disgust. "Never thought you did. Too bad, too, because I could have used the ready money, might not have all that many years left to live it up during retirement." He gave his dry chuckle. "So we'll have to make the best of things, won't we? Now, this is what I feel the business is worth, and this is about what it brings in on a good month." He shoved a paper with a careful list of figures across the desk at her.

"Way I see it, by living on bread and water and working eighteen hours a day..." He chuckled wickedly at his own wit.

Doc was in rare form this morning, Sara concluded dazedly.

"...you could probably pay me this much..." He pointed a stubby forefinger at a figure.

"But it's impossible, I don't even have a down payment," she protested sadly, not even looking at the amount he was pointing at.

Doc's fist thundered down on the desk, and his raspy voice was filled with exasperation.

"Blast you, woman, I'm trying to tell you I'll forgo a down payment for a full year. See this figure here?" He rapped an impatient forefinger on the paper.

"In the course of a year, with hard work, you'll be able to establish the business in your own right, and I'm quite sure the bank manager will agree to loan you the money at that time to pay me this lump amount. Interest included, young woman, I'm not a charitable institution," he added grumpily.

Afraid to hope even yet, Sara took the paper with trembling fingers and studied the concise figures.

The amount he'd arrived at as a purchase price wasn't outrageous, but it made her gulp all the same. Doc wasn't giving her anything...except an unheard-of opportunity to own her own practice, which Sara wouldn't have dared even to begin dreaming of for at least another five years.

"Take the damned paper away with you and go over it carefully. Nobody should buy anything without giving it time," he ordered. "Not too much time, however. If you decide it's what you want, then the business is yours as soon as I get the papers drawn up, and I'm through on Friday." He glanced beyond her to the door, where they both knew

Floyd was probably hovering, hoping to hear what was going on, and Doc's voice lowered until she had to lean forward in order to hear.

"There's one thing, not a condition, of course, but...I'd be grateful if you could see your way clear to keeping Floyd on. I know he's drinking heavy again, but I'll throw the fear of God into him for you if you agree. He does need the job..." Doc was embarrassed, avoiding her eyes as he made the request.

"Of course." If she hadn't met Judy, would she have agreed so readily to keeping Floyd on? Sara didn't pause to think about it right now.

She understood a great deal more than she had before about Doc, and about Floyd, too.

She looked at the old vet, her heart full of gratitude, unable to say anything of what she felt because she knew he would wave it impatiently away with some caustic comment or other.

"Thank you, Doc," was all she managed, and sure enough, he waved a hand at her as if he were brushing away a pesky fly.

"Don't you have calls to make, girl? You young vets seem to waste an awful amount of time having coffee breaks and lunches," he harrumphed, and Sara couldn't resist. She walked behind the desk and boldly planted a hearty kiss on his cheek.

Doc turned magenta and glared at her until she left the office.

"See you phone me the minute you make up your mind," he all but snarled after her. She heard him snort, "Women," as she shut the door behind her.

SARA COULDN'T REMEMBER afterward just which farms she visited that afternoon or even what animals she treated.

Once she was out of the office, her brain went from Mitch and his proposal to Doc and his, and the more she thought of both, the more uncertain and confused she became, and the more anxious she felt.

Mitch had already complained in a good-natured way about how little time they had together because of her job. If she accepted Doc's offer and bought the vet practice, she was practical enough to admit that even the small amount of free time she now had would most likely be sacrificed to work—she wouldn't be able to afford any assistant other than Floyd, and financially, she needed all the work that opportunity presented.

In other words, she'd be forced to work as many hours a day as possible.

Would Mitch be able to accept that?

The alternative was to refuse Doc's offer, which would result in the practice selling to someone else, and more than likely, with Sara having to move away if she wanted to go on practicing.

She couldn't refuse, she simply couldn't.

Doc was making a dream come true for her. Somehow, she'd balance her job and her love for Mitch.

Just before she drove home to Bitterroot, she phoned Doc.

"Could you have the lawyer draw up those papers, please, just the way you suggested this morning?" she asked with a catch in her throat. "I want very much to buy the business."

Doc snorted. "Damn well took you long enough to make up your mind, young woman" was all he said before he hung up.

Sara found that she was shaking as she drove home slowly to Bitterroot. Too much had happened in just two days, too many changes were imminent in her life.

At Bitterroot, too, things were changing rapidly. Instead of Jennie or Gram calling out a greeting and having a leisurely cup of tea with her when she came home and giving her an opportunity to discuss what was on her mind, the place was a maelstrom of frenzied activity.

A new dishwasher had been installed that afternoon in the kitchen, and a huge freezer had been delivered, as well. Gram was already busily stirring an immense pot of chili while Sara's mother tossed a salad in a bowl nearly large enough to bathe in when Sara walked into the kitchen.

Mitch hadn't arrived yet.

Should she tell her family about buying the business, or should she wait for Mitch and announce their engagement first and her business dealings second? she pondered.

Or should she tell Mitch privately about the business, and then...

"Sara, grab that pot holder, child, and get those rolls out of the oven, will you? And then take these plates out and pile them with the cutlery on the buffet—we're serving things casuallike tonight. Jennie, d'you figure we've got ample dessert made or should I whip up some more?"

Jennie gave Sara a quick hug on her way to the fridge.

"We've got plenty, Mom, barring an army invasion. Hi, Sara, Ruth was here till half an hour ago—that woman's an absolute treasure. Her husband finally phoned and she had to go home to make supper. Do you think he's going to mind her starting work here tomorrow? She was just wonderful, helping us today, and she said she hadn't had such fun for a long time."

That gave Sara pause for thought. On top of everything else, she started thinking about Wilson's reaction when he found out his wife had a job at Bitterroot and his son was engaged to the woman vet.

Wow. If both Ruth and Mitch broke their news tonight, Wilson was in for a bad evening, Sara mused with a wicked grin, setting out baskets for buns and getting roped into three more jobs before she finally managed to slip away to her own cabin to shower and change into a sleeveless top and a brightly printed cotton skirt before Mitch arrived.

IT WAS NEARLY MIDNIGHT before Sara and Mitch even had a chance to exchange more than a few words with each other, and they didn't tell Jennie, Dave and Gram about their engagement at all that evening.

In fact, everyone was too tired to do more than grunt, anyway, by the time the crowd cleared. Mitch planted an exhausted kiss somewhere to the left of Sara's mouth and went home without giving her an engagement ring.

"I'll come by tomorrow and pick you up at the office after work," he promised her a little grimly. "If you can be finished by five, that is. I want to do this properly, without fifty million starving people watching me put a ring on your finger."

Sara agreed and wearily apologized for what had happened that evening.

Things at the lodge had gotten quite out of hand, because about thirty rambunctious and hungry young men had descended on the place expecting supper.

It seemed that Gram, in an excess of enthusiasm, had told several customers on Saturday that there would be an all-you-can-eat chili dinner on Monday night, same price as the spaghetti feast had been, and they'd eagerly spread the word among their friends.

Mitch had barely climbed out of his truck when he was hauled into the lodge and put to work helping Dave fashion makeshift tables out of boards and sawhorses.

Sara wasn't waiting for him in her cabin, anyway. She was up to her elbows in dishwater in the kitchen, washing plates because the new dishwasher had sprung a leak the moment it was turned on.

It was the only night at Bitterroot that she found herself wishing desperately for a veterinary emergency so she could insist she needed Mitch's help and spirit them both away, and it was one of those rare times when the phone didn't ring for her services even once.

More and more hungry people arrived, Sara's hands shriveled from hot water and detergent, and there wasn't a chance for a stolen kiss all evening, much less a proper time to receive a ring and announce an engagement.

It was unbelievable how much people could eat at an all-you-can-eat chili dinner.

"MITCH, IT'S GORGEOUS."

Sara stared down at her left hand, admiring the antique ruby ring Mitch had finally slid onto her finger moments before.

"Best of all, it fits," he answered with practical satisfaction.

They were in the veterinary office with the doors safely locked. It was after hours, and Sara had carefully switched on the answering machine and made sure Floyd was gone. She'd even insisted the cats go outside and stay out. After last night, she wasn't taking any chances.

"It was my grandmother's ring. She had two, this and an emerald. Mom gave one to Bob and one to me years ago, to give to the women we'd marry someday," Mitch explained, wrapping his arms around her and holding her close. "Mine's never been out of the safety deposit box, because there's never been anyone like you before," he told an enthralled Sara. A pleased, little-boy grin spread across his rugged features. "I'm glad you like it, Doc."

"I absolutely love it. I'll treasure it as long as I live, and that's how long I'll love you," Sara assured him, planting a kiss on his chin and then gasping as he took over and made a much more thorough job of the whole thing.

One thing led to another, and soon they were making good use of the couch in the waiting room.

Sara could never look at that couch again without feeling a blush rise in her cheeks.

Mitch told her much later that his father nearly had apoplexy when his mother broke the news about her job at Bitterroot.

His mother had never worked outside of her own home before, and Wilson considered this a blow to his male ego.

Mitch didn't tell her that Wilson also blamed Sara for the whole thing. And that he'd nearly had a seizure when Mitch announced that he was about to marry her.

As a result, he and his father had had another massive blowup.

What with one thing and another, Sara never did find exactly the right moment to tell Mitch she was buying the business from Doc Stone.

JUST AS SARA HAD EXPECTED, Gram and Jennie were beside themselves with excitement over the engagement. They saw it as an ideal opportunity to invite the residents of Plains and outlying areas to a celebration at Bitterroot, which would introduce the entire community to the new restaurant.

A barbecue, held outdoors by the pool.

And, of course, it was to announce that Sara and Mitch were to be married, but wasn't it superb timing on their part, getting engaged just when publicity for the Bitterroot Resort and Dining Room was most needed?

"EVERY POT HAS A LID," Gram declared firmly to Sara when they finally had a quiet moment together. "I knew right off when I met him that Mitchell was the right lid for you."

"Gram, for heaven's sake, you make us sound like a set of cookware or something," Sara protested.

"Stainless steel," Gram pronounced. "That boy is steel through and through. I know quality when I see it. And no question about you, dear. You come from good stock. Stubborn, but good stock all the same." She narrowed her eyes and peered at Sara over her glasses. "You gotta remember, though, honey, any marriage is sixty-forty. You give sixty percent, the man gives forty. That's why I never married again after your grampa."

"Not anymore, Gram, it's been renegotiated. It's straight fifty-fifty now."

Gram snorted eloquently. "Bull," she stated succinctly.

The engagement party was planned a week from Sunday. On Wednesday, Sara signed on the dotted line, the scared-stiff new owner of Stone's Veterinary Service.

The lawyer's name was Martin Leskey. He was contemporary to Doc Stone, and he talked and moved so slowly every single thing took twice as long as it ought to take.

He was determined that Sara should understand all the aspects of the transaction. As one hour slipped into another, Sara found herself looking at the clock first curiously and then with growing concern as the lawyer went on and on in excruciating detail about every last thing.

There were still two calls she had to make before she could go home, and Martin Leskey seemed ready to prolong the meeting until midnight.

"Now, this is an itemized list of exactly what the business includes, this is the percentage of the purchase price allotted to goodwill, this is..."

Sara knew what she was buying down to the last cotton swab.

"You understand that the business leases the premises it occupies from—" Martin consulted his closely typed notes yet again "—from Equity Holdings, and that notice has been given that the owner is raising the rent beginning in September?"

Sara sat up straighter. Doc Stone hadn't mentioned that, and Sara was appalled at the amount of the proposed increase.

She thought of the decrepit old house and the faulty plumbing, and indignation took the place of boredom.

"If they're raising the rent, then I feel something should be done about necessary repairs to the building," she said firmly, and Martin dutifully noted down all the things Sara listed, from the leaky toilets to the falling-down fence at the rear of the building.

Finally it was finished. Leskey stood up and beamed at Sara, holding out his hand for a congratulatory handshake.

"I've never met a woman vet before. Never dreamed Doc Stone would sell out to a woman. Well, best of luck, my dear, and if you ever need any legal advice, you know where to reach me."

It hadn't seemed real before now. The lawyer's handshake brought home to Sara the enormity of what she'd just done.

And she hadn't said a word about it to Mitch.

WITH THE SALE FINALIZED, Doc immediately disappeared.

Floyd was surprisingly reliable for a change, calling Sara

"Dr. Wingate" in an annoyingly formal way when he congratulated her on the purchase.

"I'll do me best for you, just as I've always done for Doc," Floyd assured her, and Sara shuddered.

It was more a threat than a promise.

SARA CAME TO THE OFFICE EARLY and stayed late and answered several midnight calls that brought her back home in time to go to work again during the two weeks before the party.

Fortunately it was haying season, so Mitch was just as busy as she. They were able to spend a couple of hours together one evening, but it wasn't nearly enough.

She didn't find the right moment to tell him she was the new owner of Stone's Vet Service.

HE RANG SARA FIRST THING on Friday morning.

"Hiya, Doc." There was a note of exuberance in his greeting, and Sara smiled into the receiver.

"Hiya Doc yourself."

"How about playing hooky with me and driving down to a ranch south of Missoula this weekend? Misty's come into season and the guy down there has some of the best rodeo stock in the country. We could leave tonight, come back Sunday afternoon and go out for dinner and dancing in some fancy hotel in the city."

Sara knotted a fist with frustration.

"Mitch, I'd like nothing better, but I simply can't get away," she said bleakly.

"Surely that place will run without you for two lousy days," he said. Floyd bustled into the room before Sara could answer.

"There's a rancher from up the valley in the waiting room. He wants to talk to you, Doctor," Floyd informed her in a stage whisper, hovering.

Sara waved a hand at him. "I'm coming," she said impatiently.

"Good, I'll pick you up..." Mitch's tone was jubilant.

"Oh, Mitch, not you, I was talking to Floyd." She glared pointedly until Floyd finally inched his way out and shut the door.

"Mitch, darling, I'm sorry, I just can't get away right now."

There was silence, and then he said he understood, but Sara could hear the disappointment in his voice.

That weekend passed in a flurry of hard work, two night calls that kept her out till nearly dawn, and a constant, nagging sense of utter misery because she hadn't been able to go with Mitch.

He called her late Sunday night; she was having a cup of coffee with her mother and Dave by the pool.

"Hiya, Doc." His voice was weary. "I'm home, I'm beat. It was one hell of a lonely weekend without you."

"Same here," she said fervently. "I missed you desperately, Mitch. I hated every moment you were gone."

"Good, then next time you'll come along."

There was a pause, and she finally said, "If it's possible, yes, I will."

THE SUNDAY OF THE ENGAGEMENT party, Bitterroot was hopping with frenzied activity by 8:00 a.m.

Ruth had already arrived with a dour-faced Wilson in tow, and he'd been immediately ordered to work by Gram. The amazing thing was, Sara noted wonderingly, Wilson went meekly ahead and did what he was told, which included, of all things, washing a huge bowlful of salad greens.

Buffet tables were set up on the cedar decking all around the pool, and flowers were arranged on each. Chairs were grouped in friendly circles here and there across the grass, and by twelve, everything was ready for the arrival of the guests at one. The women were putting the finishing touches on the salads and arranging the rolls in napkin-lined baskets and growing more nervous by the minute.

"Go and get ready, Sara. We'll finish here," Jennie ordered, and Sara gratefully headed for her cabin.

She actually had a new dress for the occasion, a silky black-and-white-print minichemise with string-thin shoulder straps, about the sexiest dress she'd ever owned. Sara had seen it in the window of the smart new boutique in Plains and bought it without giving herself time to think about the leg-baring hemline or the expensive price tag.

Mitch deserved this dress, she told herself now, sliding it down her freshly showered, perfumed body and wishing she had a full-length mirror to see how it looked. He'd rarely seen her in anything but stained working coveralls, and the time had come to remind him she was female through and through.

She was just putting the finishing touches to an ambitious chignon high on the back of her head when she heard a tap on the door and Mitch came in.

He took two steps into the room and stopped, and the expression on his face was worth twice what the dress had cost.

His green eyes were sultry as he allowed his gaze to trace every inch of her, from the ridiculously high strappy sandals and sheer hose to the artfully casual curls escaping from the high knot at the back of her head.

"Are you the lady doc who's gonna marry a cowboy?" he said wonderingly, and she closed the space between them and wrapped her arms around his neck. "You look like a movie star."

"I feel like Cinderella," she said, and neither of them cared one bit that he kissed off all her carefully applied lipstick.

The guests started arriving long before one, and Mitch kept Sara's hand clasped proudly in his the whole time they greeted friends and neighbors.

Carol and Bill Forgie were among the first to arrive, Carol hugely pregnant by now.

"Not much longer," she groaned, lowering herself carefully into a straight-backed chair. "But I wanted to come and congratulate both of you even if I go into labor right here with all of Plains looking on. I feel as if our foal had a lot to do with you and Mitch falling in love. I'll never forget the way you looked at each other that day. Look, Bill, they're doing it again now," she teased. "Isn't that cute?"

Sara stuck out her tongue and Carol giggled delightedly.

The smell of beef roasting in the huge outdoor barbecue pit mingled with the pine scent from the surrounding trees and the faint mineral odor from the pool.

Laughter and voices filled the air, and Sara and Mitch shook hands and smiled and thanked more people than they would have thought even lived in the area. But before the last guests had even arrived, Dave came hurrying over and tapped Sara on the arm.

"There's a phone call for you," he said quietly.

She turned to Mitch, and the look he gave her sent a shudder of foreboding down her spine.

"Sara, not today. Please. Tell whoever it is that you can't come."

"I'll be right back," she said weakly, and hurried into the lodge.

The man on the phone was furious and upset.

"One of my cows calved out in the pasture last night, and she pushed out her uterus in the process. The neighbor's dog was running loose, and he's ripped her to ribbons. Not only that, he attacked the calf as well. I called the vet I usually use from Lynch Creek, and he's out for the day. I phoned his partner, and he's got the flu. He told me to call Doc Stone, and finally I got referred to you. Now, I'm goddamned sick and tired of trying to get a vet out here. Are you gonna come and do something about this or not?"

Sara could see Mitch standing apart from the group outside, waiting tensely for her.

In her mind's eye she saw the bloody cow and the poor newborn calf.

"Tell me where you're located," she heard herself saying. "I'll be there as quickly as I can."

MITCH SAW THE EXPRESSION on her face when she hung up the phone and started toward him, and he knew, even though he could hardly believe she'd do this to him.

Sara was about to walk out on her own engagement party; walk out and leave him to apologize and explain and act as if he didn't mind at all being deserted on such an occasion.

"Mitch, I have to go."

Impotent anger flared in him, and he wondered, not for the first time, just how much of their life together would be interrupted by those very words.

He saw her stricken look, and he tried his best to swallow his rage. "How long d'you think you'll be?"

She shook her head hopelessly.

"From the sound of it, quite a while."

He saw his father watching them, and he forced himself not to show his frustration with her in front of Wilson.

He planted a hasty kiss on Sara's cheek as she hurried off and pinned as good a grin as he could manage on his stiff features.

He wasn't about to give the old man the satisfaction of thinking he'd been right about what he'd said when Mitch had told him he was marrying Sara.

"Better learn quick how to cook and clean house, boy. These career women put their jobs ahead of everythin' else."

The afternoon stretched ahead of Mitch like an eternity.

# *Chapter Eleven*

It turned out the ranch was twenty miles away, and the tiny calf was nearly dead when Sara finally arrived in the pasture where the rancher and his men were waiting with the injured animals.

Sara'd taken a wrong turn and had to backtrack, wasting valuable time, and the rancher, Adam Mayberry, was quick to ask scathingly what the hell had taken her so long.

She took one look at the horribly mutilated calf and with nausea rising in her stomach, she quietly told Mayberry that it was hopeless.

"The calf will have to be put down."

Mayberry cursed viciously. "I hope you know what the hell you're talking about, lady, because I don't think much of letting some green vet make decisions like that about my animals."

Under different circumstances, Sara thought that the big, rawboned man might have been easygoing and friendly. Today he was as obnoxious as he could possibly be.

She met his gaze with a cold, level stare.

"You called me out here. Now decide right now whether or not you want me to treat these animals, because if you have doubts about my ability, I'll leave immediately."

He gave her a furious look. "I don't have much choice, do I, miss? You'd better go ahead."

She thought of the party she'd left to come here, Mitch's anger when she'd left him to deal with their celebration alone, and she longed to walk away. Fast. But the cow was lowing pitifully over her calf and was bloodied herself. What's more, at the end of the month, there was Sara's payment to be met to Doc Stone, and all the other payments for all the other months ahead. And the rent increase.

Neither her conscience nor her bank account could afford an excess of pride at the moment.

"Do you want to salvage the meat from the calf?"

Mayberry shook his head. "There's not enough intact to bother about," he said despondently, and Sara had to agree with him.

She administered a lethal injection to the calf and prepared a second hypodermic full of anesthetic. She injected it in the cow's tail, grimly hoping it would do what it was designed for.

"Get me buckets of hot water from the back of my truck," she ordered sternly. "I have to clean this animal before I can do anything for her."

Time disappeared as it always did when she was doing the work she'd been trained for, and afternoon waned and became evening and then night as she struggled and failed and tried again, and then again, and still again.

"SHE'S NOT HERE? Hey, Mitch, don't tell me she saw through you already and ran, buddy?"

"Where's your lady, Mitch? We drove all the way in to meet her. Can't believe you're really gettin' hitched, you old son of a gun. Introduce us..."

During the interminable afternoon Mitch parried comments, apologized for Sara's absence and endured the taunts and teasing from friends he hadn't seen for years and had rashly invited to the engagement party.

When everyone finally got in their vehicles and drove away, he stalked out to Sara's cabin, threw himself into the old rocker on the porch, and waited.

It was nearly ten before he saw the lights of her truck turn in. He heard the vehicle's door slam, saw her tall shape coming across the yard.

She avoided the lodge, making her way around the side of the building quietly and skirting the pool as she found the path to her cabin.

*Smart move, Doc,* Mitch thought admiringly, despite the outraged fury rising in him. Jennie and Adeline had been anything but pleased at her absence, and Adeline wasn't one for keeping silent.

His own mother was the only one who staunchly defended Sara's absence that day.

"She's a doctor, and doctor's go when they're needed," she'd said firmly when they were all cleaning up that evening and Adeline had made a caustic comment about Sara being absent from her own danged party.

She stopped just short of the steps when she realized he was there.

"Oh, hi, Mitch. I thought everyone had gone home." Her voice was infinitely weary. She still wore the blue coverall she'd worked in, and it was a spectacular mess. Her face was dirty, her hair sweaty and lying in ropes on her shoulders.

He tried to stop the angry retort that rose in his throat, but he failed.

"I'm not everyone, Sara. I'm the guy you're supposed to be marrying in a month. This wingding here today was to celebrate that, remember? But it's kinda hard for me to have a good time when my bride-to-be walks out on the party.''

A long, weary sigh escaped her. All the long way home, she'd hoped she wouldn't have to deal with this tonight.

"I'm sorry, Mitch, really I am. There was a cow and calf that'd been savaged by dogs...."

He cut her off abruptly. "Every single call is something urgent, Sara. What the hell is wrong with Doc Stone answering a few of his own emergencies? It's his practice. You're just playing the sucker, letting him throw all the work on you."

Here it was. She should have told him days ago, and hadn't.

"Mitch, it's not Doc Stone's practice anymore." She drew in a deep breath, hoping for courage. "It's mine now, I've made arrangements to buy it."

He was speechless. Long, pregnant moments drifted by and neither of them moved.

"You bought it, you bought a business, and never said a word to me about it?" His eyes narrowed, and there wasn't a trace of warmth in the cold, hard lines of his face.

She was bone-tired, and annoyance crept into her tone.

"I didn't think being engaged meant I had to ask permission. It came up all of a sudden a week or so ago, and I had to make the decision. It's what I've always dreamed of, having my own practice. Besides..." She was trying to figure out how to tell him all the details, but Mitch wasn't listening.

"This affects my life as much as it does yours, and yet you didn't even bother talking it over with me," he was saying in icy tones. "Your job obviously comes first with you, Sara, and that's not going to change just because we get married. So where does that leave me? Sitting around waiting for a few scraps of your time when nobody has an emergency? Being embarrassed, like I was today, when you ought to be beside me and instead you're off taking care of somebody's cow?''

Sara's fatigue was rapidly being replaced with defensive anger.

"You knew from the beginning that my job was demanding. Can't you understand what it means to me to have a practice of my own? I spent years in school, hard years, dreaming of the day I'd be able to have something like this. Can't you understand that and be happy for me?''

"Lots of us have dreams, lady," Mitch sneered. "I had dreams, and look where it got me, back here slopping pigs and rounding up sheep. Some of us don't just take what the hell we want without first considering the people we love.''

Sara's tenuous control was gone. She was trembling, and her voice rose. "So that's what this is about, that I have a career I love, a job I look forward to doing, while you go on wishing you were still the hero of the rodeo circuit. Don't you think your being a reluctant rancher will affect our life just as much as my being called out on a Sunday? What happens to me if one day you decide you just can't handle pigs and sheep anymore, and you grab your rope and take off back to the rodeo?''

She knew she sounded petulant, she knew she shouldn't attack him in this particular way, and she was sorry even before the words were finished, but there wasn't any way of taking them back again.

He took two quick strides down the steps and detoured sharply around her, careful not to touch her. Sara couldn't see his face clearly; it was getting very dark and his hat brim shadowed his expression, but by the stiff way he held himself she knew he was furious.

"Mitch, please, I..." She held out a hand to him, and she knew he heard her, but he didn't turn around. In a few moments, the truck roared and gravel spun wildly as he accelerated out of the parking lot.

Mitch clutched the wheel as if it were someone's neck.

Her words smashed through his skull, making it ache, and as he hurtled down the deserted highway at a speed far beyond the posted limit, his mouth twisted into a grimace with the bitter admission that what Sara had accused him of was only the truth; he wasn't thrilled with his role as prodigal returned, he didn't look forward to days spent working beside his father.

Maybe some of the rage that had built up today against the woman he loved was actually just what she'd said—envy because she had a career she loved, and he didn't.

So what the hell was he going to do about it?

Cut and run, back to a way of life he was already getting too old for? Climb on Misty and head on down the road, odd-jobbing here and there until something took his fancy?

His shoulders slumped, his grip relaxed on the wheel, his foot slackened on the gas. None of the reasons for his coming back here had changed. Home was where he belonged.

He was the one who needed to change.

He was no quitter, either. As a rodeo rider, he didn't give up just because a bronco threw him once or twice, or ten times.

There was a way to make this work, and by God, he'd find it.

The problem was, would he ever be happy at it?

Damn that stubborn woman of his anyhow, buying a vet practice and never saying a word to him. Hurt pride mingled with Mitch's other confused emotions.

His mind's eye pictured Sara as he'd left her back there, hopping mad at him, covered in the muck her job so often produced, and a stab of uncertainty shot through him.

Was there hope that the two of them could take the love they had and turn it into a marriage that worked?

Was love enough?

Or would they be smarter to pack the whole thing in right now?

THE ANSWER TO THAT QUESTION continued to plague him during the days that followed, and because there were no simple answers to it, Mitch stayed at the ranch, busy from daylight to dusk with haying but aware also that he was deliberately avoiding Sara.

She sent a message back with Ruth, late in the week, that she'd like to talk with him, but still he delayed.

He worked from dawn until dark in a kind of maniac frenzy, collapsing into bed in utter exhaustion and getting up before daybreak to do it all over again.

There'd been an uneasy truce between Mitch and his father since the day of the engagement party. They worked together when a job required two men, but neither sought out the other's company voluntarily. Wilson had maintained a stubborn silence about the trip Mitch had taken to have Misty bred. Mitch no longer offered any comments or suggestions about the management of the ranch. He did his stubborn best to act exactly like a hired hand, taking orders meekly.

He knew it drove Wilson nuts, and that was satisfying in some perverse fashion.

Friday morning, Mitch was already half done with the chores when he saw his father coming across the yard. Dawn was just streaking the eastern sky, and the roosters were crowing persistently from the chicken coop.

Wilson strode determinedly over to Mitch.

"You tryin' to show me up, boy, gettin' out here every mornin' this week an hour ahead a' me?"

"Nope," Mitch said shortly. "Just can't sleep, that's all."

To Mitch's absolute amazement, his father heaved a huge sigh and said grumpily, "Well, that makes two of us. Never dreamed that at my time of life I'd be havin' problems with your mother like this." He spat disgustedly, and with an embarrassed sidelong glance at his son, added, "Leave the rest of this, I'll do it. Come up to the kitchen and have some coffee."

It took a long moment for Mitch to realize that the old man might actually want to talk to him.

Wilson made heavy business of pouring mugs full of the truly awful coffee he'd brewed. Ruth was still asleep upstairs, and Wilson carefully drew the door shut at the bottom of the stairwell before he sat down.

"It's this danged fool job your mother's taken, Mitchell," he whined before Mitch had even lifted his cup. "She never worked before, in all the years we bin married. Why in tarnation would she have to go and get a job now being a cook at some fool restaurant? It's blamed disgustin', if you ask me." Wilson shook his head dejectedly. "And she's never here anymore, place is fallin' apart. Half the time, supper's late, nothin' baked."

Usually the old man's complaining tone sparked anger in Mitch, but this morning, he found himself feeling strangely sorry for Wilson, even though the urge to defend his mother ran hot.

This job at Bitterroot was changing Ruth...changing her for the better. She'd started smiling again, she chattered about the people she met, she'd stopped crying all the time.

Mitch told his father that, trying his best to make Wilson see that Ruth had good reasons for taking the job.

But Wilson couldn't and wouldn't understand. He just began another tirade about the chickens, of all things. Ruth had always taken care of the chickens, and now Wilson was having to clean out the coop. It seemed that was the final straw.

He was deliberately ignoring the fact that having a job was making his wife happy again.

Why was that?

Mitch sat back, his coffee untouched, not listening to the litany of petty complaints about unwashed socks and dishes in the sink.

Instinctively Mitch knew these weren't the things really bothering his father.

Was it the realization that Ruth had suddenly found something that interested her, Mitch mused, something that Wilson had no part of? Was Wilson jealous that Ruth could be involved in a life quite apart from the one she'd always lived?

Why, the old man was running scared, Mitch realized with a sudden burst of insight. He was scared of change, scared of losing his wife. He'd always had her all to himself, and now he didn't.

Maybe he was scared that she wouldn't want or need him anymore, of all the damned stupid ideas.

Mitch felt like grinning at that. His mother doted on the old man, always had. Wilson's ego was hurting, that was all.

But was it unimportant? Was his father's reaction that different from Mitch's resentment of Sara's job? Wasn't part of the reason he was feeling put out right now just the fact that Sara's job was consuming her, that he couldn't really be a part of it, that it took her away from him when he wanted her?

What was all that, but ego?

He absolutely hated the feeling that he and his father might have a lot in common.

"Look, Pop..."

Look, Pop...what?

The last time Mitch had tried confiding in this man, he'd had his dreams jumped on and tossed back in his face.

Well, if an ornery horse bucked him off, he'd always climbed right back on, hadn't he?

"Pop, I'm having the same kind of problems you are," Mitch finally blurted out. "With Sara. Would you believe she's gone and bought that practice of Doc Stone's, without so much as mentioning it to me? And she's always off treating some damned animal or other. Look what happened at the engagement party. Made a damned fool out of me."

There, that ought to bring on a load of complaints, for sure. The least it would do would be to divert the old man's ire from Mom to him and Sara. Wilson could get into his objections to women vets, and Sara in particular, release a lot of steam at Mitch's expense. What the hell, the old man was his father, Mitch told himself, feeling like a martyr.

"Humph." Wilson drank down half his cooling coffee without even a grimace and then set the cup down before he went on.

"Well, that's no different from what your mom did. Damned if Mother didn't up and take that job without a word to me, either. Y'know, son, like you said before, maybe they both have their reasons. Maybe we ought to try patience. We're men, after all. That Sara of yours, she's got lots of gumption, and I like that in a woman. Y'know, I think your mother's the same."

Mitch choked on his coffee and nearly fell off his chair. In the next hour, for the first time he could remember, he and his father actually tried to have a conversation.

The fact that it was about whether or not Wilson should trade the station wagon in on a four-wheel-drive unit didn't matter at all.

The fact that he asked Mitch's opinion mattered one hell of a lot.

MITCH CALLED SARA several times that day and missed her each time. Finally, just past noon, he gave up and drove into Plains, absolutely determined to snatch her away from her work for just an hour, to talk through the strain that was between them . . . and hold her in his arms and kiss her until she was breathless, until all the tension between them disappeared.

He was parking the truck in front of the vet office when the sirens started wailing down the street. A fire truck and an ambulance tore by, and when he opened the office door, Sara was frantically snatching vials and supplies from the drug cupboard in the hall and stuffing them frantically into a case.

She looked over her shoulder and saw him, and he took a quick, anxious step toward her when he saw the naked fear on her pale features.

"Mitch, oh my God, I'm so glad you're here. How did you know? C'mon, there's no time to waste, carry this . . ." She thrust another bag at him and raced for the door. "I called Doc Stone and he's meeting us out there, Floyd's gone to fetch him. . . ."

"What the hell's going on? I came to see you. . . ."

She was already half out the door.

"You didn't know? Oh, Mitch, it's Bill and Carol Forgie . . . their barn is on fire. Some of the horses are already . . ."

Her voice broke, and her face crumpled.

"Oh, Mitch, I'm so scared."

After the first, paralyzed instant, he took charge.

"C'mon, I'll drive."

Together they raced for the veterinary van.

FROM SEVERAL MILES AWAY, they could see the black smoke rising ominously over the rolling hills.

"The barn's so damned old," Mitch said fearfully, and Sara swallowed the fear in her throat and nodded.

"It'll go up like tinder," she said in a strained voice. "Horses aren't smart about getting out, either. They panic and refuse to leave what they figure is the safety of their stalls. I only hope Bill doesn't try being a hero."

Mitch remembered the ambulance racing past and cold fear overcame him. He cursed the potholed road and stepped still harder on the accelerator, ignoring the bone-crushing jolts the van made.

They rounded the final corner, and both of them gasped aloud with horror.

The stable was an inferno, with flames shooting high into the air. Several neighbors were already on the scene, their trucks parked helter-skelter in the meadow, and men ran frantically in pursuit of two horses crazed by the fire and out of control. They had huge, raw burn patches on their hides.

But it was the ambulance, and the sight of a blanketed human form being carefully loaded into it that was most horrifying to Sara and Mitch.

The instant the van stopped, they hurried over, just as the ambulance attendants were about to shut the doors.

Carol, hugely pregnant, was crouching in the back beside the stretcher, her face streaked with soot, the pupils of her eyes dilated with shock.

"It was a beam, one of those old heavy logs, it fell on Bill's leg. Sara, the colt . . ." she was saying urgently as the doors shut and the ambulance started to move.

THE NEXT FEW HOURS WERE CHAOS, and Sara could never remember them afterward without shuddering and feeling again the awful, helpless nausea that had engulfed her all that day.

The pitifully few horses that had survived all suffered varying degrees of burns, and she began at once putting packs of sodium bicarbonate on the worst of the wounds and injecting the animals with antibiotics to combat infection and painkillers to calm them and make them more comfortable.

Mitch helped her until Doc Stone and Floyd arrived, and then he left them with the animals and added his efforts to the volunteer firemen who were desperately trying to keep the flames from spreading across the grass and engulfing the old log house.

Most of the outbuildings near the barn were smoldering masses of black ash.

Sara was humbly grateful for the solid, impassive presence of the old vet working beside her, and now he had no qualms about having Sara double-check the name of any drug he administered.

Nine animals died that day, three of which Sara and Doc Stone were forced to destroy.

Floyd wept openly, and Sara wrapped her arms around him and gave him a quick hug.

Five horses survived, two of which were Scarlett and the colt, Butler.

It was Sara's turn to burst into grateful tears when someone led the tall mare and her rangy foal out of the woods and into the makeshift corral where the surviving animals were. Somehow, the two had escaped without a mark, the only animals totally uninjured.

Mitch happened to be there, and wordlessly he gathered her into his arms and held her for long moments, knowing exactly how she felt about the mare and the foal they'd helped deliver. He fought with the burning ache of unshed tears in his own throat.

Before evening, more and more vehicles bumped their way down the dusty road, bearing relatives and friends of the Forgies, but also concerned residents of the area who'd heard about the tragedy and wanted to help in any way they could.

"Bill's got a badly broken leg and a couple of burns on his back, and Carol's gone into labor," one of Bill's cousins quietly told Mitch that afternoon. "It's one hell of a tragedy for them, losing this stock and their barn."

Sara heard, and tears filled her eyes again when she remembered Carol telling her once how much she wanted Bill present when the baby came.

All those bright and shiny dreams, lost in one day.

Mitch thought bitterly about dreams as he sweated and coughed his way through the thick haze of smoke that hung over the area.

Bill's dream of a breeding stable was Mitch's as well, and the tragedy that had befallen his friend seemed a personal loss to Mitch.

The time finally came when there was nothing more to be done that day, for either Mitch or Sara, and they drove wearily back to Plains, exhausted both mentally and physically.

Mitch drove immediately to the hospital, but he and Sara weren't allowed past the nursing station.

Bill was resting comfortably, the pudgy nurse informed them, a statement Mitch seriously doubted, and Carol was still in labor. No visitors were allowed.

"Want to come out to Bitterroot with me?" Sara asked.

Mitch shook his head. "I have to get home, there's chores to do." Belatedly he remembered telling Wilson at noon that he'd be gone only an hour or so. It was now nearly ten at night. Well, they must have heard by now about the fire. All the same, it wasn't fair to leave him with Mitch's work as well as his own.

It was an excuse, however. Mitch hadn't talked to Sara as he'd planned to do that day, and now he just couldn't. Partly the problems between them seemed insignificant now, buried by the day's happenings...but partly, too, Mitch was no longer certain about dreams and futures.

All the cheerful optimism that he'd felt that morning seemed to have burned away with the fire, blown away with the smoke that was all that was left of Bill and Carol's hopes.

He kissed her apologetically, and through the bone weariness felt the surge of need she inevitably stirred in him. If only that was all there was to consider.

"You were wonderful with those animals today," he told her tenderly, wishing he had more to offer, wishing he could regain the confidence he'd had earlier that day about the two of them.

Her eyes were bloodshot, and her hair smelled of smoke.

"So were you. But our being heroes doesn't much help Carol or Bill, does it? Do you think they had insurance to cover the loss?"

Mitch shook his head sadly. "Bill told me they couldn't afford it. They had a small fire policy on the buildings, but I think the animals will be a total loss."

Sara shuddered at the memory of those dead animals.

"Life doesn't seem very fair sometimes, does it?" she said sadly.

Mitch remembered his brother as he'd been a year ago last Christmas, with his youngest daughter on his shoulders and a smile on his face that seemed never to fade.

"No," he said roughly. "No, life isn't fair. I used to think you got out of life what you worked for, but now I'm not sure anymore."

There didn't seem anything else to say.

MITCH HEARD THAT CAROL had given birth to a baby girl in the early hours of the morning; nine pounds, seven ounces, and wonderfully healthy. It was several hours before Bill could be brought on a stretcher to the nursery to see his new daughter.

Everyone in the community said what a terrible thing the fire had been, but it was Dave Hoffman who did something about it.

He called a meeting in the school gym that Friday night, and half the town turned up.

"We're a small community," he began, "and the way I see it, we can't afford to lose many more people off the land hereabout. Neighbors used to help one another when a barn burned down, and, of course, we can do that, have a barn raising for the Forgies. But seems to me these youngsters need a mite more than that, losing their horses the way they did. No use having a barn without stock to put in it. Seems to me if we could figure out a way to raise some cold hard cash, give them a new chance at some breeding stock, they could begin again."

Ideas flew thick and fast.

Someone suggested a dance, and someone else said why not a barbecue as well?

It was Millie Jackson, the postmistress in Plains, who came up with the rodeo idea. Everyone loves a rodeo, she boomed in her foghorn voice, and they could incorporate the barbecue and dance, and it would draw a much larger crowd than anything else and make a heap more money.

Everyone agreed enthusiastically.

Mitch wasn't sure exactly how it happened, but before the evening was over, he found himself in charge of the rodeo committee. He tried to explain that being a rodeo competitor didn't qualify him at all for organizing one of the damn things, but nobody listened, and he felt totally alone and less than confident about the massive job ahead of him.

Just when he needed Sara for moral support, of course she wasn't there. She'd come to the meeting with Mitch, but a call had come for her before Dave even got through his talk.

She'd whispered to Mitch that someone's horse had colic, shrugged apologetically to him and quietly slipped out of the hall. He wondered if the time would ever come when they'd make it together through one single social occasion, start to finish.

Their wedding, maybe?

It didn't look too promising.

Mitch found out in the next week that he despised and abhorred committees.

Every suggestion he made required endless discussion and hundreds of phone calls and never ended up amounting to a hill of beans in the end.

In desperation, he consulted Dave, who gave him great advice.

Put one person in charge of the others, Dave instructed, someone formidable, with a sense of order and a knack for making decisions fast, who isn't scared of having everybody else scream at them. Then just go ahead and make the major decisions yourself and tell the committee afterward.

It worked. There was a certain justice in appointing Millie Jackson head of the hive, Mitch decided. The rodeo had been her bright idea in the first place, so she might as well absorb some of the flak. And having run the post office for years, she was used to telling people firmly that certain things just wouldn't do.

And at two hundred and thirty pounds, with lungs like a drill sergeant's, Millie managed just fine at keeping the committee in perfect order as it argued over whether the rail fence should be six or eight poles high, which let Mitch get on with the important stuff.

Mitch didn't need to check the rodeo schedule to know there was a professional rodeo in Spokane, easy driving distance from Plains, the second week in August. It surprised and shocked him a bit to realize that he still knew precisely where the next rodeo was scheduled, and when. It was Saturday, August 13.

He craftily set the date for the Plains Rodeo for Sunday, August 14, and then sat down one evening with the phone, a list of his old buddies' numbers and a couple of cold beers to wash away any slight guilt he might feel at coercing those buddies into donating their time and talents for a good cause, seeing they were in the area, anyhow.

Wasn't there an unspoken rodeo code that said one cowboy helps another, he queried plaintively time after time in the next hour?

He threw in the promise of barbecued beef and cold beer and bent the truth a bit about the dozens of sex-mad female rodeo fans in the area, and the Plains Rodeo suddenly took on the shine of a major event. The best of the riders good-naturedly volunteered their talents, and an unexpected offer of fine rodeo stock came out of the blue.

"I PHONED FRANKIE. She's offered her services as bullfighter for the day," Sara told Mitch when he dropped by her office at noon one day. She was filled with excitement at the thought of seeing her sister.

Now, if only there wasn't this constraint between her and the man she loved, everything would be perfect.

The antique ruby engagement ring still circled her finger, but as each day went by Sara had the panicky feeling she and Mitch were getting farther and farther apart. She hardly ever saw him since this rodeo benefit came up, and for once, the fault wasn't hers.

Mitch seemed distant and preoccupied whenever they were together. He was like that again today, the same way he'd been ever since the fire.

They were in her office, and Sara had hastily put the Closed sign on the door outside and switched the phone to the answering service.

"It'll be great to have Frankie here, just like old times," he remarked absently.

"Are we going out for lunch, or do you want to share my sandwiches here?" she asked brightly after a long silent pause.

"Lunch?" He sounded as if it were a foreign word and shook his head. "Sorry, I can't stay, Sara, no time. I just dropped by to pick up those vitamins you said I should give Misty now she's in foal."

Sara's heart plummeted.

"Oh, sure, I've got them right here." She felt absurdly disappointed that he hadn't come by just to see her.

He took them and thanked her politely, saying he'd see her at Bitterroot probably the next night.

Undoubtedly he was only coming to Bitterroot to talk to Dave again, she raged silently as she watched him hurry out the front door and down the sidewalk toward his truck. Mitch and Dave spent more time together lately than Mitch and Sara.

And if he did have any time left over for her, he'd be in a hurry, just as usual.

Sara smashed her fist down on her desk hard enough to hurt.

Why did it seem as if she and Mitch were constantly going in different directions at the same time?

## Chapter Twelve

August 14, rodeo day, dawned clear, with hardly a cloud in the wide canopy of blue Montana sky.

Everyone on the rodeo committee breathed sighs of relief. The weatherman had obviously paid attention when Millie Jackson ordered sunshine for the day.

The last of the preparations were complete.

Huge banners tacked to power poles for miles around trumpeted RODEO TODAY, as if one single person in the entire area could forget an event that had been the sole topic of conversation and argument and downright chaos ever since the fire at Forgie's ranch.

At Bitterroot, Sara was up at dawn. She'd left a message on the answering machine at work, firmly directing emergency calls to the service in Thompson Falls, no exceptions. She'd had no choice about the matter because Mitch had arbitrarily nominated her as official vet for the rodeo and so she had to be there.

It would have been an ideal morning to sleep in for a while. Instead she got up and showered quickly, plugged in her coffeepot and crept along the path to the tiny cabin next to hers, where Frankie was still asleep.

They'd spent last evening gossiping until midnight with Jennie and Gram and Dave, but there were other, more private things Sara wanted to discuss with Frankie, things she'd rather not get into in front of Mom and Gram.

It was a struggle at first to get Frankie awake enough to do more than grunt, and Sara felt a momentary pang at waking her sleepy sister so early. But in a very short time, the whole place would be awake, and with the rodeo starting at noon, there wouldn't be another peaceful moment all day. And there was no telling when Frankie would be home again to share confidences.

The birds were sending up a chorus of song and the sun wasn't quite over the mountain as the two women settled with mugs of strong coffee on Sara's tiny porch.

Frankie's tall, bone-slender frame was still enveloped in a long blue flannelette nightgown. She tucked her bare toes up under the hem and yawned hugely, then took a deep gulp of coffee and settled deeper into the rocking chair.

"Did Gram give you that nightdress?" Sara asked, studying the decidedly old-fashioned garment.

Frankie laughed and shook her head. "I bought this myself. You oughta see the one Gram sent me for Christmas."

"Don't tell me. It's all pink froth and see-through lace, right? She gave me one exactly the same."

They shared an amused look, and Frankie said, "Poor Gram. She figures she's never gonna get any great-grandchildren out of us unless she takes some drastic measures. She must be delighted about your engagement. She's going to be asking you ten minutes after the wedding if you're pregnant yet. In fact, I'll bet she's already started knitting little clothes."

"Not her." Sara shook her head. "Gram detests knitting. She'll probably be out in the shed hammering together a cradle instead." She sighed and added, "Gram's going to be disappointed. If we do get married, it'll be a long time before we have any kids." Her expression clearly signaled her troubled feelings.

"Okay, Sis," Frankie drawled, sleepy gray-green eyes on Sara. "Spill the beans. All last evening I could tell there was something wrong. You look like you haven't had a good night's sleep in months, and if it were Mitch keeping you awake all night, you'd be smiling more than you are." She tilted her head to the side and mused, "Y'know, it's hard for me to get used to the idea of Mitch Carter as a future brother-in-law. When I knew him he was the idol of every rodeo-crazed female from Calgary to Texas. He left a lot of broken hearts behind when he packed up and came back here."

Frankie grinned at the sudden scowl on Sara's face and added, "Don't get homicidal, Sis, it was definitely a case of women chasing Mitch most of the time. He never resisted all that much, mind you. But he never made any great effort with any of them, either, that I could see. That's probably what attracted them to him."

"He did with me," Sara said pensively. "Make an effort. He's been so patient and understanding. Till just lately." She looked past Frankie, at the pine trees just catching the sun on their highest tips and added, "I'm not sure he even wants to get married anymore, and I'm scared to ask him right out."

Frankie studied her sister, and a worried frown creased the tanned skin on her forehead.

"What d'ya mean? What's changed? The few minutes he was here last night there was some pretty heavy electricity going on between the two of you."

Sara grimaced. Mitch had come to Bitterroot with a crowd of cowboys, old friends of his here for the rodeo that he said he wanted her to meet. She'd felt farther away from him than ever with so many people around.

''That electricity was because he hadn't bothered to tell me until last night that he's competing in nearly every single event today. I found out accidentally, from that friend of his, Tom Coleman.''

''Is that what's got you upset, that Mitch's riding today? Heck, Sara, he's an old hand, one of the best. There's no need to worry about him.''

''I know that, I guess. It just bothers me that he'd want to ride. He's not a rodeo cowboy anymore. And the thing is, he didn't even tell me he was going to.''

Guiltily she remembered not telling Mitch about the vet practice, either.

But that was different, she rationalized. The reason she hadn't told Mitch was because it meant so much to her, and she'd been afraid he wouldn't understand or approve.

A shock of recognition ran through her. Was that exactly why Mitch had kept quiet, too?

Did rodeo competition still mean as much as that to him, as much as her vet practice meant to her?

She met Frankie's gaze and all her worries boiled to the surface and spilled out in a confused mass of words. ''Frankie, I'm not certain anymore that Mitch wants to get married and stay here. I know he misses the rodeo life, I just didn't realize till now how *much* he misses it. And then there's my job. There's never enough time for us to be together. Before, it was my fault, the darned practice keeps me busy day and night. But since he got involved with planning this benefit rodeo, it seems he's the one who's always busy and hasn't time for me. And on top of that, I deserted him at our engagement party,'' she added with completely irrational logic.

Frankie frowned and stretched her legs out.

"Maybe it's good for you to know how it feels to get put on the back burner, then," Frankie pronounced with a wry grin.

One look at Sara's stricken expression sobered her.

"Look, Sis, I'm no expert on relationships, heaven knows. My one stab at marriage left a lot to be desired. I was all of fifteen when I got married and Brian was killed before I really had a chance to grow up much," she said thoughtfully. "But I learned one thing. Marriage has a lot better chance at success if both the man and the woman have jobs or interests of their own, something they enjoy doing. You're great at your job and you love it, and that's wonderful. I was like a burr on Brian's chaps, trailing around after him all the time with not one thing of my own to do. Looking back, we'd have made out a lot better if I'd taken up pottery or something." She reached over and took Sara's hand in hers. "What I'm trying to say is, if Mitch decides he wants to give the rodeo life another go, you'd better send him off to do it with a smile rather than try to keep him here, feeling lassoed. Maybe he needs to take another crack at it, just to find out it's not what he wants."

Sara's head bent forward despondently and her hair shielded her expression. "It seems lately there's never time to really talk with him and find out what he does want."

Frankie shrugged. "If it's just a matter of time, for heaven's sake take some out of your busy schedule, make time for loving the way you would for anything else. Now," she said, getting to her feet and stretching her long arms over her head, "how about a dip in that pool before breakfast? It's liable to be the last time I'm really clean all day. Bullfighting's dirty work."

As Sara tugged on her bikini, Frankie's advice went round in her head.

"Make time for loving," Frankie had ordered.

If only it were that easy. Time was a commodity that seemed in short supply, and you couldn't just mix up a batch the way Mom did baking powder biscuits. Didn't Frankie realize that?

CHOKING CLOUDS OF DUST, blistering sunshine and a booming loudspeaker joined the bawling of cattle and the din of an excited crowd at the rodeo grounds that afternoon.

Brightly colored lawn umbrellas shaded tables set up in a pasture off to one side of the arena where the women of Plains had set up refreshment stands. The stands were Gram's idea for the day. Lemonade, iced tea and soda drinks were going fast, along with mouth-watering home baking.

Sara was beside the stock pens in case an animal needed her, close to the chutes where the cowboys prepared for their events. So far she hadn't had to do too much, but she'd been staying conscientiously near the animals just in case.

Near Mitch as well, she admitted to herself.

In case he needed her?

The microphone blared.

"Ladies and gentlemen, from the end chute we have Leo Anderson on Good Times. Leo needs seventy-two points to reach top score today ahead of local favorite Mitch Carter. Now to get the lead in the bucking event . . ."

Sara listened to the announcer, knowing that Mitch would be next out of the chutes after Anderson.

As it had done all day, her stomach knotted into a nauseous mass and her fists clenched helplessly as she watched the man she loved clamber up the sides of the chute and casually get into position over the heaving, frothing bulk of the maniacal horse he'd drawn in the bareback riding competition.

The animal was named Last Chance, and by the look in his eye, he wanted nothing more than to kill any man who dared to climb onto his back.

Sara felt about Last Chance the way she had about most of the animals Mitch had ridden here today.

They ought to be humanely put down in the interest of human survival. Mitch's survival, to be exact.

Rodeo always drew criticism from animal rights groups about cruelty to the stock, but in Sara's opinion, Mitch was the one who'd endured most of the punishment all day in the bone-wrenching moments he'd spent in the ring. Her own body ached in sympathy and she'd flinched with every blow.

But Mitch didn't feel that way at all.

Sara knew that for certain. If he did, he'd stop doing it, wouldn't he?

He'd already competed in calf roping, steer wrestling and saddle bronc riding. Either he or the professional cowboy called Leo Anderson had won most of the events, and it looked as if Mitch might be the overall winner of the day if he kept it up, an astounding feat considering he'd been away from rodeo for so long.

The announcer was introducing Mitch.

For a split second, Sara caught her fiancé's eye, and he gave her a cheerful, carefree wink and then settled his Stetson tight and low on his forehead.

He was enjoying himself. He was doing what he longed to do.

A sense of foreboding rose in her, a sick certainty that he'd already gone far away from her in some way she couldn't explain.

This was very much his world, and none of hers. The signal sounded, the chute opened, and her fingernails bit

deeply into her palms as the man she loved erupted on Last
Chance and the crowd went wild.

"WANT SOME LEMONADE, DOC?"

Mitch held one of the Styrofoam cups he was carefully
balancing out to Sara. His brown-checked shirt was covered in ground-in dust and torn at the elbow from the tumble he'd taken off of Last Chance a few moments before,
and there were sweat stains under the arms. He'd recovered
his hat and dusted it off, jamming it back on his head first
thing. It didn't quite hide the long, angry scratch that started
left of his eye and disappeared under his hat into his hair-
line.

Sara's worried gray eyes seemed to engulf him as he took
long, thirsty drafts of the cold drink, and he did his best to
avoid her troubled gaze.

He'd already had an upsetting few moments with Ruth,
and he sure didn't need more of the same from Sara, he
thought irritably.

Hell, he'd been a rodeo rider most of his adult life, didn't
these women of his understand that? Airplaning off of Last
Chance before the buzzer sounded was embarrassing
enough without tears and lectures about broken bones from
both his mother and his woman. The only slight consola-
tion was that Leo Anderson had failed to stay on his mount
for the allotted time, either.

"What's your next event, Mitch?"

Her voice was only a little unsteady, and she was doing
her best to smile at him. Maybe she wasn't going to say
anything after all. A rush of gratitude and tenderness filled
him, mixing with the other complex and confused emotions he'd been experiencing all day.

How he loved her, this woman of his.

"I'm finished for a while, maybe for the rest of the rodeo. I'm not certain yet."

The judges were still adding up the scores, and if he and Leo were tied the way Mitch feared they probably were, then he'd have to ride once more. But he didn't tell Sara. He wasn't sure he wanted to think about it himself.

Not telling her was the right idea, he decided after a minute. Relief showed in her long-lashed eyes, and she relaxed as she sipped the lemonade he'd given her.

Mitch didn't feel relaxed. With all his heart, he wished the rodeo was over and he could take Sara away somewhere so they could talk. He needed to talk with her.

Mitch had felt exhilarated and happy when he awoke at dawn that morning, with excitement and anticipation sending adrenaline pumping through his veins in the intoxicating way he remembered from his earlier rodeo days.

This was what he did best, this was what he loved doing.

Then, as the day progressed and he competed in one event after another, doggedly determined to make a good showing for his hometown crowd, he gradually came to the realization that something had changed in him over the past months.

In stray moments he found himself, against his will, comparing the hectic, physically dangerous rodeo scene with the quiet, purposeful life he led on the ranch, and the rodeo was somehow less appealing than it had seemed.

Then there were the cowboys.

There was something touching and infinitely sad about the older cowboys here today.

Older? They were Mitch's age.

They began to remind him, for some crazy reason, of the herd of wild horses he and Sara had seen that memorable day up in the canyon: tough, beautifully free in their way, but fighting a losing battle with time and civilization.

These cowboys were fated for extinction just as the wild horses were, and it made Mitch sad.

It seemed that every one of Mitch's old buddies today had gotten around to telling him that they knew their time as rodeo competitors was passing by, and with many, their dreams centered around exactly what Mitch already had: a "spread," a woman they loved, who loved them back, and a little town like Plains where everyone knew who they were and where they lived.

A home of their own.

Mitch listened.

He thought about hot summer days spent haying, early mornings doing chores, long star-studded evenings when he wandered out to check the horses and have a quiet cigarette under the moon.

He remembered sitting at the kitchen table, having coffee with his father and discussing women.

Most of all, he watched the admiration and envy on his friends' faces when he proudly introduced Sara as his fiancée.

Like all simple truths, the one Mitch arrived at was both profound and endlessly comforting.

Sometime when he wasn't looking, he'd come home.

It was a disturbing thing, this finding out that he'd really come home at last, and he wanted to tell Sara, he wanted to take her somewhere quiet and try to put into words what he'd learned today. He longed to share it with her.

He wanted to share everything with her from here on in, but it didn't seem the right time or place to start now, right beside the stock pens with cowboys and animals and spectators milling around.

"Have you seen Frankie?" Sara was asking anxiously, shading her eyes and peering around.

"She's getting ready for the bull riding, it's coming up next."

Sara's nervous system went into overdrive all over again as she turned to look at the pen of deceptively sleepy-looking bulls with the distinctive Brahman humps and large drooping ears.

"I hate the thought of her getting in the ring with those monsters," she said and shuddered.

Mitch studied the massive animals, and a shiver ran down his spine, as well.

He hadn't ridden bulls since his earliest days in rodeo. Bull riding was easily the most dangerous of all the competitions.

It was a young man's sport, a young man's challenge.

"If we're tied for points, Carter," cocky young Leo Anderson had declared moments before, standing with widespread legs and thumbs hooked in his pockets, "then I'm challenging you to a tiebreaking ride, and I bet I'll beat ya, ya lucky old devil."

Other competitors were crowded around the chutes where the conversation took place, listening with interest to the exchange.

They were Mitch's friends, real old-fashioned cowboys in Mitch's estimation.

They'd learned their skills growing up on ranches, practicing on their fathers' stock, learning their trade as a vital part of earning their living... as Mitch had.

The young rodeo competitors like Leo were a different breed entirely. Many of them had never rounded up a cow in their lives and had only seen a real working ranch on television.

Instead, they were professional athletes who attended riding schools where they were simply taught to stay on a bronco or a steer for the required eight seconds in order to win the huge prizes available at commercial rodeos.

"Well, Carter, what'ya say?" Leo had persisted.

Mitch had grinned good-naturedly at the confident young cowboy. "You're free to try and beat me any way you like, Leo."

A calculating look came into the aggressive young man's eye.

"Don't guess an old guy like you would dare take me on with the bulls, eh, Mitch? See, bull riding's my specialty."

For a moment, Mitch considered simply saying no. He had too much to lose to risk his life on a Brahman just to prove a point.

But a quick glance around showed the resentment his friends felt about this newcomer and his half-veiled contempt for their older generation.

So Mitch gave Leo what he hoped was a cool, unconcerned stare and said the only thing possible, especially because he knew in his heart that this was the last time he'd ever be competing as a rodeo cowboy.

And damn it to hell, he was determined to go out a winner.

"Sounds fine to me, Leo. If we're tied, that is. Maybe you ought to give an old guy like me some pointers first, though, eh? I've forgotten a lot since the days I used to ride bulls," he drawled.

The crowd of men guffawed at Leo's expense. Mitch was effectively saying that he'd forgotten more than the young cowboy ever knew, and they loved it.

Now all Mitch could do was hope against hope that there wasn't going to be a tie after all.

He finished the last of his drink and leaned over to plant a kiss full on Sara's lips, for love and for luck. She tasted warm and sweet, and he longed for a quiet place and time.

The announcer's microphone blared.

"Ladies and gentlemen, we have a tie score here today," he began excitedly, and Mitch frowned and reached out and took hold of Sara's shoulders as if he could shield her from the words booming out of the loudspeaker.

"Sara, love, I . . ."

But his attempts to explain were drowned out by the blaring sound system.

"We got a real show here for you today. I've just been informed that Leo Anderson and Mitch Carter are gonna ride for a tiebreaker—" the announcer paused for dramatic effect "—and believe me, this ride will be somethin' to see. They're ridin' bulls, ladies and gentlemen, Brahman bulls. The roughest, toughest animal there is. So put your hands together and let's hear it for Mitch Carter and Leo Anderson."

SARA FELT SHE MUST be in the midst of a truly awful nightmare as she watched her sister cartwheel flamboyantly into the arena, wearing red-striped tights and outsized blue-jean cutoffs, held up by purple-striped suspenders over a fluorescent-yellow T-shirt. Frankie and another clown were now performing slapstick tricks for the audience while they waited for the first bull rider.

Would it be Mitch? Sara agonized.

Even in her worst nightmares, she'd never envisioned a situation like this one, with the man she loved riding a bull and her sister out there to protect him, if she could.

Frankie had long ago explained to Sara the role the bullfighters played in the arena.

The other events used riders on horseback—pickup men—to rescue a competitor after a ride, but bulls attacked men on horseback as readily as they did anyone on foot, so bull riders relied on the agile ability of the clowns, or bullfighters, to rescue them after their duel with the crossbred Brahmans.

The "barrel man"—in this case, Frankie—teased and taunted the bull with a red cape to distract the animal from the cowboy who had either slid or been bucked off. Frankie's task was to attract the animal's attention until she or the other clown could help the sometimes-dazed rider to safety, and if the bull tried to gore her, which he usually did, she hopped into her barrel.

To hear Frankie tell it, the whole thing was as simple as could be. But every single spectator who witnessed the daring rescues the bullfighters made knew exactly how dangerous and complex the performance was.

It called for split-second timing, an athlete's agility and monumental courage.

Eyes riveted on the arena, Sara felt her throat close with terror as the whistle sounded and the first man riding a bull exploded from the chute.

It was Leo on a bull named Panda, and Sara watched anxiously as the bull corkscrewed. But she relaxed a tiny bit as the bull slowed, looked around in confusion and then, like a huge, docile cow, gave two halfhearted kicks and subsided, panting a little before he moved over to the exit chute standing open on the far side of the pens.

Leo was frantic, trying desperately to spur the animal into action, but Panda wasn't playing the game today.

Leo stayed on the animal's back for the required eight seconds, but the ride wouldn't score him the required high points he desired, and also the crowd was laughing.

"Ladies and gentlemen, this is a unionized bull," the announcer quipped gleefully. "He only works for three seconds at a time."

The crowd guffawed again, and the moment Leo was out of the arena, he snatched his hat off and threw it to the ground in a fit of frustrated temper and hurt pride.

Sara thought the ride was the best it could possibly be.

*Please, God,* Sara was praying, *please let Mitch's bull be just as tame as Panda.*

Drawn closer to the chutes against her will, she shaded her eyes and watched as Mitch cautiously tried to climb into position atop the pen that held the bull he'd drawn, an enormous gray beast named Rambo.

Sara's heart sank and dread filled her. The snorting, fighting Brahman was doing his best at knocking down the walls of the narrow pen, and twice Mitch was forced to retreat quickly as the maniacal bull heaved and twisted. The cowboys helping him were doing their best to wrap the braided rope loosely around Rambo, with a weighted cowbell underneath, so the rope would fall free after the ride was over. There was a weighted handhold on it that pulled tight around the rider's hand.

Sara suddenly wished her sister hadn't been as graphic when she explained the details of bull riding.

"Bull riders all have their little tricks to ensure a win," Frankie had explained. "Some of them pull the strap up between their fingers on the second wrap to secure the grip, and almost all of them use resin to keep their hands from slipping."

Frankie's face had been somber as she added, "When a cowboy does stick the full time on a bull's back and then gets his hand tangled in the rigging and can't release it, it's as close as he ever wants to come to suicide."

Just getting on a bull was suicidal, Sara agonized while Mitch struggled into position.

She jumped as the chute suddenly opened and Mitch exploded out on Rambo, right arm held high, left hand stiffly clinging to the belly cinch.

Rambo erupted into the ring like a primeval force, galloping far from the chutes into the middle of the arena, snorting and pawing the earth right in front of the barrel where Frankie crouched.

Sara clasped her hands in front of her and moaned, feeling in her own body each sickening jolt as the bull went wild, twisting, corkscrewing and gyrating, changing direction with lightning speed.

She could see the wild red eyes of the animal, hear the awful snorts and choking grunts of effort that were forced out of Mitch as the bull hit the ground, reared, turned and gyrated like a dervish.

*God, let it be over. Please, God, just let it be over soon,* she prayed fervently.

And after an eternity, the horn blew.

A horrified gasp from the crowd mingled with Sara's choking cry of terror as she realized that Mitch was still half hanging on the animal's back.

He was tugging desperately at the strap that held his hand firmly trapped, and he was being dragged this way and that as he slid helplessly down the animal's side.

*Let go, Mitch, oh please, let go.*

Sara was unaware that she was screaming and running toward the arena.

The clowns were already in action. Frankie's partner raced to within a foot of the bull's nose, waving his arms in a brave, futile attempt to distract the animal. He was forced to leap out of the way as the bull reared and bucked within inches of him.

Frankie had already spun in close once and tried to release Mitch, but the effort failed.

The bull threw his hind end in the air at the exact moment she raced in again.

Rambo writhed as he landed, and the jarring impact twisted Mitch's arm and hand at an unnatural angle. His body flopped helplessly with Rambo's every frantic movement. Frankie danced this way and that, watching for a chance to move in.

For a split second, Frankie's partner was able to catch the bull's attention.

To Sara, it looked as if Frankie threw herself at the bull's side, supporting her weight with one arm across Rambo's back, wrenching at the cinch entangled around Mitch's hand.

Then at last Mitch was sliding free, and Sara's heart seemed to stop as she saw him tumble dangerously down between the kicking hooves.

In the moment she should have used to dance away, out of the Brahman's path, Frankie grabbed desperately at Mitch's shirt and yanked him to safety.

At the same instant, the bull's massive head jerked back toward her, the long blunted horn connected with her cheek, and Frankie's scream was drowned in the terrified cries of the crowd.

Her body flew weightlessly through the air, the full force of the bull's mighty head and neck tossing her like a rag doll up and down again into the dust.

Sara felt the world begin to spin, felt blackness at the edges of her vision as the terrible scene stretched on and on, and she tried to get her legs to move, to carry her toward her sister, lying motionless and bleeding in the dust, toward Mitch, trying dazedly to struggle to his feet, arm hanging helplessly at his side.

Cowboys and clowns were filling the arena in a frantic attempt to run Rambo into the exit chute, and after several abortive tries, the Brahman finally charged out of the arena and the gate was shut firmly behind him.

"Doctor, we need a doctor," the announcer was gabbling hysterically. "Where's the ambulance? First-aid people, please, to the arena immediately."

Then Sara was over the fence and inside the ring. First-aid people were converging on the area where Frankie lay absolutely still, and Mitch was running across the ring, ignoring two men who tried to restrain him.

Horror washed over Sara in waves as she drew closer to Frankie.

Her sister's face had a jagged tear, starting under her eye and laying the flesh open all the way down to her throat. Bright red blood was welling up and pulsing rhythmically out.

Sara's legs threatened to buckle as she got nearer and nearer to her sister.

Was Frankie even breathing?

The blood, there was far too much blood...

An ambulance screamed to a halt and a medical team leaped down and came racing over, surrounding the fragile figure sprawled in the dirt, hiding her from Sara's view.

A hand closed over her arm. It was Mitch, covered in grime and barely able to walk. His other arm hung grotesquely at his side, obviously broken.

"Mitch, oh Mitch, are you...do you think she..."

But the anguished look in his eyes silenced her.

"It was all my fault, every damn bit of it," he said through clenched teeth, agonized remorse evident in every syllable. "I was a fool, a bloody fool to even try...oh, Sara, I'm sorry. I'm so damn..."

Before she could find breath to reply, he staggered and had to close his eyes against the red-hot band of pain that shot through his body.

"C'mon, Mitch, you need to see a sawbones, old buddy," one of his cowboy friends urged, and several more all but carried him over to a waiting car.

They didn't try to load him in the ambulance; most cowboys were superstitious about riding in what they labeled the "meat wagon."

Sara made a move to follow them, but Jennie and Dave and Gram were suddenly all around her, and Gram was holding Sara's arm as if she couldn't stand up alone. Frankie's inert body was being loaded onto a stretcher, and Jennie was sobbing in Dave's arms.

Ruth and Wilson came running, and behind them half the town poured into the arena. Everything was chaos.

The car containing Mitch and the ambulance began to move away, siren wailing.

Before Sara could think clearly again, both Frankie and Mitch were gone from her.

# Chapter Thirteen

At the hospital, a part of Mitch welcomed the agonizing pain of having his dislocated shoulder put back in place and his broken forearm set and put in a cast.

The physical hurt consumed him, so that at least for a while he didn't have to think about anything else, and when the procedure was finally over with and Mitch growled that he wasn't staying in any hospital, he was going home, the doctor simply gave him a shot of something that knocked him out until an entire night had slipped past without his knowing.

He opened his eyes and Sara was there, sitting beside him holding his good hand.

He closed them again and saw vividly the crumpled form of Frankie, body broken and what had been a lovely face split open now, bleeding into the dust.

With sick and awful certainty, he knew that he'd destroyed the chance he'd had for happiness. How could Sara go on loving him, knowing what he'd done to Frankie?

Worst of all, how could he live with himself?

He'd wrecked it all the moment he'd climbed onto that bull. He'd been playing some macho game at the rodeo, and a beautiful woman had paid. Sara's sister had paid.

"Frankie? Is Frankie...?" he demanded urgently, opening his eyes and forcing himself to meet Sara's gray gaze.

"They flew her to Spokane. She has a broken collarbone, a couple of fractured ribs, and she needs..." Sara's best efforts to control her voice failed, and she dissolved into exhausted tears.

"She needs plastic surgery for her face. It's a mess. Mom's gone with her, and we won't know for several days whether..." Sara couldn't go on, and she didn't have to.

Mitch knew exactly what she was trying to say.

They wouldn't know whether or not Frankie's face would be deformed for life.

Because of him. Because he'd been a proud and stubborn fool, thinking only of himself. She'd paid for his stupidity, and he wasn't sure he could stand the pain it caused him now.

The deep, sick ache in his shoulder and arm grew incredibly worse as he swung his legs over the side of the bed and wound the sheet around himself. He cursed in a low, steady stream as he moved, head swimming alarmingly, toward the locker in the corner of the room.

"Where're my pants?"

"Mitch, what are you doing? Get back into bed, the doctor..."

Sara tried to hold on to his good arm, but he shook free and moved away from her.

"I'm getting out of here, Sara. Can you drive me back to the ranch?"

His voice was remote and cold, as if she were a stranger.

"Mitch, your arm—I'm calling the nurse." She moved to press the call button by the bed, and he turned on her so ferociously she froze before she could touch the button.

"Don't treat me like some stupid kid," he grated at her. "If you can't drive me home, say so and I'll call a cab. But get it through your head that I'm leaving. Now."

Sara swallowed hard and told herself not to be hurt. After all, he was in pain and most likely still groggy from whatever the doctor had given him. Silently she helped him retrieve his clothes, his boots, his Stetson.

"Your mom and dad were here till late last night. Your mother said she was going to help Gram at Bitterroot this morning and would come by the hospital about noon to see you. Why don't you let me take you there? We could have some lunch, relax by the pool..."

He shook his head impatiently and cursed under his breath when she had to carry some of his things for him.

When he'd paid his bill and signed himself out, she flinched in sympathy when his lips grew white and his face stiff as he bumped his shoulder slightly climbing into her car.

"Mitch, darling, I'm sorry," she said, and leaned across to press her head comfortingly against his good shoulder, and he moved deliberately closer to the window and turned his head away from her.

"What the hell have you got to be sorry for?" he snarled, and she missed the pain in his voice and heard only the sarcasm.

After that, she simply drove him home.

When they arrived at the ranch and she made a move to get out of the car, he said, "Don't bother coming in, Sara," and then climbed painfully out and slammed the car door.

"Thank you for the ride," he said, already moving away, just as if she were some stranger he was dismissing.

Sara spun gravel all the way down the drive, her feelings shifting from fury at his rudeness to raw hurt at his cruelty.

Her face burned with embarrassment at the way he'd treated her, and her chest hurt with suppressed emotion.

She'd left Floyd to manage everything alone at the office just so that she could be at the hospital. She'd wanted to show Mitch that for once she was there beside him when he needed her.

And this was how he reacted.

By the time she stormed through the door of the clinic, anger had the upper hand. Floyd was waiting at the front door.

"Doctor, I'm so glad you're back, there's a terrible emergency," he announced, and Sara snapped impatiently, "For heaven's sake, Floyd, skip the dramatics and just tell me what it is."

Dozens of possible calamities with animals raced through her head, and it took a moment to adjust when Floyd said dolefully, "It's the electricity. I plugged in the sterilizer and every fuse in the place blew. I tried replacing them, and the whole panel started smoking, so I had to turn everything off. I've called the electrician, but he's not come. There's no lights and the instruments aren't sterile, and the fridge holding the vials of medicine needing to be kept cold is starting to defrost. And you can hardly see your hand in front of your face in here."

"Call the electrician again, right now."

She shut the front door and leaned her back against it. A glance into the murky waiting room revealed half a dozen pets waiting patiently with their owners despite the gloom.

"The man says he won't come unless you personally guarantee him payment. He says the last time he was here, he never got paid for the job," Floyd announced, holding one hand over the receiver.

"Tell him . . . tell him I'll pay him. Just tell him to hurry up."

If the electrician charged very much, she wouldn't have enough for her other expenses. But she couldn't manage without electricity. Sara glanced up at the stain on the ceiling where the roof had been leaking. In the bathroom, the plumbing was faulty. The roof needed replacing.

She'd listed all the things wrong with this place the day she'd signed the lease, she remembered now. Nothing had been done, although her invisible landlord was still raising her rent.

All the frustrations of the morning suddenly became focused.

Sara marched into her office and dialed the number of the lawyer, Martin Leskey, and when he came on the line, Sara didn't give him a chance to launch into any long-winded speeches. She related the message from the electrician, reminded Leskey that she'd asked for repairs and coolly demanded that something be done immediately...this morning, before she paid any electrician's bill.

"I understand your concern, my dear, but I must warn you that my past dealings with the owner have been less than satisfactory, and I'm very much afraid..." Leskey droned.

"Who, exactly, is my landlord?" Sara interrupted.

"The property is leased from Equity Holdings..."

"Damn it all, I know that," Sara exploded. "Give me the name of the person. I'll phone and deal with him directly."

There was a rustling of paper, and Sara could imagine Leskey meticulously sorting through his voluminous file folder.

"Very well, I see no reason, even though she doesn't want to be bothered. After all, these are emergency circumstances, ahhh, here we are." Martin cleared his throat and Sara chewed her thumbnail impatiently.

"Crenshaw is the name, E. Crenshaw."

Ugly visions of a cat named Queenie made Sara shudder.

It couldn't be the same Emily Crenshaw, it was impossible. The name was just coincidence.

Emily Crenshaw was nearly destitute. Wasn't she?

"What does the E. stand for, Martin?" Sara inquired fearfully. An incredible, unbelievable suspicion was growing within her.

"It stands for Emily. She's an extremely eccentric elderly person, I must warn you..."

"I know her," Sara said weakly. After a long pause, during which her painful dealings with Emily Crenshaw flashed before her eyes, Sara finally became aware again of Martin, breathing patiently... and silently, for once, into the other end of the receiver.

"Mr. Leskey, you told me once that if I ever needed legal advice, you'd be happy to help me. Well, I do now."

"Yes, my dear?"

"Is it possible for you to inform Emily Crenshaw that my business is suing her for the bill she hasn't paid for treating her cat, and also that the amount of the electrical repairs will be deducted from my next quarterly payment on the lease?"

"I see no reason why not. I'll get on it immediately." Martin actually sounded as if he might enjoy the hassle he'd undoubtedly endure with Emily Crenshaw. "I admire your spirit, Dr. Wingate."

"One last thing. Did Doc Stone know that Emily Crenshaw owned this building?"

"Oh my, yes. Doc had numerous problems with the lady over the years. Yes, he knew indeed."

Sara hung up slowly.

She'd been made a proper fool, and Doc hadn't said a word.

With shaking hands, she dialed again.

"Stone here." Doc's raspy, impatient voice sounded in her ear, and Sara had to take a deep breath before she could say a word. She felt like going over and giving Doc a shot of something lethal, she was so furious with him.

Without any preamble, she blurted, "You knew Emily Crenshaw wasn't poor, you knew she owned this damned building. For all I know she probably owns half of Plains. How could you let me make such a fool of myself?"

Doc's dry chuckle came over the line. "So you found out about poor Emily, did you? I wondered how long it would take. She's a bad one, a proper con artist." He sounded amused and absolutely unconcerned. "Everyone in Plains has had some dealing with Emily over the years, and every one of them got stung."

"It was vile of you not to tell me. Why, I never got a red cent out of her for that operation, and Floyd and I got scratched half to death by her rotten cat." Sara's voice was trembling with barely controlled passion.

"Yes, well." Doc's voice became serious. "It was bad of me, I'll grant you that. But you see, young woman, I was making so many mistakes just then and you were so self-righteous. Half the damned county was telling me what a wonder the new woman vet was. I felt it was only fair that you made a mistake that one time. So I instructed Floyd not to say a word, and old Emily and her cat did the rest." Ironic amusement filled his voice again. "Don't feel too bad, young woman. I spayed the damn thing for free, years back. Still got a scar on my wrist."

It took a moment, but Sara's sense of humor finally surfaced.

The joke was on her, and she probably deserved it. Like all young people starting a career, she'd thought at times that she knew everything.

A giggle escaped her, and suddenly, she and old Doc were laughing uproariously. It was the first time she'd ever heard Doc Stone really laugh hard.

When it was over, Sara ventured to ask Doc about his eyesight.

"There's some newfangled technique they're going to try on me. I'll either end up instantly blind or have fairly good vision again. They put permanent lenses right in your eye, or something. The procedure's slated for next week."

Sara quickly thought of all the encouraging things she might say and discarded them. Doc would just grunt and hang up in her ear.

"Well," she finally said, "if it works, I warn you I'm not selling you this business back again. But if you ever want a job, you could try me."

His grunt came, but it was amused rather than angry.

"You need an old, experienced vet around there, young woman. Keep you from being taken in by the likes of Emily Crenshaw, if nothing else." His voice sharpened. "I heard about young Mitch Carter and his tussle with that bull. Your sister was injured too, wasn't she? How are they?"

All the laughter that had filled her moments before disappeared.

"Frankie needs plastic surgery, and Mitch...he broke his arm just above the wrist. He's, ahh, he's fine, though."

He wasn't fine at all, and neither was Sara, but that wasn't anything she could explain.

Doc grunted, and then, as if it was hard to get the words out, he said, "Hear you're plannin' on marrying that Carter boy. When the time comes, and if this danged thing works on my eyes, I'll take over the practice for you for a week or two. As a wedding present," he added gruffly. "Just don't delay the marriage too long, I'm not getting any younger," he added in a sour tone, and then, before Sara could say a word, he hung up.

Floyd came to announce the arrival of the electrician just then, adding that the man wanted a check in advance.

By the time the lights went back on, Sara owed him fifty dollars more than the rent plus the proposed increase.

Emily had probably won another round.

Floyd came into her office late that afternoon.

Sara was slumped at her desk, utterly drained and on the verge of tears. She was physically exhausted; she'd been at the hospital until the small hours of the morning, and after only a couple of hours' sleep, she'd hurried back early so she'd be there when Mitch woke up.

She was emotionally exhausted from mentally going over and over the way Mitch had acted that morning.

For some reason, she'd been certain that he'd call her sometime during the day to apologize, and he hadn't.

His behavior hurt deeply, even though she kept telling herself she shouldn't let it. He'd had an accident, he was likely in a great deal of pain.

But why had he been cruel to her? Why had he treated her the way he had?

The tears spilled over just as Floyd knocked and opened her door. He took one look at her and his ruddy face softened.

"If you want to leave early, go on. I'll tend to the animals in the infirmary and lock up for you. Is your man still in the hospital, Doctor? I was at the rodeo yesterday, it was a terrible thing that happened."

Floyd's kindness brought more tears, and she tried to sniff them away, unsuccessfully.

"He's home, Floyd." She gulped back a sob. "I drove him home this morning."

"And your sister? She's a brave one, that girl. I heard she broke her collarbone."

Sara listed Frankie's injuries and told him about the surgery she'd need, and Floyd nodded thoughtfully.

He seemed to consider carefully before he added, "He'll be feeling bad about it, you know, causing the accident. He'll be feeling responsible."

Sara shook her head impatiently. "That's ridiculous. Mitch would never have hurt Frankie deliberately, the whole thing was plain and simply an accident. She was doing her job, and Mitch was, as well. No one in his right mind would blame Mitch for what happened to Frankie. She certainly doesn't. The first thing she asked when she regained consciousness yesterday was how Mitch was."

Floyd nodded thoughtfully. "Has he talked about it with you, then?"

Miserably Sara shook her head, giving up all pretense at control and sobbing openly.

"He was absolutely hateful to me this morning, and he hasn't called or anything all day."

Floyd awkwardly patted her arm. "I'll make you a nice cup of tea, and then you ought to go home to bed, you're tired out, Sara. I'll finish tonight, and I'll be sure to come in early tomorrow, so don't hurry in the mornin'."

It was such a relief to have him back to calling her Sara again.

She blew her nose hard, told him so and gave him a watery smile.

"Thank you, Floyd."

"And Sara?" His broad, ruddy face creased in a frown. "Don't worry your head over me maybe bending my elbow one too many times and not making it in tomorrow. I've joined a group. I've decided to turn over a new leaf."

"Oh, Floyd, I'm so glad. That's wonderful news, just wonderful."

He seemed to puff up with pride, and then he added ingenuously, "Yes, well, Doc said it was either that or he'd sign me into a clinic."

Sara didn't know whether to laugh or begin to cry again.

She'd bet her stethoscope Floyd's new leaf wouldn't last till autumn.

SARA BROKE DOWN AND PHONED Mitch three times the next day, but there was no answer at the ranch.

She hurried through the afternoon's farm calls and then drove hesitantly up the Carter driveway.

Ruth answered her timid knock, and she greeted Sara with a warm smile. She'd had her hair cut and styled recently, and she was wearing a bright turquoise cotton pantsuit that brought out the blue in her eyes.

"Sara, dear, come in. I was just making soup and a sandwich for Wilson and me. You'll have some with us, of course."

"Thank you, Ruth."

Where was Mitch?

Ruth took Sara's hand fondly and drew her into the kitchen, then busily went about making thick ham sandwiches and stirring a pot of soup as she talked.

"I'm sure you're as upset with Mitch as I am, going off like this when he's barely out of the hospital. Honestly he's more stubborn than even Wilson ever was. I told him so before he left, too."

Sara could hardly get her breath. She felt as if she'd been hit in the chest.

Mitch hadn't said a single word to her about going anywhere.

But then, he hadn't said a single word, period.

"I . . . I didn't even know he was gone, Ruth," she finally stammered. "When did he leave? Did he say where he was going or when he'd be back?"

The desolation that filled her must have shown clearly on her face, because Ruth hurried over and put her arm around Sara's shoulders.

"I'm sorry, Sara. I was sure he'd have . . . you see, he was all ready to leave when I got home today at noon. I went over early this morning to help Adeline at Bitterroot, with Jennie gone there's so much to do. Anyway, a friend of Mitch's who owns his own plane came to get Mitch right after I got home, and all Mitchell said was that he had some business to attend to and not to worry about him, he'd be fine. He wouldn't say when he thought he'd be home or anything. I'm very annoyed with him, he was as cross as a bear with me last night."

The back door opened and slammed, and Wilson's voice called from the hall, "Mother? When's supper going to be?"

Ruth shook her head fondly and gave Sara's shoulder a final squeeze as Wilson came into the kitchen.

"Well, hello there, Sara," he said jovially. "Gonna stay and have some supper with Mother and me?"

"Wilson, dear, I'm not your mother," Ruth said gently but firmly, and even through the pain Sara felt about Mitch's behavior, she had to marvel at the change in Ruth Carter.

A new confidence shone from the older woman—she even walked differently than she had a while ago. Even with the strain of the past few days and the shock of Mitch's accident, Ruth was firmly in control of her emotions.

"We're discussing that son of yours, Wilson," Ruth added briskly. "He's gone off with not a word to Sara, and you said he wouldn't talk much with you, either."

Wilson removed his straw hat and hung it on a peg by the door. He ran his fingers through his hair, setting it on edge just the exact way Mitch was in the habit of doing, and pain tore at Sara's heart.

If he loved her, how could Mitch go off like this without a word? She remembered his coldness yesterday morning, and her heart plummeted.

Perhaps it was all over between them. The ruby ring on her finger suddenly felt as heavy as lead. Perhaps he was avoiding her until he figured out a way to tell her.

Wilson sat down heavily at the table, and Sara noticed the worried lines around his eyes, the deep grooves beside his mouth. Wilson was deeply concerned about his son, Sara realized.

"Don't go getting upset about the boy, now, Moth... Ruth," he said with an obvious effort at using her name. "Every so often a man has to get away, sort himself out. Mitchell's gone through a lot of changing, last few months, and now he feels bad about this accident and all. He just needs a bit of time."

Surprisingly Wilson made a touching attempt all during the simple meal to keep conversation going. He asked Sara about her work and actually passed on a nice remark someone had made at the auction about a horse she'd treated.

When it came time to leave, he walked companionably across the yard with Sara to her car, telling her in minute detail about a sow he thought might be getting sick. She had some weird mark on her back, and she was off her feed.

Sara offered to look at the animal, but unexpectedly, Wilson changed the subject.

"Gonna surprise Moth... eh, Ruth... and take her on a holiday," he confided almost shyly. "Her birthday's comin' up. I bought the tickets already, thought we'd go visit our daughter-in-law in Seattle, get to know the grandkids again. Haven't seen 'em since after—" he swallowed hard and tried again "—after our Bob died. Think you could warn Jennie and Adeline that Ruth'll be gone awhile?" He scowled and added morosely, "She's likely to refuse to come with me if she thinks that blamed job won't be waitin' when she gets back. Never saw a woman so set on a job in my life."

"Of course I'll tell them, but they'd never hire anyone else, they couldn't manage without Ruth," Sara assured him.

"Yeah, well, neither can I," Wilson admitted baldly. "Thought we'd take off as soon as your mom gets back."

"If Frankie's okay, Mom will probably be home in the next few days. It all depends on the surgery," Sara said. "I'll be sure and let you know as soon as I hear anything."

"Drive careful," Wilson ordered sternly as she started the car and began to back up. "Women drivers, none of you ever could drive sand down a rat hole."

Sara just gave him a tight-lipped smile. Wilson was incorrigible, but he'd also touched her heart tonight, the gruff old chauvinist. She'd gotten along with him better than she'd ever thought possible.

Ironic, wasn't it, that she'd lose Mitch just when Wilson seemed to be ready to accept her as a daughter-in-law? The hurt that she'd been holding tightly inside all evening stabbed at her, and the empty road shimmered as the tears came.

*Mitch, I love you. Why, why are you doing this to us?*

ABSOLUTELY THE LAST THING Mitch wanted to do was walk into Frankie's hospital room in Spokane that evening. Clenching his hand around an enormous bouquet of flowers he'd bought in the lobby, he tried to swallow the dry fear in his throat as he checked the numbers on the doors he passed in the long hallway. He stopped before the one with the right number.

Hesitantly he moved through the half-open door.

There was only one patient in the small room, and Frankie's mother, Jennie, was sitting on a chair beside the high bed.

Mitch forced himself to look past her, at the bandaged figure lying there.

Horror caught at his throat, and for an instant he was afraid he was going to be sick. The terrible guilt that had been eating at him ever since the rodeo engulfed him all over again, and he fought against it.

Frankie was a mass of bandages, bruises and intravenous tubes, and the certain knowledge that she looked that way because of him totally unnerved him.

He wanted nothing more than to turn on his heel and run, head for the nearest bar and spend the rest of the night…the rest of his life… purging his guilt with alcohol.

Just the way Floyd O'Malley had done.

Floyd. Who would have ever thought that Floyd would be the only person to really understand how Mitch was feeling?

The phone call had come late the night before, and Mitch had already drunk over half a bottle of Scotch when his father tapped on the door of his cabin.

"Tell whoever it is that I'm not here," Mitch had ordered rudely, and pain twisted and turned inside of him because he knew it had to be Sara, and he couldn't talk to her.

He couldn't talk to anybody.

"It's Floyd O'Malley, son."

Awful terror filled him, and he lurched for the door. Something terrible had happened to Sara. Why else would Floyd be phoning him at this late hour?

His heart was hammering wildly when he picked up the phone, and he cursed Floyd in a steady vicious stream when he finally believed Sara wasn't injured.

He was about to slam the receiver down when Floyd said evenly, "You're feelin' bad over what happened at the rodeo, aren't you? I hurt someone one time, y'know, just the way you've done. Everyone said it was an accident, but I never thought it was." There was something in his voice that caught Mitch's blurry attention and held it against his will.

He listened without a word as Floyd told him the same story Sara had heard from Judy... brother and sister taking the horses, racing them and colliding, Judy falling; but Floyd believed the injury his sister had sustained was totally his fault.

Even now, years afterward, it was plain he believed it implicitly.

"First, I drank to live with meself," he admitted baldly. "Then I used what happened as a reason for drinking. It's terrible hard, you understand, to forgive yourself when you see a person in a wheelchair because of something you've done."

He paused and added apologetically, "I'm fond of Dr. Sara and I'm not one for preaching usually. But she was crying her heart out this afternoon, and I had to try to help. I'd not like to see you destroy her and yourself over this. She's a fine lady, is Dr. Sara."

Mitch had hung up the phone and spent most of the rest of the night sitting out by the corral, smoking one cigarette after another and trying to think instead of feel.

The upshot of that sleepless night was the knowledge that he had to come and see Frankie before he did anything else.

Now that he was here, he wasn't sure it had been the right decision, either, but he couldn't just walk out again.

Frankie turned her head toward him, and recognition dawned in her unbandaged eye.

"Hiya, cowboy," she said in a thin, reedy voice not at all like the one he remembered. "What are you doing here?

You're supposed to be back in Plains taking care of my big sister.''

Mitch cleared his throat, tried to speak and had to try again. ''Came to see you,'' he finally managed.

''Hello, Jennie,'' he added, and then he stood there, feeling stupid, clutching the damn flowers in his one good hand and not knowing what to do with them or himself.

''Mitch, you shouldn't have come all this way. You look as if you ought to be in a hospital bed yourself,'' Jennie chided. ''Frankie's fine. We've just talked with the plastic surgeon and he says she won't have hardly a scar to show for this.'' She said softly, ''Here, give me those flowers and I'll go find a nurse and see if we can beg a vase for them.''

In a moment, Mitch was alone with Frankie.

He had to get through it quickly, while his courage held.

''I came to apologize, Frankie, for all the good it'll do,'' he burst out harshly. ''I'd do anything to change what happened out there, but there's no way I can, so all I can say is I'm sorry. That's about all I came to say. That I'm sorry, damned awful sorry for what happened to you. It was my fault, my pride, see, that caused the whole thing. I never should have climbed on that fool bull at all. And I want to thank you, for what you did for me.''

He'd already made arrangements to have all her medical bills sent to him, but he wasn't going to tell her that. He half turned to leave, but her angry voice stopped him.

''What the hell kind of garbage is this, Mitch Carter, walking in here and thanking me for doing my job? Acting like a martyr because I happened to get hurt a little? You know as well as I do that every bullfighter gets hurt sooner or later.'' Her furious voice rose higher as she went on, ''You macho cowboys make me sick. First you give me a bad time for being a female doing what you consider a man's job, and then you act like it was your duty to protect me instead of the other way around." She was breathing heavily, and Mitch took an anxious step toward the bed.

"Frankie, don't get yourself..."

"Shut up. If I were a man and this happened, you'd be making jokes and smuggling in a beer for me instead of whining. So help me, Mitch Carter, if you ever say one more word about this to me, I'll...I'll spill the beans to Sara about that redhead in Dallas." She closed her one eye and took a few deep breaths to calm herself. "Now get the hell out of here and go make love to that sister of mine. You're wasting time—mine and hers both."

Her words hit Mitch like a bucket of ice-cold water dumped on his head.

He was halfway back to Plains in his buddy's small plane the next morning before he managed a weak grin.

That was one mean-mouthed lady, all right. Bringing up Lucy back in Dallas was definitely hitting below the belt.

He loved Frankie for it.

And he loved her sister in quite a different way altogether.

THE PHONE CALL CAME just after noon hour. Floyd took it and came hurrying into the infirmary where Sara was just working on a German shepherd pup. She'd been at the clinic since dawn, not even stopping for coffee or lunch, forcing Floyd to keep up with her.

Floyd took a deep breath and said, "There's a terrible emergency, Dr. Sara."

She looked at him with swollen eyes and sighed.

"Don't dramatize, Floyd, please. Not today. Just tell me what it is."

"Mr. Carter phoned, and there's somethin' terrible wrong with that whole herd of pigs we tested that time. He says would you get out there on the double."

"But I was out there just the other day. There was nothing wrong then."

*Only that sow. Wilson had mentioned that sow.*

"Well, Dr. Sara, there is now. He sounded wild, he did."

All the way out to the ranch, Sara went over and over the diseases pigs could get. It had to be something bad, if Wilson was as upset as Floyd had indicated.

She forced her tired brain to concentrate only on the problem, just as she'd done ever since Mitch left, in an effort to keep herself from thinking of him.

Pigs. What diseases did they get?

Erysipelas, she suddenly remembered, and a cold shudder ran down her back.

Hadn't Wilson mentioned a mark on that sow's back? And she wasn't eating.

As if she were reading a page in her thick veterinarian's guide, Sara listed the dreaded symptoms in her mind.

Erysipelas, an acute infectious disease of pigs.

Diamond-shape skin lesions. High fever, prostration, vomiting, refusal to eat.

It could quickly kill an entire herd. Why hadn't she insisted on looking at that sow the other night, she might have caught it in time?

Wilson would be livid.

Worse, he needed those pigs as income. And she was his vet. She should have insisted...

She drove in at a furious speed, tearing across the yard and pulling up in front of the pigsty.

Sara didn't bother getting into her coverall. She didn't wait for Wilson, either. She hurried over to the fence and opened the gate, stepping in among the squealing, milling Yorkshires.

She stood there, trying to keep the pigs from upending her and watched intently for the obvious signs of illness she expected.

There were none. As far as she could tell, these were healthy hogs.

She glanced up in confusion, and there was a rangy cowboy, one arm in a cast, perched on the rail fence watching her.

*Mitch.*

Shock waves went through Sara as their eyes met and held. His were shaded a little by his Stetson, and his face looked somber. He motioned toward the gate and she slowly began to make her way to it.

He was waiting a short distance away. Apprehensively Sara walked on, wishing that she'd taken time to pull on her coverall and boots.

Her jeans were stained and her shoes were filthy from the pen.

Had she even brushed her hair this afternoon?

She drew herself up straighter, reminding herself that she was here on a professional basis. She'd act like a doctor of veterinary medicine, damn it.

"Mitch, hello. Your father called the office, he said there was something wrong with the pigs, and I . . ." Her voice trailed off. She just couldn't do it. She loved him far too much. Everything melted inside when she got near him.

"Hello, Doc."

The deep, intimate tone of his voice thrilled her, told her that whatever had been bothering him the past few days was gone.

He reached out and touched a piece of her hair that had come loose from the bun at the back of her neck, and the roughness of his fingers on her cheek made her shiver.

But she drew back and waited for whatever he was going to say next. She needed explanations.

"I went to see Frankie," he began, holding her gaze with his. "I was coming apart inside, after the rodeo. See, it finally dawned on me that day that I had everything in the world a man could want: you, this ranch, this big, beautiful country. I didn't want to ride that bull. I let myself get cornered into it." He looked away from her, out over the rolling fields to the mountains. "I felt responsible and guilty as hell for what happened to your sister." His green eyes came back to hers. "And I hurt you as well, because I was hurting bad." He took a deep breath.

"Will you forgive me, Sara?" He added in a hoarse whisper, "I'm home now for good, and I love you."

She nodded uncertainly, still making herself hold back. "I love you, too. But nothing's really changed, Mitch. There's still this demanding job of mine. There'll always be times when I'm called out at exactly the wrong moment. Can you really live with that? It won't be easy."

He tipped the brim of his hat back with one finger, and grinned his crooked one-sided grin. "If it gets too bad, I can always saddle Steamboat and take you up Wild Horse Canyon, can't I?" His grin faded, and his voice was earnest and compelling.

"It won't be easy for us, Sara, I know that. But I've been thinking a lot, and there's changes we can make. Maybe we can set up an office for you in the house I'm going to build us, so at least you're working from home. And Floyd said there's students in the summer who'll work more for experience than money. There's ways, Doc. We'll find 'em."

He was right. Where there was love like this, there would also be a way around problems.

They'd find it together.

She moved toward him, and he caught her fiercely against him with his one good arm. He reached up and tossed his hat away, and then he bent his head and kissed her, slowly, passionately, with the promise of forever.

It was a long time later when she thought to ask about the pigs.

"Your father said there was something terribly wrong with them, Mitch. I really ought to..."

He drew her firmly back into his embrace, cursing the cast on his arm.

"I made the call, Doc. I figured you'd come quicker if you thought there was an animal emergency," he admitted brazenly. "The only thing wrong with those confounded pigs is that they're pigs."

He kissed her again, more insistently this time, and put his lips close to her ear.

"Have I ever told you there's no telephone in my cabin?"

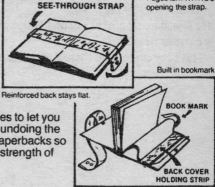

# BARBARA DELINSKY

## THROUGH MY EYES

Smuggled diamonds . . . a desperate search for answers . . . a consuming passion that wouldn't be denied . . .

This May, Harlequin Temptation and Barbara Delinsky bring you adventure and romance . . .

With a difference . . .

Watch for this riveting book from Temptation.

HARLEQUIN *Temptation*

# *Harlequin American Romance*

## COMING NEXT MONTH

### #293 APPEARANCES ARE DECEIVING
### by Linda Randall Wisdom

More than anything, Caryn Richards wanted two things: to keep her
personal secret forever and to catch the culprit whose pranks troubled her
magazine. When security expert Sam Russell arrived, she was grateful for
his help—but she didn't plan on him capturing her heart. If he discovered
her secret, would it destroy or strengthen the love a man felt for
a woman?

### #294 PEPPERMINT KISSES by Karen Toller Whittenburg

New lawyer Dana Ausbrook learned fast that the candy business was
anything but sweet. Her first job was to sue for custody of a candy
recipe—a wedding gift given to her mother forty years before. But the
wedding had been called off, and since then the bride and groom had
founded rival confectioneries, each fighting for the wonderful secret to
Peppermint Kisses. And now Rick Stafford had come to plead the
groom's case and stayed to court the bride's lawyer. The candy business
would never be the same again.

### #295 THE SHOCKING MS. PILGRIM by Robin Francis

Staid and sensible Libby Pilgrim would never have kidnapped Joshua
Noon without a very good reason. And what better one than the
protection of her beloved Maine coastline? But now, after a broken
rudder and strong currents, Libby, Josh and their little boat were drifting
out to sea, and Libby was quickly learning the hard way that crime did
not pay.

### #296 FIRES OF SUMMER by Catherine Spencer

Five years ago, Susannah Boyd's husband had lost his life rescuing their
infant son from kidnappers. Now Susannah was trying to make a new life
for herself and her boy in the safety of the rural Alaskan Panhandle. But
fire-fighting pilot Travis O'Connor challenged her isolation. Would she
refuse his love to protect herself—and her son—or could she find the
strength to risk, and love, again?